CHAOS
UMPIRE SITS
KEVIN KNEUPPER

CHAPTER ONE

"Chaos umpire sits, and by decision more embroils the fray by which he reigns..."

—John Milton, *Paradise Lost*

T HE SCREAMING HAD GONE ON for hours, longer than anyone could have expected. A master torturer knows his victims' limits, and none of them would be blessed with an early escape. The fortunate servants had either fled into the city in the confusion after the tower's collapse, or had been granted the relative blessing of being cut down at random by one of the surviving angels going about their rescue efforts. But these poor souls had crossed paths with Ecanus, and he had no interest in humanitarianism.

"Louder," said Ecanus, pressing his foot onto the chest of a man impaled on a nearby piece of scrap. He'd arranged them in a circle, men and women and even a few children, using nearby wreckage to crucify them through their hands and feet and pin them to the ground. He stood in the center, conductor of the chorus, directing their anguish and amplifying the screams as he thought would best improve his grotesque symphony.

"I should have hunted down a tenor," groused Ecanus, the scars on his face twisting into a scowl. "There's no harmony to your hosannas. The Maker will never listen to you, not if you can't be bothered to work at it. Now scream some more, and see just how much he cares for you. See if he'll save you, if only you're loud enough for him to hear."

He spread his wings, their black feathers turned grimy with dust from the clouds that had enveloped the area, and looked down on his victims with glee. He was strutting at the center of his orchestra, waving his hands to the tune of their cries and entertaining his audience, such as it was. Most of the able-bodied angels were off scouring the debris for survivors, but a few loafers had stayed behind at their camp, feigning illness to avoid hunting through the remains of the tower with the rest of them. It was a credible excuse; none of them had come off well from the blast. Those at the back of the Hunt had fared best, sick and stunned but soon to recover. Those towards the front bore the brunt of things, and were still being accounted for by the search parties. And as for those who'd been in the tower itself, nothing had been recovered but bodies.

"And now, the grand finale," said Ecanus, drawing his flaming dagger from its hilt. The sight of the fire inspired the performers, and they shrieked and wailed together in a fury, bringing enthusiastic applause from the malingering angels. There was no more sympathy for the servants, not after what they'd done. Not that there'd been much to begin with, but Ecanus had once been something of an outlier in the extremity of his cruelty. In recent hours, though, he'd become a favorite even of those who thought themselves above him. Their views of his stature were unchanged, to be sure, but dark times call for a dark jester, and the surviving angels welcomed a little levity.

His performance complete, he disposed of each of the players, thrusting his dagger into them one by one, taking his time to savor the moments of anticipation the rest of them endured as they waited their turn. He took a bow at the end to clapping and laughter from the angels, and sat down with the rest of them to dream up new entertainments to pass the time.

He didn't have to wait long. Motes appeared in the dusty skies, black spots floating in the distance and growing larger as they approached. They lit down next to him one by one: Uzziel, followed by one of his search parties, carrying back corpses they'd dug out of the rubble. His beard was grey with soot, and it had crept into every corner of his armor, leaving him looking like he'd been dumped in water and rolled in flour. But that was par for the course for anyone who'd been dredging through the tower's ruins.

Despite his appearance, Uzziel was in fine form, better than he'd been in years. All eyes had turned to him for leadership, once they'd regrouped. He alone had predicted the threat, and though none of them had listened, they were closely following his every raving now. He'd stepped into the role with ease, an experienced commander from his duties up above, barking orders and haranguing the dispirited into action. It brought back some of his old stability, and cleared his head of bogeymen, if only for a time.

"Ecanus," said Uzziel, eyeing the recent massacre. "Cease this waste of time! Our brothers lay buried in ash, and all you can busy yourself with are these antics. Threats abound from all sides, and every hand is needed to turn them away. We must go back, and continue looking until all of the missing have been found."

He waved the search party forward as he spoke, directing them as they dumped their cargo to the ground. They'd recovered more bodies, and Uzziel was adamant that they be laid to rest with martial honors. Likely none were warriors, but that was no matter. Pomp and circumstance were point enough themselves for a general, regardless of who was being honored or whether there was any particular basis for bestowing the honors.

"Why, Uzziel," said Ecanus, "that's the very reason I occupy myself the way I have. The things they whispered to me before they passed! They're scampering around the city now, those servants of ours. You better than anyone should know the danger in that. You should have heard them. You were right all along, you know. About the walls."

"The walls," said Uzziel, tugging at his beard nervously. He hadn't forgotten them, nor the threats he'd heard from within them.

"The walls, the ramp, the very roof," said Ecanus. "Plots everywhere, and only you could see them. And all that was needed for me to lay them bare was a little bit of pain."

"We've no home left for them to attack, and there

are more pressing matters," said Uzziel, though he didn't sound like he quite believed it.

"There can be no more pressing matter than our own safety," said Ecanus. "And the threats continue, believe you me. We should talk, you and I. About what the servants have been saying, and what's to be done about it."

Uzziel's pupils widened, and he started again to dwell on his fears, but only for a moment. "What matters now is what they've done already," he said. "And what's been done to our brothers in arms." He motioned to a group of angels behind him, who came forward with one of the bodies, laying it gently on the ground before them.

It had been charred, flesh burned and shrunken in on itself so that it resembled a blackened mummy. Its arms were withered and gnarled, clutching at its chest but not quite making it all the way there. The body had to have been from a male, judging by its size. His wings had no more feathers, and no more flaps. They were nothing but bone and a little skin, laid up loosely beside him. His face was a permanent sneer, lips pulled back and burnt away to reveal large, angry teeth, and hollow sockets where his eyes had been boiled from his skull.

"He was at the front of things," said Uzziel. "Closer than the rest, too close."

"More's the pity," said Ecanus. "We'll mourn the fallen, once their corpses have been accounted for. And give them the revenge they deserve."

"He's not to be mourned," said Uzziel. "Not just yet."

The body gave a quick twitch, and what was left of the wings poked up and down. A little rattle came from inside the mouth, coughing its way up from somewhere within, and the arms shook slightly and moved closer to his chest. It horrified even them, and stirred what little empathy was left within their calloused shells. The angels averted their eyes, unwilling to look at the thing before them directly, and they all stepped backwards involuntarily.

"There's still life in him," said Uzziel. "Curse the Maker for what he's done. All he can speak of is mercy, but here he's gone and left this one alive."

CHAPTER TWO

"TRAITOR," MUTTERED THANE. "FUCKIN' VICHY." He was in and out of consciousness, and Jana preferred it when he was out. He put her on edge, with all the fire and anger in him that spilled out at the mere sight of her. She'd been afraid to be alone with him at first, until she'd seen him try to get up. So much of him was broken that he could barely wriggle on the table, and he'd screamed in pain at the effort. Now he was passive, except for the cursing, and in any event he spent most of his time asleep.

"I don't know how your friends stand you," said Jana, wiping his forehead with a damp towel. He'd been afflicted by fevers since he'd been injured, and one of the few things they could do for him was to keep him cool.

"Fuck you," said Thane, before passing out again.

"I can't say I like you much, either," said Jana. "But until you can help yourself, you don't get to complain about who helps you."

How she'd become a nurse was a mystery to her, though everyone out here seemed to be called upon to perform the most eclectic collection of tasks, regardless of their actual competency at them. It all came back to Peter, in the end. She'd done so well with him over the last few weeks in the tower that the others thought she might have a knack for nurturing. Besides, there was nothing to clean here, and no food to prepare, and none of them much wanted her around.

It was what she'd done with Rhamiel that made them treat her so, and what he'd left in her belly. They all knew, now, and they were all afraid of it and uneasy around her. People fear the unknown, and can't help but conjure up all manner of fantasies of the horrible ways an unfamiliar situation could turn out. Something primal inside forces them to obsess over it, running through the worst possible scenarios and mulling over the things they'd do if it came to that. Not even a day had passed since the tower had fallen, and already they were at it, the other servants keeping their distance and whispering among themselves.

Maybe it was a valuable instinct to have, and maybe those grim simulations would help the ones who performed them survive someday if their fears ever came to pass. But for now, all they accomplished was to keep Jana apart, and keep her lonely, with only the injured for company.

There were hundreds of the servants there, hiding underground. They'd huddled aimlessly at the city's edges for almost an hour after the blast, without the slightest notion of what to do next. No one had planned this far, not even the ones who'd set it all in motion. The servants themselves were hopeless, a body without a head. They needed direction, or they'd have stood there for days, paralyzed by indecision.

Ultimately, it was one of the ones from outside who'd gotten them moving. Holt, the one who'd led the others there. Jana thought he must fancy himself an angel, the way he expected everyone to follow his commands. He'd told them to hide, to make their way into the city and then find their way out again once it got dark.

He'd gotten more than he'd bargained for. The servants didn't know the way, with the exception of some of the older ones. Even they were cautious, wary of leaping into the unknown without someone telling them where to land. Some had left in small groups to try to escape on their own, latching themselves onto anyone who thought they remembered their way through the city. Others simply sat there, refusing to move and immobilized by shock at seeing their home destroyed. And a large number of them had taken Holt at his word, following behind him as he tried to lead his own group to safety.

Jana was fortunate in that respect. Cassie and Sam had convinced him to bring her with them, though not without a good deal of cajoling. He'd had a long, spirited discussion with Faye, the only one who seemed to be genuinely sympathetic to Jana. Finally they'd agreed to let a few of the servants come with them, just to the city's edge. But the few had been followed by the many, and there had been no way to stop them short of violence.

They'd all ended up underground, hiding by torchlight in a subway station and waiting for things up above to calm down. It was crowded and dirty, decaying from years of abandonment. Being stuffed to the seams with servants didn't help the matter. They looked like the homeless they were, filthy from the ash outside and fighting for space anywhere it could be had. Jana had been blessed with access to an enclosed booth, a place for the sellers of tickets and sundries before the Fall. But she didn't have it to herself. It had been commandeered as a resting place for Thane, and she was expected to care for him in return.

"Is he up?" The voice came from behind her. It was Faye, come partly to check in on her friend, and partly to check in on her.

"Sometimes," said Jana. "He's hurt. More than Peter was. He needs more than I can give." She'd tried to treat him, as best as she could. He was stable, at least, and wasn't bleeding from the inside, not as far as they could tell. But he was in pain, and bones had been broken, and they wouldn't be able to do much about it until they got him out of the city.

"You're going to be fine," said Faye, feeling at Thane's forehead for his temperature. "We're going to get you some help, and you're going to be fine." He wasn't conscious, and couldn't hear, but then, he wasn't the one the words were meant to reassure.

"I know he's your friend," said Jana. "But he's not a very nice person. All I'm trying to do is help, and all he does is insult me."

"It's not you he's mad at," said Faye. "It's who he thinks you are. The people out here, they're not like the ones from the tower. Especially the ones who serve them. All of you are just afraid. The servants who live out here, the Vichies. They're mean. You don't understand how mean."

"I know everything about mean," said Jana. "Ask Peter what I know about mean."

"We've been talking," said Faye. "Holt and I. You know we can't stay here, don't you? Not for much longer."

"I have to find Rhamiel," said Jana. "Or one of his friends. I can't leave, not 'til I find him." Tears were welling in her eyes, and her cheeks were flush. She hadn't been happy to leave the tower, and she certainly wasn't happy as a refugee. She'd thought she'd finally be safe, living with someone who cared for her and had the power to protect her. Now her haven was gone, and he was off who knew where.

"He'll be fine," said Faye. "I've been talking to your friends. They tell me he wasn't there. He was away on his own business, and he wasn't there."

"He was trying to find the man who scarred him," said Jana. "The man who attacked him. He was trying to punish him for it."

Faye just looked at her, taking her in, trying to read what Jana knew and what she was thinking. Finally she spoke. "He wouldn't want you here," she said. "He'd want you to leave, to come with us. He'd want you to get out of the city. It's dangerous. His friends are dangerous. Angry. They can't tell one of us from another. It's not pretty up there. We've found bodies. And you're not the only one you have to keep safe anymore."

They both looked at Jana's stomach, and then looked back at one another.

"Will I be able to come back?" asked Jana. "I have

to. When it's over, and they stop fighting, can I come back?" Her hands clutched at her belly, and she started to sniffle, until Faye interrupted her with a shush.

"You can go anywhere you want when the fighting stops," said Faye. "Your angel might even find you before then. If he's one of the good ones, he won't leave you out here alone."

"He won't," said Jana. "He'll find me."

"I know he will," said Faye. "I know he's fine. Now you just stay in here, and keep Thane company for a few more hours. We'll come get you when it's time."

"I can help everyone get ready," said Jana. "I can help with Peter. You don't have long, and you'll need to get everyone prepared. They just don't know what to do with themselves without the angels to tell them." She started towards the door to the booth, but Faye barred the way.

"Jana," said Faye. "They're not coming. None of them even know. We're leaving, just a few of us, to go to the mainland and find a real doctor. And everyone else is going to have to stay behind."

CHAPTER THREE

"I KNOW WHO IT IS," SAID Ecanus. "I can tell, from the armor he wears."

They'd tried to make the wounded angel comfortable, but there was little they could do. He couldn't see them, and he couldn't hear them, and all he seemed to be able to do was twitch and cough. They'd given him some water, but he started to choke, and in the end they all felt it best to let him be and keep their distance. Brotherhood was one thing, but it had its limits, and the sight of him was unsettling. He was a vision of what they could have been, if they'd flown a little faster, and it gave them shivers if they allowed themselves to think on the matter for very long.

"You see it, the little bits of silver around the edges," said Ecanus. He ran his finger along what was left of the angel's armor, a battered chunk of melted metal that was now one with its bearer's flesh. "They're melted to a trickle, now, but I know them. And the insignia, just there, of the ladder. Only a miracle worker would wear it."

"Zuphias," said Uzziel, shaking his head. "He was

the first to believe me, and the first to defend his home. I never ranked him among the real warriors, not with his softness and snobbery. But he was one of us, when things mattered, and now he's been reduced to this."

"This is why we must not delay in killing the ones who caused it," said Ecanus. "And if we entertain ourselves in the process, well, it's no sin to find pleasure in your work."

"You shall come with us," said Uzziel. "You shall do your duty, and you shall hunt for the fallen. The servants will answer for their crimes. Believe me, they will answer. But on another day."

"I thought we were done with dictators," said Ecanus. "The very reason for our rebellion was so we could do as we please."

"Then you may do as you please alone," said Uzziel. "None of us deserve the fate of … that." He looked at Zuphias, and looked away just as quickly. "And any who would leave one of us in such a state is no brother of mine."

"Oh, spare us the melodrama," said Ecanus. "Zuphias was no brother to any of us." He squatted down next to Zuphias, wings out and smile broad. There was no sorrow in him for the thing before him, only schadenfreude, and he didn't even attempt to hide it.

"He thought himself better than you, and better than me," said Ecanus. "He was so very high, back when there was a tower. Perched above us all, sniffing his wine and sniffing at us. And now where is he? Lying in the dirt, with no tongue to sing his own praises, and no eyes to take offense at the sight of those below him." Ecanus bent low towards Zuphias's burnt skull, smirking as his jaw ground the air in helpless clacks. He leaned in towards his ear, and spoke to him in an exaggerated whisper. "Do you still hear me, dear Zuphias? I know my words would wound you, if you weren't all wound already."

"Show him respect," said one of Uzziel's warriors. "He was turned to this, in defense of his home. He deserves honor, not opprobrium."

"I'll show him all the respect he's due," said Ecanus. "He was quite fond of droning on about the scars of others, though we too acquired them in defense of our liberties. You were ever the one to insist on treating the scarred as the scum of the Seraphim, weren't you, Zuphias? And now you're a stub of your former self, a burnt offering at the altar of the Maker. Zuphias would want us to mock him so, to do justice to the memory of who he was. He'd tell you so himself, if he weren't indisposed."

Zuphias gave no response other than to jerk his wings, though whether he had heard any of it, none of them could tell. Finally it was too much for Uzziel, who began to roar. "Put a tarp above him, and preserve some of his dignity! And you, Ecanus! It's time we return to our digging. Stay if you please, or come if you've any honor."

"I have none, and so I shall be about my business," said Ecanus. "Honor is nothing but pride in one's own moral pompousness. It's the sort of self-indulgent thing that Zuphias here would truck in, but it's not for the likes of me. I'll be on about my interrogation of the servants instead. I'll be sure to let you know the results, and what dangers you've ignored to root around in the dirt for the remains of fools."

With that, he took to the skies, laughing all the while. The others didn't pursue him. There would have been little point; the chain of command was precarious as it was, and the return to some semblance of military discipline was an artifact of the crisis at hand. It was hard enough keeping them together to complete the search, and it was easier for Uzziel to ignore the challenge to his authority, such as it was. He gave a harumph, beckoned to his soldiers, and took to the skies himself.

He led them to the epicenter, the shattered ruins of their former home. Chunks of it remained roughly intact, though they'd been toppled on their side as the tower had broken apart and collapsed into itself. They'd searched the larger sections first, as the most likely places to find survivors. But all they'd found there were bodies, of servant and angel alike. The heat of the blast had been conducted through the tower's metallic frame, and anyone they'd recovered had been badly burnt. Piles of human corpses were lumped next to each section, and a few of the angels with more morbid inclinations had taken over the responsibility of examining the bodies to determine which were angels to be buried, and which were humans to be left to the elements.

"Spread outwards, and poke around the periphery," said Uzziel. He directed them hither and thither, bidding one to dig through a pile of slag, and ordering another to lift hunks of metal to see what lay beneath. Still others he instructed to circle the skies and scan the ground for movement, going lower and lower as they went. Ash swirled around them all, and they couldn't see clearly for more than a few yards in front of themselves. It made precise coordination an impossible chore, and kept them uncertain as to exactly where they'd already searched. Uzziel's paranoia didn't help things. He ordered checks, and then re-checks, scouring the same areas over and over to try to satisfy himself that nothing had been missed.

The searches produced nothing, though many were still unaccounted for. Uzziel's frustration mounted, and finally he decided to act for himself where others had failed. He began flying over the wreckage, looping in a gyre above it and darting through the clouds of dirt that stormed around him. His area of inspection grew wider and wider, touching the bounds of what was left of the city. It all seemed fruitless. He'd see movement below him, and wings, but each time he would swoop down only to find one of his warriors going about their orders.

He'd almost given up, when a glint of something caught his eye from below. He could see it shining through clumps of concrete, strewn around where one of the old buildings had once stood. It could have been nothing, and odds were he'd be chasing wild geese were he to investigate. But Uzziel was prone to assigning meaning and motive even where none could be found, and his feverish imaginings began at once. He descended, losing sight of the glimmer as dust and wind battered his eyes, and then catching it again as he circled.

He lit down next to a pile of rocks and soot. He couldn't tell what it was he'd seen, but it had to be in there, somewhere. And so he dug, tearing at the edges of the pile and tossing pieces of rubble behind him. Dust devils swirled around him as he worked, and added ash even as he pulled handfuls of it away. Then he saw it again.

The light was dim, under the clouds of dust, but when it caught it the thing seemed to glow. Uzziel flapped his wings, lifting himself up and landing directly above it. He scraped at the dirt, and then saw it. The lion, melted into the armor it had adorned, its carefully molded face now dissolved into a golden mush. He worked furiously, then, tossing aside rubble and stones until he'd revealed what was lying before him: Rhamiel, motionless and limp, cloaked in a mask of soot and grime and covered in the rocks that had buried him.

CHAPTER FOUR

THEY WAITED FOR THE SERVANTS to fall asleep, before they began to sneak away. The refugees were clustered together, laying on the floor of the station in groups, a mass of sad, homeless souls lingering there for lack of any other place to be. They'd been told this was the way to salvation and to safety, if only they'd follow. And now they were about to be left behind.

"Get him on the stretcher," said Holt, his voice a whisper. They'd found a solid sheet of metal, the remnants of an old bench, and it was serviceable enough. It would hold Thane, so long as they could keep their hold on it.

He moaned as they lifted him, and began spitting out scattered bursts of profanity. They tried to go more slowly, and more gently, lest the noise draw the attention of those they were about to abandon. Holt had his shoulders, and Faye and Cassie his legs, while Jana stood to the side in silence.

"Jana," said Holt. "We'll carry him. You lead the way. But stay quiet, and stay slow. We have to go, but we can't move fast and still keep him balanced."

She didn't like it, but she did as she was told. She took up a torch and weaved them through a maze of sleeping servants, lying on the floor and getting some well-needed rest. Most were fast asleep, exhausted from the trauma of losing their home. A few had lost more, and couldn't help but keep their own vigil through the night. They passed a boy and a girl, not more than six years old, clutching each other in the dark and sobbing softly together. They'd lost someone dear, though who it was none could tell. Family, lovers, and friends alike had stayed behind, according to their own sensibilities. It was all a matter of what they feared most: death if the rumors of the outsiders were true, the wrath of the angels if they were discovered as they fled, or the prospect of living under their thumbs forever if they stayed.

Some of the servants stirred as they passed, looking up and following the glow of the torch as it wound its way between them. Holt would have had them creep away in the darkness if they could have, but they would have been sure to trip over someone along the way. As it was, they were conspicuous, but only to the few who were awake.

"Take my spot," said Cassie, as they approached the stairway leading out of the subway station. "Hand me the torch." Jana complied, and eased her hands under the makeshift stretcher to relieve Cassie of her portion of the burden.

Cassie turned back towards the station, as some of the servants who'd been roused from their sleep were starting to stand and edge closer. "Now go on," she said. "Careful up the stairs."

"You're not coming?" said Jana. She was frightened, and more than a little suspicious. She didn't know these strangers she was being sloughed off onto, not well. She didn't particularly trust Cassie anymore, either, but at least she was a familiar face.

"Someone has to help the rest of them," said Cassie. "Someone has to help Peter, and someone has to lead these people somewhere else. I did this to all of them. I opened the door and let in the outside, and now here they are. It wasn't any way to live, how we were. You'll understand that once you're out there and free. What we had wasn't a life at all. But they still deserve a chance, and they won't find their way out of here on their own."

"Let them come with us," said Jana. "Let's bring them along."

"We can't," said Faye. "We have to move fast, or he's not going to make it. He'll just get worse without medical attention. And you might need it, too."

"Me?" said Jana, dumbfounded. "There isn't anything wrong with me."

"Just to be safe," said Faye. "There's nothing wrong, but we just want to be safe. Have you seen a pregnancy, where you're from?"

"No," said Jana. They hadn't been very common, not with the servers. There weren't any places to sneak off to and do the deed, and many of them had grown up together and felt like family, too familiar to ever feel the tug of attraction. Sometimes things still happened, on occasion, but none of the girls had ever been allowed to stay. The kitchens weren't a place to raise children, but where they ended up, none of the others knew.

"Well, where we come from, you have to see a doctor," said Faye. "Everyone does. It doesn't mean anything's wrong, it's just to make things easier. More comfortable."

"Okay," said Jana. She didn't trust them, not really, and she wasn't entirely sure what a doctor did. But she wasn't entirely sure how pregnancies worked, either. She'd had no formal education, and certainly not on those matters. What little she knew came from adolescent whisperings, from sources with little more knowledge than she had. She knew the outlines, but not the details, and she didn't want to try to handle things on her own.

"Well go, then," said Cassie. "Get moving. And good luck." The ones who'd noticed them were starting to wake others, and starting to cluster together. The servants were working up the courage to approach and ask what was going on, and if they waited much longer, they wouldn't be leaving on their own. Cassie turned, went towards the nearest group, and began giving them her best and most reasonable explanation for the sudden exit. The rest of them started up the stairs, carefully balancing Thane as they went.

The city was dark, lit only by the moon. They were close to the water, and close to where they needed to go. Holt had made sure of that. Carrying the wounded was slow, and it would have been better to do it underground. But the subway tunnels wouldn't lead them all the way out, so they'd have to make the last dash to the ferryman under the open skies. He'd be there, if all went well. He'd promised to be near the shores each night, for at least a week after they went in. But promises are an easy thing to make, and an easier thing to break. The world was chaos now, and whether he wanted to be embroiled in their affairs was ultimately up to him.

They walked next to the buildings, slowly, watching the skies as they went. Angels tended to sleep at night, but it was just a tendency. The events of the last day had wired everyone up with excitement, and they had no reason to expect the angels would experience things any differently. So they crept quietly, and tried their best to keep from jostling Thane.

They finally saw the shore in the distance, and they quickened their pace. When they reached the water's edge, there was no ferryman. But nautical navigation had gone from art to science, and back again. They knew the general area he was supposed to be in, but it was dusty and dark, and they had no better option than hope. So they sat Thane down, and Holt began to run up and down the coast, trying his best to spot the boat.

Jana was in awe, staring out at the water. She'd never seen so much before, one giant puddle splashing back and forth on its own without anyone even touching it. She stood watching it, working up the courage to get closer. "Go on," said Faye, and after a little hesitation, she did.

Her feet sank into the dirt, the first unsteady ground she could remember stepping on. It scared her, but the soil managed to hold her weight, and so she pressed ahead. She felt the water lapping at her toes, and jumped away in fright. Faye's laughter from behind her steeled her courage, or at least her determination to keep going. She went in up to her knees, and cupped a few sips in her hands to drink before spitting it out at the briny taste. To her the place was a wonder, one she couldn't get enough of, even if others would have thought it a drab urban nowhere.

It took almost half an hour before Holt began waving wildly, signalling out into the sea. He'd found the ferryman, and grabbed his attention, and was guiding him in towards land. He made his way back to them, sitting there on the beach, and reached down for his end of the stretcher.

"Let's go," said Holt. "Jana, you're going to meet one of our friends. He's a little rough, but don't let him fool you. He's good at heart, and he's going to get us out of here." They picked up Thane, and started him towards the shore as the ferryman brought in his boat. They were nearly there, before they heard the clamor behind them.

Cassie's efforts to take the reins hadn't gone well, not from the look of things. A trickle of servants moved towards them from the city, yelling at them to wait, and as more and more of them emerged it grew to a mob. They were scared, and desperate, and the little boat would never hold them all.

"Double-time it," said Holt. "Let's go, let's go." They waded into the water as the ferryman eased his boat into the shallows. Jana almost lost her footing in the mud, and for a terrifying moment they all thought that Thane would be dumped into the sea. But she steadied herself, and the ferryman got closer, and after a bit of effort they managed to lift him into the boat.

The servants were sprinting down the beach, and as the first of the mob approached the water they could hear their cries. "Don't leave us!" yelled some. "We're coming with you!" yelled others. The ones at the front thought they were sure to make it; the ones just behind them grew more aggressive with each other as they saw their own chances slipping away. Fearful that they'd lose a spot in the boat, they pushed each other aside as they ran, knocking over their competitors as they worked themselves into a frenzy at the prospect of an escape.

The boat had been boarded and had pushed away before the first of the servants made it into the water, splashing their way towards it as they begged and pleaded to be let inside, or offered to just swim along.

"Only you," said the ferryman.

"Only us," said Holt.

The ferryman started to row, but it didn't stop the servants from following. Some of them turned back to land once the boat started to move out into the sea, just as fearful of the water as Jana had been. Only the older ones knew how to swim; the rest had no reason to have ever learned. But then a roar came up from the crowd behind them as it massed near the shore, and everyone pressed into the water all at once.

It was hard to tell through the darkness what had set them off, until the screaming started, and the air began to whoosh with the beating of wings.

CHAPTER FIVE

"**I**S HE ALIVE?" SAID UZZIEL, as one of his lieutenants conducted an inspection of their fallen comrade. "He hasn't moved an iota, not since I found him."

"He certainly isn't moving," said the lieutenant. "He must have been close to the blast, very close."

The lieutenant had been a healer before the Fall, wandering the Earth to help the lame to walk and prod the sick to health. It was thankless work. None of his patients had ever even known he was there, and all the credit went to others, humans blundering over the ailing with their leeches or their pills. Such remedies didn't help much, not in the cases he took. But they were something the patient could see, and something their human doctors could explain. And so he'd toiled unknown for centuries, until the time finally came when it was fellow angels who needed his aid.

"The important thing is whether he's alive," said Uzziel. "And whether he can recover."

The prospects on that front looked grim, if one was

to go by appearances. Rhamiel's face was covered in dirt, and he would have been unrecognizable if it hadn't been for his armor. He didn't move, and didn't seem to breathe, and his skin was clammy to the touch. His limbs drooped, and nothing stirred inside as far as any of them could tell.

"Only just," said the lieutenant, opening Rhamiel's mouth and pressing his head beside it for a listen. "He's alive, but only just. The hellfire, it's a scourge to any in its path. The energy is too much, the havoc of creation unleashed and uncontrolled. It's weakened him, almost to the point of passing. He likely won't survive much longer, if nothing else is done."

"Something must be done," said Uzziel. "Something must be done about all of the wounded, no matter how distasteful it may be."

"Then we must take him to the camp," said the lieutenant, "and then take him to where he may be helped."

Uzziel himself heaved Rhamiel over his shoulder, and they all began to fly. They made haste to their destination, moving through the dust storms as if pursued by some demonic foe, and when they arrived they laid him down among the ones who were wounded and the ones who were merely pretending to be.

The pretenders suddenly found their strength at the commotion, hovering around and above to watch. The lieutenant began to prepare a salve of foul-smelling glop, one he insisted would awaken his patient. It certainly awakened the senses of the others, who turned their noses away in disgust as he mixed goo with powders and a sprinkling of water. Once done, he'd concocted a lime green poultice which he liberally applied beneath Rhamiel's nostrils.

The medicine worked its magic almost at once. A few seconds in, and the life had returned to him, though it came at the price of a violent coughing fit. "Hold him down!" yelled the lieutenant, and the nearby angels obliged. Rhamiel thrashed and kicked, shouting things that sounded like words but weren't quite fully formed, and he knocked more than one of the well-meaning away as they tried to contain his violent outburst. He sent up puffs of ash from his lungs, hacking them out as he slowly regained himself. Finally he managed to sputter out something the others could understand.

"Where am I?" said Rhamiel. He tried to rise, and nearly tipped over as the angels around him lunged forward, grabbing his shoulders to steady him and keep him standing.

"The outskirts of the tower," said Uzziel, looking in the distance at the ruins of their former home. "It's gone, all that we built. All that we had, laid waste by those without the sense to serve."

"Where is she?" said Rhamiel.

"Nefta is dead, we think," said Uzziel. "Identifying the bodies precisely is an arduous task, and mostly guesswork. They're in a poor state, if they were in the tower."

"He means the servant girl," said the lieutenant, his wings primming up behind him at the thought. "The one from the party."

Faces all around tightened into suspicion. Many of

them had seen her, and seen how Rhamiel had looked at her. Cavorting with one of them had been an indiscretion even before, something to be tolerated in the privileged, but barely. Now it amounted to something closer to a treason, and the angels expected more from their leaders.

"Most of them are dead as well," said Uzziel, bristling at the question. "Certainly all of the loyal ones are. If she was loyal and true, she stayed and died a noble death, one to be commended. If disloyal, then her whereabouts are of no concern, unless you plan another Hunt. There are traitors scrabbling about in the ruins of their old city, ripe for a harvest once our rescues are concluded."

"And Isda?" said Rhamiel. "I'd speak to him, if he made it."

He showed a hint of pain, buried beneath the layers of soot and his own efforts to mask it. But the others could still see, and it was beginning to agitate them. They were tensing their wings, and complaining amongst themselves, though not quite so loudly that he could hear.

"Isda was a victim of the servants' duplicity," said Uzziel. "Him, we could identify with certainty, owing to his girth. The entire tower came crashing down upon him. None of us could have survived it."

"I must look," said Rhamiel. "I must begin a search." He spread his wings, and pulled himself away from those keeping him in balance. He immediately started to stumble, though not in the direction of the tower.

"Such affection for Isda," came unhappy mutterings from the crowd. "I never knew them to be so close." Titters of laughter surrounded Rhamiel as he struggled to find his bearing, and then they turned to grumbles. "He'd search for a servant before one of his brothers," came one. "His mind must be melted, along with his armor," came another.

His mind was hazy, to be sure, for he fell to the ground in a bout of dizziness almost as soon as he'd separated himself from the ones who'd been holding him up. The lieutenant returned to his side, and motioned for the others to restrain him.

"We must free him to breathe, and keep him idle," said the lieutenant, as he pulled out a small knife and sawed at the straps supporting what was left of Rhamiel's armor. They came away easily, having been weakened by the blast, but the armor itself did not. The lieutenant pulled at it, slowly, carefully removing it from the skin it had been meant to protect. Finally it came off, but what lay beneath the melted gold produced a gasp from all around.

Rhamiel was no longer the only one of them without scars. His face had survived, but the rest was a different story. The blast itself hadn't scathed him, but his armor had been heated until it had branded him, ending the perfection his physique had once displayed.

A human might not have thought so, according to human tastes. A human might even have admired it. It was a scar, to be sure, but with a distinctive shape: the lion's head of the creature that had once adorned his armor. Some might have considered it decorative, a primitive tattoo of the sort tribes had long employed before they'd learned to wield ink instead. A human certainly wouldn't have compared it to the burns that covered the faces of the rest of them. But the angels were no humans, and had nothing but disgust for decorations of the skin.

"He's been disfigured," they whispered. "He can hide it all he likes beneath his clothes, but he's worse than any of us, now." Perhaps he was and perhaps he wasn't, but the angels were always ready to make excuses to tear apart those above them. Their thoughts were devoted to their relative positions, and they'd spent years thinking of little else. They coveted what he had, and hated where they were, and they would be only too happy to pull him down below them if it would free up a little more space at the top.

Rhamiel started to protest, and started to push himself up to confront them. But weakness overcame him, and he collapsed backward into a beaten heap of feathers.

"He won't last, you know," said the lieutenant. "Not with what I have here, he won't."

"Then we mustn't stay here," said Uzziel. "We must move him, and Zuphias, and all of the rest. It fills me with disgust, to involve the others in our affairs. But we are lost, and we are scattered, and we have no other choice. We must take them to the Cherubim."

CHAPTER SIX

IT ONLY TOOK AN INSTANT, and the entire shore was overwhelmed with panic. The servants had been aggressive, but they'd also been focused on whether they'd win their race with one another. Now they were running amok, governed no longer by reason but by terror. The lower parts of their brains had taken over, leaving them hostage to their instincts. The result was anarchy, a frightened mob breaking against the water and willing to do whatever might get them away.

At first all they could hear in the boat were screams, piercing the darkness. They came from the back of the crowd, forcing the rest forward to avoid their source. Then came the laughter, and with it recognition.

"Ecanus," said Jana. "Let's go. Please go. Please."

"You're fine," said Faye, putting a hand on her shoulder and trying to calm her nerves. "You're going to be fine."

"We're not fine," said Jana. "You don't know him. None of us are going to be fine."

"Then punch it," said Holt, nodding to the ferryman

as they both paddled. "I'm less worried about angels, and more worried about them."

The servants were thrashing through the water, clumsily making their way to the boat despite their lack of swimming skill. The ferryman was doing his damnedest to outpace them, but though he had the oars, they had the incentive. The only saving grace was that the crabs kept pulling back anyone who tried to leave the bucket. Hands would grasp at the boat from out of the water, just touching its sides, only to be dragged into the darkness by someone else behind them.

They saw something on the beach, blinking on and off like a lightning bug. They didn't recognize it at first, but as the screams moved along with it, they recognized it for what it was: a flaming knife, scything through the crowds around its bearer, disappearing as it went into them and reappearing as it came out. The laughter grew louder, more manic, and soon they could see him clearly as he stood at the edge of the shore, wings stretching out behind him and fire tickling the air before him. They stopped rowing, and all of them ducked down low into the boat. They hadn't yet distanced themselves from land, and while it was dark, they wouldn't be hard to spot if the angel looked closely enough.

"We shall play a game," he said loudly, and Jana shuddered and whimpered as they watched him grab hold of a man and woman who'd stumbled before him as they fled.

"I've recovered my fondness for worship," said Ecanus, "and it's been so long since I honored the Maker. I grow convinced we should honor him in our play, as well as in our labor. I call this 'Forty Days and Forty Nights.'"

They could hear him even in the distance, practically shouting the words. He hadn't seen them, bobbing in the darkness among the throng of swimmers, but he knew a crowd was listening, and he wanted them all to hear.

"Now you shall play as Noah," said Ecanus to the man, "and I shall play as the flood." Then he thrust the man's head beneath the waves, holding him under as he waved his arms in a fury of splashing and desperation.

"Count, dear," said Ecanus to the woman. "A second for a day, and a second for a night." She couldn't seem to get herself going, and just sat there in shock, trying to avoid his glare as he held her by the throat.

"Be quick about it, and he might survive," said Ecanus. "Tarry, and he'll drown with the rest of the sinners." That broke the dam, and the woman began counting out the seconds as she'd been told. She was muffled at first, and too quiet for them to hear. But he growled something to her under his breath and she grew louder, counting upwards and outwards for the benefit of all around.

"Fuck it," said Holt, sitting up in the boat and picking up his set of oars. "Let's go. Before this asshole comes looking for someone else to toy with." He and the ferryman began pushing against the waves, as hard as they could, while Ecanus continued on with his merriment.

The count reached eighty, finally, and the woman looked up at Ecanus with pleas in her eyes and on her lips. "Please let us go," she said. "Please stop." It didn't matter. Ecanus continued to hold the man's head beneath the water, letting him grow quieter and weaker. The fight in him had been reduced to a lethargic flopping, and the woman was left to watch helplessly as his energy faded.

"I can't very well stop," said Ecanus. "I love it so. The looks on your faces, the fear. It's a terrible thing, thinking your place in the universe is at the bottom. But it's all relative, in the end. There's always someone below you, if only one knows where to look. There's such joy in knowing that, and in making sure everyone else does, too. Wouldn't you agree?"

"Please let us go," said the woman.

"I shall," said Ecanus. "I shall, once the game is done. But I'm afraid we've both made an error, a terrible one. We've broken the rules."

"I counted it right," said the woman. "Please."

"You did, you did," said Ecanus. His expression turned to mock sadness, and he gave the woman a pat on the head with one hand even as he kept the man submerged with the other. "It's an error of my own making, I'm sad to say. We must follow the will of the Maker, to do him any honor. And he was very clear. There were to be two of every animal. Including man."

She didn't have time to respond before he'd shoved her in as well, renewing the splashes even as the man beside her went still. Ecanus kept the count himself this time, loudly and slowly, booming the numbers out into the night for all to hear.

While he busied himself with his entertainments, the boat was moving further and further from the shore. But along with it came a chain of swimmers, clasping at each other and linking their limbs with a few who'd managed to grab hold of the boat itself. It was slowing the escape to a crawl, and both Holt and the ferryman were turning sweaty and red with the effort of dragging them all along.

"Let go," said Holt, moving to the rear and confronting the swimmers. They cried out their pleas again and again, begging for him to help them escape, and they all tightened their grips as he grew nearer.

"They'll die if we don't take them," said Jana. "They'll drown, or he'll kill them. You can't just let them die."

Holt looked at her, and looked at Ecanus, and looked at all the rest. After a pause, he spoke, softly. "Dax died, because I sent him up. Thane might die, because I sent him, too. And neither one of them had to. We could have just gone in, and done it quietly, and we'd all have gotten out before anyone knew. But we tried to save them all, and where'd we end up? Try to save everyone, and everyone dies."

"It's not your fault," said Faye. "You can't blame yourself. It's not anyone's fault. Dax knew what he was doing. He knew, he knew what was going to happen."

"But it didn't have to happen," said Holt. "He only had to do it because of the choices I made. I chose to try to evacuate them. I chose the risk he died over, because I didn't want to just do good, I wanted perfection. And I'm not going to sacrifice the good to the perfect ever again." His hand went to his side, and it came back with his taser. He rolled it over in his hand, weighed the burdens he'd have to live with, and then he chose again.

He jammed it into the hands that were clasped to the boat, pumping electricity into the swimmers who'd thought they'd found a refuge. It was a risky business. Each shock brought a flash of light, and yelps of pain, and either one could have given them all away. But Ecanus was occupied, and after a few zaps all Holt had to do was brandish the taser and the rest of the swimmers let go in fear.

The ferryman began to build up distance, and both shore and swimmers faded away behind them. As they escaped, they could still hear the counting echoing through the darkness, until it turned to screams mixed with mad laughter, and finally to nothing at all.

CHAPTER SEVEN

T HE PLACE HAD ONCE BEEN called Toronto. It had been a fine location for a city when it was founded, and it was its fine location that had gotten it destroyed. What the powerful want, they take, if it's in the hands of the weak. And no one there could have defended the city against those who came to covet it.

The skies were still and clean, as Uzziel led his flock towards the structure that abutted the coastline where a city once sat. They couldn't see much of it; the bulk of the thing that had replaced it was buried underground, with only a few metallic domes poking up to the surface. They surrounded a gaping hole, more than a mile wide, lined with spirals of silver curving down into a small, black dot of an entrance at the center.

They called it the Nest. The nickname had spread from the servants to the Seraphim, whose fondness for tweaking its residents had made them delighted to adopt it for themselves. Some said the name stemmed from its resemblance to the nest of a bird. It looked like one, in a way, with ridges of metal guarding the sloping plain of silver that drained its way into the entrance. Others attributed it to the lifestyle of the residents, who burrowed beneath the earth like ants and left their home only for scavenging. In either event, it was the closest clustering of angels, and provided the best prospects for medical attention for the wounded.

They landed at the perimeter, waiting for someone to come out to greet them. "They'll be watching us, if not with eyes of their own," said Uzziel, and he was right. Little dots moved around the ground at their feet, dark against the waves of light reflected from the metal surrounding them. None of the dots came close enough for them to get a good look, but some of the angels were interested enough themselves to approach for a peek.

What they saw were insects, or parts of them. The Cherubim had been meddling with them, and none had been left as the Maker had created them. They'd been fused with tiny bits of machinery, trading legs for clockwork contraptions or wings for glowing pieces of fabric. None of them looked quite like the others, and there was no consistency to their design. They looked as if someone had simply hacked off pieces of the originals, replacing them with a diverse array of mechanical implements salvaged from some celestial junkyard. They buzzed or crawled around the angels, keeping their distance and keeping watch.

"I know you listen," said Uzziel loudly, to no one in particular. "I know you hear. Now show yourselves, and speak to us in person. We come not to quarrel, but for aid, and there are those among us who need it at once."

The only response was silence, for a time. The insects

stood guard, but didn't approach. The angels waited impatiently and tended to the wounded as best they could. Finally there was a cranking noise, emanating from the entrance, and something rose to greet the visitors.

There were three of them, standing on a platform that slowly approached the surface from down below. The angels recognized them at once, but no human would have. The place of the cherub in human mythology had long ago descended to farce. They'd come to be depicted as children before the Fall, and indeed they were small, not more than half the size of a normal adult. But they bore no arrows, and stole no hearts, and there was no cuteness or cuddliness about them.

They were scarred in places, just like the others, but it was their faces that were the most unsettling. They changed, according to the angle at which one was looking at them, dissolving into a shimmering mass of colors as they realigned into something else depending on how the light hit them. One moment they would appear human, but for their wings. The next their face would be an unrecognizable rainbow blob, only to glisten and reappear as the head of an eagle, or a lion, or an ox. And if one were to stare too closely, it all turned to a glowing blur, perched atop their squat little bodies and fizzling with strange energies.

"Zephon," said Uzziel, as the first of the three walked towards them. He was bigger than the others, though that was a battle of inches which had no victors. His face was cold and without expression, when you could see it. His human side was the best looking of the four; the others were scarred extensively, with large patches of missing fur or feathers. Likely he'd protected the one he favored most as best he could, during his fall. He wore a small brown loincloth and little else, with no concern for the blotches and blisters from the Fall that it exposed.

"What brings our erstwhile masters to this place?" said Zephon. "We heard you've had a second fall from grace."

It was an odd sound, to hear them talk, if it could be called talking at all. They didn't so much speak as they chanted, releasing the words in short bursts that droned out in a mechanical monotone. There was no emphasis and no emotion, and one sentence sounded just the same as the last. The Seraphim were used to it, but it made the intentions of the cherubs uniquely difficult for outsiders to discern. Their every utterance was methodical, and they were quite partial to verse. The mechanics of it fascinated them, as did its orderly rules, and they composed it on the fly in lieu of the unstructured speech of those they considered beneath the practice.

"We've been attacked, and by men, no less," said Uzziel. He gestured towards the dozens of wounded angels lying on the metal behind him, some wailing, some shaking, and some not moving at all. "An act of infamy, done under cover of darkness when the best of our warriors were away. Many have died, and many more will, if left untreated."

Zephon responded only with a grunt. "And so our betters drop their chins at last, and stoop to dealing with a lesser caste. But why should those who've always had to serve, pay heed to cries from one who has such nerve?"

"An attack on one is an attack on all," said Uzziel.

"Even now, men plot against us. Soon, they shall plot against the Cherubim as well. And the death of a seraph is no small matter. Our tower has fallen, but others yet stand. What will the rest of the Seraphim do, if they hear that our injured were turned away at your doorstep?"

"No son of Adam can approach our home," said Zephon. "We've planted spies along this field of chrome. And what of seraphs, hiding in the clouds, with so few triumphs, yet so very proud? So little effort it would take to crush, those weakened by a life so very lush. Yet we're your betters, from our constant toil; we'll keep your friends tied to this mortal coil. Now come along, and come beneath the earth; we bid you welcome to our humble hearth."

Zephon turned, without awaiting reply or other pleasantries, and walked back to the platform with the other cherubs. There they stood, staring blankly at their visitors, until the hint was taken and Uzziel ordered his party to the platform as well. They carried the wounded onto it, as gears below began to grind and they all slowly descended into the darkness beyond.

CHAPTER EIGHT

HE'LL LIVE. AS LONG AS you make sure he gets some rest, he'll live. We set all the bones, and patched everything up. But he'll probably be feeling the aches from this one until the end of his days." The surgeon pulled off his gloves with a loud snap, and left them waiting there, outside what currently passed for an operating room. It had been a classroom before, but now the school was a hospital, if only a few times a month.

The ferryman had shown them pity, though none of them had believed he had it in him. Likely it was because they'd be his last customers for some time. The city was all danger now, and while there were plenty who cared to leave it, they had nothing to trade and had shown no qualms about attempting to ride for free. He wasn't coming back, he said, and so he'd take them as far as they needed to go. He made Holt do most of the work, but fair's fair, and it got them to the mainland, down the coast and within a few miles of where they knew they'd find help.

They'd had to wait another day for the hospital to arrive, even after they'd made their way to where it was supposed to be. It was all mobile now, a roving caravan of modern gypsies who'd pledged the Hippocratic Oath. Some were doctors, and some were nurses, and some just claimed to be. But they had enough expertise to treat most anything, and it was a valuable enough service that even the Vichies normally let them alone. They moved from place to place, healing for their supper and trying to avoid the attentions of angels who had no need for their skills and no need for them.

Eventually the doctors came, the surgery started, and so did the waiting. They'd sat there on a bench in the hallway for hours. Holt had just slept, exhausted, and Faye had been dying of boredom. Only Jana was enjoying herself, digging through the lockers in awe of the things she found left inside them. There were still books, hundreds of them, about subjects she'd never even heard of. There were pictures of students who'd once spent much of their lives there, left haunting the inside of the only space in the building that had truly been all their own. There were clothes, and binders filled with scrawled notes and drawings, and even a few toys. They were trash to the rest, but marvels to her, a treasure trove from times past and a life she could have lived herself had history taken a different path.

"Can we see him?" said Faye to one of the nurses passing by, a short woman in blue scrubs with hard lines on her forehead from years of worrying over the angels' victims.

"No," said the nurse. "You can't see him, yet. But we're ready to see her."

It sent chills down Jana's spine. She'd known the moment would come, eventually, but she'd preferred not to think of it. She didn't want to be poked at, or sliced to pieces and stitched back together. She'd seen the instruments after the doctors were done with Thane. They'd gone in silver, and come out red, sticky with blood and gauze and things that were meant to stay inside you. She didn't want any part of that, but she didn't seem to have any choice.

"It's okay, dear," said the nurse. "We're just going to talk, and do a little ultrasound."

Her expression was blank and confused, and so the nurse tried again. "It doesn't hurt. We just rub some gel on your tummy, and then you'll see the baby. Do you want to see the baby?"

"I suppose," said Jana hesitantly. In truth, she still didn't understand, but she put on a brave face and pretended to. She wasn't even certain she knew what a baby looked like. She knew they were small, and knew they'd have to be taken care of. She thought there might have been one, somewhere in all the magazines she'd read, but then, maybe it had been an older child. As for how they would see inside her, she hadn't an inkling.

"Come here, darling," said the nurse, and took her by the hand. She led her into another of the classrooms, a few doors down and past a pile of old broken school desks. Faye followed, and Holt was wise enough to know it wasn't his place. Inside was a machine, connected to a monitor and buzzing with electricity. Extension cords snaked around the room and out into the hallway, linked up with portable generators some distance away. Jana wasn't sure what it was, or what it would do. It was covered in knobs and buttons, and after seating her on the top of a student's desk, the nurse began to push away at them.

She'd never seen something like this before. They hadn't had much technology in the tower, and certainly not much in the way of electronics. The thing made little noises, humming in the air, though no one but her paid them any mind or even seemed to notice them. They just ignored this fat grey box with its angry beeps and its strange glow, an electric elephant in an abandoned room.

"Lift up your shirt," said the nurse, and it only made her clamp her hands at its edges to hold it down tighter.

"It's just for the gel," said the nurse, spreading some on her gloves and holding her fingers up to the air so Jana could see. "It won't hurt. You'll feel cold, and that's it. You see the screen? We're going to show you your baby, right there. We might even find out if it's a boy or a girl."

"You'll be fine," said Faye. "They just want to take a look. It uses sound, just like a bat. Then you can see what things look like inside someone, without having to hurt them. I'll hold your hand. Come on."

She held out her hand, and Jana clasped on tight. The nurse lifted her shirt, and started to apply the gel, and it was as cold as they'd warned her it would be. She clenched her eyes closed, and kept them shut while the machine did its work. She thought of Rhamiel, and where he might be, and what he'd think if he knew he was to have a child. Her mind began to wander, brushing

46

against the one thing she wanted most to know, but wanted least to ponder.

She knew deep within her that there was the chance he hadn't made it through their attack, and that was why he hadn't come to find her. These people had gone there to kill angels, and angels they had killed. But still she denied it, pushing the thoughts away when they clattered against her consciousness, pretending all was well because it had to be. She turned to her old mainstay, the fantasies that could distract her from anything, and she lived a few pleasant moments inside them before the gasps from around her brought her back to the world she'd been trying to escape.

She flipped open her eyes and saw them staring at it, the thing on the monitor. She'd never pictured a baby like that, if it was one, though she hadn't the slightest idea of what she should expect to see.

"I don't know what's wrong," said the nurse. "The machine must be broken. I don't know why it looks like that. Are you sick? Maybe you've eaten something that made you feel bad, or caused something with your stomach?"

"No," said Jana.

"What about the father?" said the nurse. "Any family history of illnesses?"

"I don't think he gets sick," said Jana. "He's—"

"He's a health nut," said Faye, putting her arm around Jana. "She never asked him about that sort of thing. But now we're not really sure where he is. It's kind of a sensitive subject. You know what it's like, these days."

"I'm sorry," said the nurse. "It's just. Well, it's not supposed to look like that."

It wasn't, indeed. They could see her insides, all around it, but they couldn't see anything of the child. It was all light, a bright, glowing star at the center of the screen that pulsed along with her heartbeat, expanding and contracting rhythmically as the blood pumped through her. It was beautiful, in its own way, but it was no baby as far as they could tell.

"Jana, why don't you go see what Holt's up to?" said Faye. "Maybe you can keep him company."

"Okay," said Jana. She didn't want to be there, any more than they wanted her to be, and was glad of the excuse to leave. They stood in silence while she left, and she could hear them talking in low voices as she walked away down the hall.

There was no one watching the door to the surgery, and Holt had fallen back asleep. She thought that if they'd wanted her out, they'd have kept her out, and so she opened the door, slowly and quietly. The desks that had once lined the classroom were now pushed into one corner, clearing the way for a single bed at its center. It was an island of cleanliness in a sea of trash. They'd sanitized the area around it, but hadn't bothered to clean up the broken pencils, notebooks, and other assorted junk that littered the corners of the room.

Thane was lying there, his arms and legs set in plaster casts. His hair was a mess, a wild blonde jungle that had outgrown its usual trim from neglect. Small fragments of bone lay inside a metal cup next to his bed, trophies from his injuries that the surgeon had removed from inside him. He wouldn't be moving for awhile, not on his own, and she thought it likely that the burden of tending to him would fall entirely on her shoulders.

"I wish they'd covered your mouth, and not just your arms," said Jana, as she sat in a desk beside him. "If you keep calling me names, I'll tape it up, and there'll be nothing you can do."

He didn't wake, and didn't respond, and so she continued to talk, more to herself than to him. "He wasn't there," she said. "He was gone, and he probably doesn't even know it happened. He'll come back home, and he'll take charge, and everything will be peaceful again. He'll come and find me, and then we'll rebuild the tower, as a better place. The mean ones can leave, and the good ones can stay, and everyone inside will be happy, this time. You won't be there, or maybe you will. Maybe you won't be so cruel, when you don't hurt quite so much."

He offered no response other than a heavy wheezing, but she hadn't expected any. It helped to talk, even if she was only pretending someone was listening. She had no friends now, and maybe she never had. The stress was getting to her, chewing on her nerves in the background even when she tried to pretend that it would all be okay. With nothing to occupy her, the facade began to crumble. She started to sniffle, and then to sob, and soon tears were streaming down her face and muffled moans escaped her lips no matter how hard she tried to hold them in. She let it all out, the ball of grief at loss of home and lover that had been growing and growing the more she'd tried to suppress it.

She felt relief, though only for an instant. It turned

to embarrassment as she heard the door creak behind her, and she rushed to compose herself, wiping the tears from her face as best she could. It didn't do much good; her eyes were still bloodshot, and she was still flush. But she was fortunate, as she wasn't the only one willing to pretend. Holt stood at the door, with Faye behind him, waiting for her to pull herself back together.

"The hospital's leaving," said Holt. "We are, too. We're not going far, but I don't want to stay here. Other people might know about it."

"You don't have to rush," said Faye. "But we want to move out before dark."

"I'm ready," said Jana. "Whenever you're ready, I'm ready."

One of the doctors moved in from behind them, and gave Thane a final check. "I wouldn't move him," said the doctor. "But that's medical advice, not survival advice."

"We're going to have to," said Holt. "Things are getting nasty out there. We need to put some distance between us and the old city."

"If you have to," said the doctor. "We can give you a stretcher, a real one. And a wheelchair, though I wouldn't leave him in it all the time." He motioned to a nurse, who went off to gather what they'd need to take Thane with them.

"We need something else, if you've got it," said Holt. "Some pills."

"I'm fine," said Faye, bristling. "I haven't felt anything for a while."

"You're fine now, but you might not be later," said

Holt. "We need to find some Thorazine. It's not what you're probably thinking. We talked—"

"Glossolalia," said the doctor, writing on his clipboard. "We've seen it all, trust me. But that can get bad, real bad. Thorazine isn't great for you, either. Ever heard of the Thorazine Shuffle? Take it too long, and you could regret it."

"We've got to do something, and for now, this is what's working," said Holt.

"You might not have much time," said the doctor. "You have to understand. It's all about the angel, the one that did it to you. The one that's speaking through you. The pills can keep them out, mostly. If they don't care, or if they're not strong, or if they're busy. But they're always in there, in your head. Just a little piece of them. I've seen crazy stuff. Scary stuff. You could go for years, and then one day, bam. It starts getting worse and worse, and then it all goes to hell."

"I'll handle it," said Faye. "And if I can't, we'll deal with it then. I can't be on that stuff all the time. I can't be some drugged out zombie. I need to be on form. Otherwise it's just you trying to take care of the three of us. Pills aren't a cure. You know they don't cure it. And I don't feel like myself, not when I'm on them. If I'm going to go out, I want to go out as me."

"I get it," said Holt, "but we don't exactly have a choice."

"Well," said the doctor. He bit his lip, thinking to himself, and then leaned in towards Holt. "If you're going to move him anyway, you might want to try something else. There's rumors, and I don't know if they're true. But people have started talking, about someplace that might be safe. Someplace you might get some help for both her, and for him."

"If it'll help her, we'll go," said Holt.

The doctor looked them up and down, sizing them up. Whatever he saw in them seemed to satisfy him, and then he spoke. "Maybe it's just a rumor, but maybe not," said the doctor. "What do you know about archangels?"

CHAPTER NINE

THE ROOM WAS VAST, AN elliptical chamber with solid silver walls, constructed so finely that no seams were visible anywhere along them. It looked like it had been poured into place, forged as a single unit all at once. The center was dotted with slabs of grey metal, and upon each of them lay one of the wounded angels, in various states of injury. Cherubs wandered back and forth between them, attending to the victims of the blast.

At the front of the room were the healthiest, still conscious but weak enough that they needed rest, sipping from slushed vitamins that the cherubs had blended and dispensed in mugs to any able enough to drink. At the back of the room were those who'd suffered heavy burns, mostly unconscious, though a few of them were moaning and screaming for however long they could stay awake. Metallic orbs buzzed through the air around them, their surfaces a swirl of blue and white, feeding data to the cherubs as they scanned their charges.

In the middle of it all was a cluster of seraphs surrounding one of the wounded, the one whose fate could be most disruptive to their social hierarchy, and as such the one they were most interested in. Little cherubs and their orbs tried to weave between them to do their work, but found themselves blocked by indifferent wings or gossiping heads.

A cherub perched over Rhamiel. The little creature's dumpy body was a mess of scar tissue ill-covered by a meager loincloth, his long toes firmly clamped onto the shoulder of a gilded automaton. The machine stood inert at Rhamiel's bedside, awaiting instructions from the cherub, a silent guardian at the edge of the slab he was laid out on.

The automaton was a hulking thing of gold, looming over even the seraphs, if nothing else a tool for pushing them aside and making room to work. It was shaped vaguely like a man, though one who'd been pumped full of some heavenly steroid and grown to the size of an ox. Its arms ended in thick logs of fingers, perfect for hard labor but ill-suited for the type of dexterous tasks the cherubs reserved for themselves. It had no face, only a golden block fixed atop its shoulders, though the cherub had faces enough for both of them.

The Cherubim had long displayed an obsessive interest in golems, practicing the art of animating inert materials into various constructs of their own design. They'd claimed it was an homage to the Maker himself, a dedication to the art of creation, even if the results couldn't technically be counted among the living. But there had always been whispers among the other orders of angels, that perhaps they were less interested in adulation and more interested in wielding some of the Maker's power for themselves.

The cherub mused as he worked, pondering ways to improve the design of his patient. "We could replace his arms, with something new; machines in place of what the Maker grew."

"We did not bring them here merely for you to disfigure them further," said Uzziel, as he oversaw the cherub's activities. "Had the Maker wanted us to sport rocks or pearls for limbs, he would have made us so. Simply heal him, as best you can, and make him as he was."

The cherub went about his business, chanting at Uzziel even as he worked. "So odd to bow before a tyrant's will; he cast you out, yet you obey him still. He wanted you a slave, and nothing more, a perfect general for his holy wars. If you'd reshape your body, you would find, you'd snip the puppet strings that knot your mind."

He ran his fingers over Rhamiel's chest, examining the scars. The cherub had many of his own; his skin was a loose mass of wrinkles, leathery and brown, and his little wings had been singed to a soft grey. It didn't seem to concern him, nor indeed any of them. Vanity was for seraphs; the cherubs were mindful only of practicality.

The cherub's face flashed from lion to human, and he picked at his nose as he continued the examination. He withdrew his finger after an elaborate dig and flicked the contents at the floor, oblivious to the disgust on the faces of the nearby seraphs. Social niceties were beyond the Cherubim. It was less that they didn't care for them, and more that they didn't seem to understand them, no matter how often they might be reminded.

When he had seen what he could with the naked eye, he fluttered across the room to a row of instruments hanging from the opposite wall. All looked complicated, a diverse collection of designs hung in no discernable order. Many of them glowed, powered by energies unknown that the Cherubim had managed to harness. The other angels had found much to criticize about the Cherubim, but even their harshest opponents acknowledged that their curiosity was unrivaled. Many thought that was precisely why the Maker had created them, though the more popular opinion among the Seraphim was that he'd recognized that the maintenance of Heaven's underworks was a task beneath the stature of the other angels.

Regardless of their original purpose, they'd taken to anything technical. They could not resist the urge to tinker, with anything and everything. Many a seraph had come to choir only to find his harp restrung, improved in tone by some modification or another but rendered unplayable without years of additional practice. This had been considered a nuisance up above, but then, no angel up there would have admitted to feelings of hostility towards another. Down here, it was free rein, and centuries of buried animosity had been loosed all at once. The Cherubim didn't seem to mind. What emotion they had went mostly unexpressed, and some doubted they had any emotion at all.

After selecting a lengthy metal rod with an orb of pink light rotating above its tip, the cherub floated back to the examination table. He used it to poke at Rhamiel, who lay still and asleep. He'd been in and out of consciousness, alternating between resting and wild thrashing, but for now he was most certainly out. The cherub pressed a button on the rod, projecting a cone of light across Rhamiel's chest, and after he had satisfied himself with the results he spoke.

"The problem's plain to any who would see; his life force drained while buried in debris. They bathed him in creation's burning light; exposing weakness in his frantic flight. And even now life ebbs from out his pores; a victim of your petty human wars."

"Can it be stopped?" said Uzziel. "Him, and the others. It's all a dishonor, a despicable dishonor. To be felled by mere servants, who blundered into power they could unleash but could not control. We must save our brothers, both for themselves and for our very dignity."

The surrounding seraphs murmured their agreement, though not without a few muffled digs at the indignity and dishonor they'd already suffered from watching one of their own chase after a servant like a love-struck puppy. That spot was still sore, and their feelings restrained only because their brother lay injured before them.

"Servants come, and sometimes servants go," said the cherub. "But our affairs aren't for their like to know. You waste your time on worries such as these, afflictions of an aimless life of ease. Why bother with such things as dignity? Why should I care what servants think of me? A golem doesn't speak and won't rebel; a golem won't complain about my smell. You filled your tower with redundant pests, and come here begging us to clean your mess."

"Matters of philosophy are no concern of mine," said Uzziel, his voice rising to an angry pitch. "Nor are petty arguments over how our respective chores are done. My concern is warfare, and a war needs warriors. I need mine restored to health, that we may right the wrong that's been done to us. Your words are the words of someone who sympathizes with our enemies. They make me wonder, wonder about your motives, wonder about your connections, wonder about your walls. Now be about your work, else I'll speak to Zephon of your intransigence."

Uzziel was growing unhinged, and the other seraphs could see it. The cherub couldn't, and started into yet another series of rhymes, oblivious to the scowl on Uzziel's face and the suspicion in his eyes.

"Don't press the matter," said one of the seraphs, hand moving to the hilt of his sword. The cherub understood that gesture at least, though it began cycling through each of its faces, a puzzled look upon all of them. Why the Seraphim cared so much for such things as dignity or revenge were beyond him, as was the reason for the sudden threats. But he understood danger, even if he didn't emotion, and so he quietly went back to his work.

After poking and prodding at Rhamiel again, and bathing him head to toe in the pink light, the cherub turned back to Uzziel. He stared at him blankly for an uncomfortable amount of time, thinking the thoughts of a cherub, and finally he spoke.

"He can be healed, if that is what you'd like, but not in time to aid your vengeful strike. Recovering from this wound is something slow; I can't just snap my fingers and say 'go.' You'll have to give him time and let him heal, to see him fighting with his former zeal."

"Damnation, for all of you," said Uzziel. "It is as it always was. You hide here while the Seraphim do battle for your benefit. And what of the others, more grievously wounded? What of Zuphias?"

The cherub flapped across the room, leading them to another of the slabs, back among the rows of the injured. On it sat what was left of Zuphias, his charred remains looking no different than the corpses they'd pulled from the ruins. Yet still he twitched, and still his jaw clicked and clacked, opening and closing in an endless scream that none of them could hear.

The cherub's face fizzled into a shapeless cloud of color, shifting like a manic kaleidoscope as he floated over the body. "You ask too much, to undo fire's flash; he is no phoenix borne anew from ash. There's only so much healing arts can do, to bring the wounded back to life anew. He'll never be the angel that he was, no matter what an able cherub does."

"Is there anything of him left?" said Uzziel. "Or is his body merely lingering, tethering him to this plane to no end?"

The cherub's face reassembled into a stern looking ox, and he delivered the best news he could. "There's something there inside this blackened husk; his night has yet to fall, though it's his dusk. His mind is trapped within this lonely shell, consigned by fire to live a private hell. The best I offer is that we'll pursue, a way for him to hear and speak with you. We'll need both luck and talent I'm afraid, the stuff of which a miracle is made."

"Then we will wait, and leave him to your care," said Uzziel. "For if anything would bring Zuphias back to us, it would be one of his miracles."

CHAPTER TEN

THEY WERE COMPLETELY EXPOSED, A target ripe for the plucking, out on the open road and with little hope of defending themselves. But the Vichies didn't even stop. There were about a dozen of them, riding motorcycles and toting guns. But they looked scared, even for the Vichies, and whatever business they were on was too urgent to indulge in plunder. So they just zoomed past, coming within yards of them but doing nothing worse than shouting a few insults along the way.

Holt had been sure they'd be in for a fight when Faye had spotted them, and they weren't in any state for one. They'd commandeered a pickup, powerful enough to get them around off-road and with enough room in the bed to lay Thane out for the trip. With Jana and Faye in the back to keep an eye on him, they wouldn't jostle him too much so long as they went slowly. They needed to find a place to stay, and they needed to move west, if what the doctor had said was true. He hadn't been able to give them much. A rumor, and a name, and little else.

Suriel.

He wasn't like the others, or so the rumors went. He'd kept to himself, after the Fall, and had avoided politics both angelic and human. Now he was gathering something of a following, a flock seeking a shepherd. And if what the doctor had heard was true, he had both the power to heal and the disposition to use it.

The rear window slid open, and Holt shouted through the wind to the rest of them. "We're pulling off, and taking a break. Dark's coming." He took the next exit, weaving around abandoned cars and following the road until they chanced upon an apartment complex, old and decaying but still standing. He pulled inside the parking lot, and pulled open the pickup door.

"Faye," said Holt. "You're on watch. I'm going to do a little recon, and find one we can live with for the night."

"Go on," said Faye, pulling her rifle out of its case and checking to make sure it was loaded. "We'll make some noise if we need you."

He disappeared among the buildings, alert for signs that anyone else had decided to make the place their home. Faye got out to stretch her legs, but Jana was too nervous to venture beyond the familiarity of the pickup.

"What is this place?" said Jana. It looked so strange to her, box stacked upon box, with windows all covered in cloth so no one could see in or out. The buildings were made of something flimsy, not solid metal like the tower had been, and already they were starting to fall apart. A few of the units were caved in at the roof, and graffiti was scrawled across the sides of most of the rest.

"People lived here," said Faye. "It looks like shit, but

there's no one here to take care of it. It's all fallen apart, just like everything else."

"Just like the tower," said Jana.

"This all used to be filled with families," said Faye. "Before the angels and their tower. You know we used to run things, not them. They were just stories. Most people didn't even believe in them. The ones who did thought they were these saints. And they turned out to be worse than any of us."

"They aren't all that way," said Jana. "Even the ones who are don't all want to be. There's more of them up there, too. Up in the clouds, where they came from. They told me so."

"What are they like?" said Faye. "What are they like up close?"

Few outside the angels' strongholds had ever interacted with them, other than to fight them or flee from them. There were stories and rumors, but most were told to entertain or to brag, and they had a tendency to grow in the telling. Mostly the angels were an enigma, a dark spot seen from the distance among the clouds or a traumatic memory formed from brief glimpses during combat.

"They're mad," said Jana. "Most of them, most of the time. But some of them are kind. Some are better than kind. It's like people, I suppose. But you can't cross them. They like things the way they like them, and you must make sure they get what they want."

"That's the problem with them," said Faye. "They can just do whatever they want, and nobody gets to say anything about it. Nobody can."

They saw Holt in the distance, waving them forward into the mess of buildings, and Faye drove them around the parking lot towards the place he'd chosen. He'd found an apartment, nestled in the middle of the complex where they weren't likely to be spotted by any strangers passing by. There had been a family there long ago, with space aplenty, and it was perfect for their needs. They lifted Thane out of the pickup and carried him inside, installed him on a pull-out couch in the living room close to the exit, and then each staked out a place to sleep of their own.

"Jana," said Holt. "You need to stay here. It'll be safe, and we'll be close by. But we need to check around for supplies while it's still light."

"I don't want to be alone," said Jana. "Let me come with you. I want to help. And I don't want to be here, not by myself."

"You will be helping," said Holt. "And you won't be alone. You'll be taking care of Thane. It's better this way. Safer. You haven't ever been someplace like this. You need to take your time, adjust."

"I'll teach you, once Thane's up and on his own," said Faye. "But we can't leave him on his own. We'll be right nearby, really close. And we can find you something to do. There's toys, in one of the bedrooms. And books, if you can read. Some of them might have pictures if you can't."

"I can read," said Jana. "We'll be fine. Go do your search, and we'll be fine."

She wasn't happy about it, but she saved anything that could be considered pouting for after they'd left.

They already treated her like a child, and she didn't want to give them any more reason to. But it was still frustrating, going from the bottom to the top, and then right back down again. She'd gone from serving angels to serving humans, and none of them were particularly grateful for her troubles.

Thane was sleeping, and so she turned to finding something to do. The apartment's library was massive by her standards—a full three shelves, filled to the brim with books. She browsed through them until she found one that caught her eye, and then took a seat near the living room window where she'd have some light to read by. It was difficult going. There were so many references to things from a life she had no experience with, and so much she had to guess at from the context alone. Such is the way of ancient texts, though this one was ancient before its time. But she made the best of it and made it a game, concocting imagined meanings for the words she didn't know, and she kept at it until Thane started to stir.

His eyes opened, and he let out a groan. He tried to move his arms, to scratch some itch he couldn't reach, but everything was too constrained by the casts. He actually seemed lucid, for the first time since they'd left the hospital, and after rustling around the couch for a bit he finally noticed Jana sitting nearby.

"You're that Vichy bitch," said Thane.

Jana didn't say anything; she was both frightened and fuming. But silence didn't seem to satisfy him, and so he poked at her again.

"Y'all are all traitors, and here we bring you along. You're helpin' out the enemy and now we gotta help you."

That did it, as far as Jana was concerned. She'd had her fill of abuse, from both angels and humans, and she wasn't inclined to take any more from someone safely plastered to a couch.

"You haven't helped me at all," she spat. "You blew up my home, and now I don't have anywhere to go. And I've been taking care of you ever since. All I do is help you. And all you do is moan."

Thane turned his head away, as far as he could manage given the circumstances. His normal outlets for anger denied him, all he could do was curse. "Help kill my friends," he said. "Help kill everyone I know. Help a bunch of assholes who shit all over our country. I used to have a home, now where's that? Gone. New York used to be a bunch of people's home. Where's that? Gone. People like you helped it happen. Fuckin' traitors."

Jana bit her lip, clamping down on the agony within. It hurt her so, listening to these assaults on her, more than it ever had coming from the angels. The angels were what they were, creatures from a different plane, and their very strangeness was at least some excuse for their indifference to the pain they inflicted. But a human had no such alibi.

"All I did was clean," said Jana, sobbing in frustration. "All I ever did was clean."

Thane responded only with profanities beneath his breath, and Jana was moments from hurling her book at his head when the others returned, laden with bags of clothes and household items of all sorts, along with a few newfound guns strapped to their shoulders. They walked into a maelstrom of accusations and emotion, and were bewildered by the sudden quarrel.

"I'm tired of him," Jana cried. "I'm not taking care of him anymore."

"She's a traitor, and you left me alone with her," said Thane. "A lot of good men died for this country. Dax died for this country. This bitch sells us out to the angels, and you want to bring her with us? She betrayed all of us. She betrayed America."

"I don't even know what that is," said Jana. "I don't even know what America is."

With that she lost all control, releasing a flood of tears and rushing into one of the bedrooms to hide her pain. She slammed the door shut behind her, and they could hear her weeping through the door. Thane just grunted, though he didn't seem at all satisfied with himself. He couldn't meet their eyes, and turned his head to the side to avoid their glares.

"Thane, you're being a complete jackass," said Faye. "If you weren't hopped up on painkillers I'd smack you myself. She couldn't help it. They had her locked up in there, her entire life. They—"

Then it happened, again.

Faye started to stammer, losing track of what she'd been saying. She soon found words again, but they weren't her own. She began to chant, more furiously than ever before, screaming in languages none of them knew.

Before she had clenched up or spasmed, but now it was worse, far worse. Her limbs were moving, jerking about clumsily, animated with purpose but unable to enact it. She looked like a puppet entangled in its strings, stumbling forward and groping around to find its bearings. Holt tackled her to the ground, holding her there as her flailing and shouting finally died down and she became herself again.

"I could hear words," she said, shaking. "Real words. In my head. I can't remember what they were, but I could hear them." She looked terrified, peering into a fog inside her head at something she couldn't quite make out.

"It's okay," said Holt. "We're going to cure this."

"There's not going to be a cure," said Faye. "It's just going to get worse and worse, and then there won't be any of me left."

"That's not going to happen," said Holt. "We're going to find this archangel. Find him soon. And we're going to make him fix what they did. We're going to make him kick that angel out of your head."

CHAPTER ELEVEN

"**B**EAUTIFUL GIRLS. THE PICTURE OF perfection, I should say. Your daughters? If so, they've done their mother quite proud."

Ecanus leered over them, the woman and her two teenagers. He'd found them hiding inside the back of an old sedan, given away by the curious eyes peeping out at the window's edge. She'd told them to stay down, but the young must make their mistakes for themselves, no matter how many warnings they're given. He'd ripped the door from its hinges and pulled them out into the city street. Now they lay huddled before him, the girls crying and the mother pleading for their lives.

"Don't kill them," she said. "Do whatever you want to me. Please. But don't kill them."

"Oh, I won't," said Ecanus. "Not both of them. Not if you indulge me, in a little entertainment."

"Anything," she said. "Let them go, and I'll do anything." She edged her way between him and the girls, working her way closer to him as she spoke, hoping to give them some chance to flee, however faint it might be.

"Well, then," said Ecanus. "I'm a reasonable person, and a generous one. I love my little diversions, and this one is special to me. One I've been meaning to enact for some time, but hadn't yet found the proper players for. I call it 'The Wisdom of Solomon.' He was quite renowned in his day. Have you heard of him?"

The woman stuttered something unintelligible. Whether she had or she hadn't, she was groping for the answer he wanted to hear, rather than the truth. But Ecanus was a hard one to read, not the least because his extensive scarring made his facial expressions an enigma.

"No matter," said Ecanus. "It's trivia, in the end. The game is simple. All you have to do is answer me a question, and I'll set one of your daughters free. It's a fair deal, I should think, for one in your position. Don't you agree?"

"Yes," she said softly.

"Splendid," said Ecanus. "Then think on this, but not for long, and speak truly. Which of your daughters do you love the most?"

The woman's eyes widened, and her face contorted in horror. Her daughters were wailing, both looking to her for their salvation. She looked back and forth between the two, paralyzed, unable to answer other than in muffled sobs. She knew the game, but not the rules, and she was consumed by thoughts of what he'd do with the daughter she didn't choose.

"Go on," said Ecanus. "If you love them equally, as a mother should, that's a fair answer. A fine answer. Then I'll simply split the baby, and slaughter the both of them." He drew his fiery dagger and began to walk towards them, brushing their mother aside as she clawed at him and wailed.

"No!" she shouted. "I'll pick. I'll pick."

She looked down at them, and they looked up at her, pleading. They both knew the stakes. They began begging, weeping at her and professing their love as loudly and as enthusiastically as they could. They clung to her sides, holding her tightly, each trying to outdo the other in affection. It was a barbarous competition, and Ecanus was lapping up their pain. The daughters were both terrified, pressing for their own survival and for assurances that their mother's love was more than mere sham. It ripped the woman apart inside, and it was all she could do to utter a few words.

"I love you," she said between tears. "I love you both."

"Choose," said Ecanus.

"Her," said the woman, grabbing onto one of her daughters and turning from the other. "I pick her."

The abandoned daughter started to scream, a look of shock and betrayal on her face. She pushed away from her mother, and started to make a break for it, launching herself into the street and making a run for one of the buildings. But she didn't make it far.

"I'm sorry," said her mother, as Ecanus grabbed the girl by the wrist and cut her escape short. "I'm so, so sorry. I love you. I love you so much."

It all turned to babbling anguish that he only seemed to feed off of. He milked the moment, twisting the metaphorical knife before turning to the actual one. The pain was the part he loved, not just the violence, and he wasn't going to let it to end quickly.

"Now tell your mother what you think of her," said Ecanus, holding the girl close. "Tell mommy dearest what she's done to your love."

"I hate you," said the girl quietly. "I hate you all."

"Please," said the woman. "Please."

"I'm afraid you've already chosen," said Ecanus. "But I'll let her go, if you'd really like me to."

"Please let her go," said the woman. "Please just let her go."

"I will," said Ecanus. "I'll let her go. And I'll let you go, too. I'm always one to please, when I'm asked nicely." He dropped the girl's arm in an exaggerated gesture, and flashed his teeth at the three of them as she ran back to the others, hiding behind them and avoiding her mother's attempts to reconcile.

"I've no interest in killing a daughter you don't love," said Ecanus. "I want to kill the daughter you do."

He lunged forward and snatched the neck of the other girl, yanking her from her mother's embrace. He held the knife to her throat, close enough to leave a black slit of singed skin, and he laughed and laughed.

"The fun part's not just in the killing," said Ecanus. "It's in knowing you'll be left alive, with a daughter who scorns you until the last. No matter what you say, she'll always know. She'll know you don't love her, not really. She'll know you would have picked her sister, if you'd had your way. It will gnaw at the both of you until your dying days, and your daughter will never truly love you again."

"Please," said the woman.

"Maybe I'll see you again, before you meet your

Maker," said Ecanus, "and you can tell me which was the more painful: watching the death of the daughter you loved the most, or living with the hatred of the one who came in second place."

He started into the act, and the mother screamed out a last, desperate gambit.

"Wait!" she said. "I can tell you something. Something you'll want to know, if you let them go."

"I want my fun," said Ecanus. "I'm not one for knowledge. A waste of energy, and a waste of my own peculiar talents."

"I'll give you another child," said the woman. "A better child. An angel's child."

His ears would have perked up, if there had been enough of them left to do it. As it was he loosed the knife, and held it back from the girl's throat as his eyes narrowed.

"There isn't any such thing," said Ecanus. "There can't be any such thing, I'm afraid. We were made to be servants, and meant to stay that way. We've the equipment, but not the fuel, as it were."

"It's true," said the woman. "There's a girl. She was with an angel. And now she's with child."

"What girl?" said Ecanus. "What angel?"

"I don't know her name," said the woman. "I know him. I know who they say it was. Everyone said it. It's not me, it's what I heard."

"Who?" said Ecanus. "Spit it out. You've more to fear from silence than from speaking his name."

"They say," said the woman. "They say Rhamiel. They say she seduced him. That she stole his honor. That she threw herself at him, again and again, until his will was weak. And she hasn't had her period since."

"She did?" said Ecanus. "She did, did she?"

He let out a long hyena's cackle, and the amusement so overtook him that he didn't bother giving chase when the three of them fled. They ran off into the distance, seeking refuge in the buildings, but Ecanus just stood by and watched.

"Run all you like," he called after them. "You won't escape the truth laid bare, of how fragile the bonds of love between you were. It will niggle at you, no matter how you push it down, and worm its way upwards and into the open. You'll never love each other the same, not now. Not knowing who she'd sacrifice, and who she'd save. It's a pain worse than any other I could have inflicted. You'll see."

They disappeared into the doorway of an old building, and he stood alone in the street, pondering what he'd heard.

"A world without a tower's a surprisingly pleasant one," said Ecanus. "No ties to bind me, no trifles to lord over me, and no place to put me in. Poor Rhamiel won't like this, if he's survived. I must be the one to deliver the news, and in person. There's simply no way, no possibility of the thing. I've only ever heard of one angel siring a child, and Rhamiel would hardly be the second. His girl's a cheat, and he a cuckold, and I'll be there to watch when his smug face collapses in anguish."

CHAPTER TWELVE

"THEY'RE REAL FRIENDLY PEOPLE, NO matter what you might think. Where you want to go is Cleveland, or thereabouts. You'll see signs. On the highways. They're getting pretty big, and they're out in the open now."

The farmer was a stout man, well fed even in these hardscrabble times, but then, he'd chosen his occupation wisely. They'd found him by the side of the highway, running a market in miniature of his very own. Crates of fruits and vegetables were stacked beside him, and he nestled in a lawn chair waiting for travelers interested in trade. Evidently there was a brisk traffic, as he had a large truck parked nearby with boxes of looted goods piling up in the back.

It was a dangerous line of work, but he'd found his own way to minimize the risk of violence: next to a few crates of misshapen produce was a handpainted sign, announcing the availability of "Free Food." They weren't the choicest picks, nor were they the freshest. But it gave the starving an out, a way to eat their fill without having to pick a fight. He had to tolerate a little theft despite the gesture, but the losses to an occasional passing robber were well worth the gains.

"Is it true?" said Holt. "What they say, about this Suriel. That he's healing people."

"It's what they say," said the farmer. "Never saw a friendly angel myself. People say he's different, though. Lot of folks believe it, and a lot of 'em are hanging around him. They pass through here sometimes. They say God still talks to him. That he's going to fix all this, and make things right."

"It's a chance," said Holt. "It's something."

"Just look for the signs," said the farmer. "They're taking all comers. All you gotta do is get there."

They carried crates of food back to the pickup, along with a few containers of gas, and they loaded it all up. It cost them nearly everything they'd scavenged from the apartments, but all things considered they were getting a good deal. Then they waved goodbye and headed along down the road, keeping the pace slow but steady.

It was days before they saw the first sign in the distance. It was just where the farmer had said it would be, a white placard fastened atop an old highway sign and pointing the way forward with a spray painted arrow. They wouldn't have known what it meant, if he hadn't told them. All it said was a single word: "hope."

Below it there were two figures, standing together near the side of the road. Holt pulled over, and they watched and waited. Whoever they were, they didn't move, and didn't approach, and didn't do much of anything other than mill around underneath the sign.

"Jana," said Faye. "Stay here with Thane. We're going to go see what's up."

The two of them disappeared into a knot of cars, and from time to time Jana could see them as they reappeared, moving between vehicles for a better position or taking a closer look through the scope of Faye's rifle. Whoever was beneath the sign, they didn't seem to notice. They just stayed put, allowing the stakeout to proceed at its own leisurely pace.

Jana sat quietly, watching them for as long as her interest held. But after a while, their cautious maneuvering lost its shine, and boredom took over. Thane was out of it, and wasn't much of a conversation partner when he wasn't. She had a few books, but she'd already been through each of them cover to cover. She turned to her fantasies, but soon found Rhamiel inside them, and she turned away just as quickly.

Finally she started to hum a repetitive old jingle to herself, an ode to a hot dog that she'd learned from some of the older servants. She knew the tune, and knew all the words, though she wasn't quite sure what any of it really meant. Her hands drifted towards her stomach, probing it with pinches and nudges. She didn't show, not through her clothes, but every day she thought it felt just a little bigger. She hummed her little song, and wondered whether it would be a boy or a girl, and whether it should have a human's name or an angel's, and what one was meant to feed a baby, anyhow.

She'd kept it quiet, but not quiet enough. A few too many bars into the song, and Thane awoke, as grumpy as ever.

"Cut that crap out," said Thane. "Where's everyone else?"

"They're seeing what's up," said Jana.

Thane gave her a glare, or tried to. He didn't have much control over what he looked at, not with all the casts, and presently he was pointed upward with only a cloudless sky to entertain him.

"Lot of help you are," said Thane. "Why the fuck are we stopped?"

"The sign," said Jana. "They saw one. But there's people there, and they need to go take a look. They're hiding in the cars."

Thane just cursed to himself, and stared at the sky, and after a few minutes of awkwardness Jana went back to her humming. It calmed her down, and reminded her of home, the good parts of it, when everyone was happy and sang around the fire as friends. But those moments didn't last, and neither did this one.

"I'm hungry," said Thane.

"I thought I was a traitor," said Jana. "I thought you didn't want me here."

"You are," said Thane. "And I don't. I want them to toss your ass out and let you fend for yourself."

"Then you can get your own food," said Jana.

"Thought so," said Thane. "You'll help one of them, but not one of us. You don't care who they kill, or how."

"I do care," said Jana.

"You kept on helpin' them anyway," said Thane. "You helped them live how they did. It's the Vichy way. Burnin' towns, lootin' everywhere. Killin' people just for the hell of it, and then blamin' the angels for what you did."

"I didn't kill anyone," said Jana. "You did. I just washed dishes. So did most of the people in the tower. And they didn't all make it out."

"That ain't an excuse," said Thane. "Just did the dishes, just followin' orders. Not my fault what the others do." He was turning red as he spoke, working himself into a frenzy, and his brow scrunched into a solid wall of furious wrinkles. He started to yell, only to find himself cut short as Jana wielded their produce against him. She interrupted him with a carrot, shoving it into his mouth and shutting down his tantrum.

"I like you better this way," said Jana. "You wouldn't be so mean, if only you couldn't talk."

Thane took a bite and spat it out, spraying his chin with chunks of orange glop.

"I'm gonna be out of these in a few weeks," said Thane. "You damned well better be gone by then."

"They're taking you to an angel, you know," said Jana. "A healer. He'll probably be the one to make you better. What'll you do then, when one of them has to help you?"

"I'll shove his halo up his self-righteous ass," said Thane.

"They say he's one of the good ones," said Jana. She ran through the angels she'd known in her head, and what they were like, and wondered which kind of angel he might be. None of the ones she'd known had ever healed anyone, but whether it was because they couldn't or because they didn't care to, she didn't know. She thought about who he must have been in heaven, and what his job had been, and whether he could help her, too. "Maybe he'll know Rhamiel. Maybe he'll know where he is."

"He ain't gonna be good," said Thane. "And he ain't gonna know about this Rhamiel."

"He might," said Jana. "You don't know anything about them."

"Trust me," said Thane. "I know plenty. I've killed a couple angels myself. They're tough, but they ain't invincible. If he was near that tower, your Rhamiel didn't make it."

"He did," said Jana. Thane was goading her, and she knew it, but it didn't stop her from chasing after the red cape as he waved it. "I'm going to find him, and we're going to leave all of you, and go live somewhere by ourselves. Forever."

"He didn't," said Thane. "And you won't. You know what happens when you die, don't you?"

"We go to heaven," said Jana tentatively.

"You go to heaven, if you're good," said Thane. "You go to hell, if you're bad. And they torture you for all eternity. That angel of yours? He's a rebel. He's fallen. Heaven won't let him back in. So you're gonna go up, or you're gonna go down, but he stays here forever."

"You're a liar," said Jana. "You don't know anything about them. You don't know the good, and you don't know the bad." She said the words, but she didn't know if she believed them. He was right about the basics; she knew enough to know that. But what kind of paradise would separate someone from their beloved?

"Ask anyone," said Thane with a snort. "Hell, ask one of them. Ask this Suriel."

"Shut up," said Jana. "Just shut up. You're mean, and nasty, and you don't care who you hurt. You think I'm just a weak little girl. You think that means you can attack me. You think—"

"Fuck you!" screamed Thane, straining against his casts and thumping up and down against the pickup bed. He'd gone from calm to totally unhinged in seconds, his nostrils flared and his face beet red. "Don't you fuckin' talk to me about that kind of shit! Don't you fuckin' dare! Fuckin' Vichy wants to talk to me like that? Wants to lecture me with what you've done?"

He couldn't move freely, but he tried anyway, roaring and pushing with all of his power. Jana leapt from the truck, watching from outside as Thane kept smashing against the pickup bed in heavy thuds. Finally he ripped an arm free, but he also ripped something else inside. The anger in his cries turned to pain. His yelps were echoing through the cars, and she could hear voices in the distance growing closer. Soon Holt appeared from between the cars, Faye following closely on his heels.

"What happened?" said Holt. "What happened to him?"

"He got mad," said Jana. "I don't know why. He just got really mad."

Faye climbed into the pickup, trying to calm Thane and undo the damage. The cries turned to whimpers, and then sobs, choked short whenever Thane could muster the strength to hold them in. Then they'd overwhelm him, forcing their way out in staccato bursts, cutting the air with a shrill mixture of pain both physical and emotional. She held his hand, spoke to him in soothing whispers, and managed to quiet him down as he regained control and crammed it all back inside himself.

"What did you say?" said Faye.

"He was so mean," said Jana. She stayed outside the pickup, watching as Thane shook in anger, and then passed out again from the pain. "I never did anything, but he's just so mean."

"Jana, he's had a tough life," said Faye. "We all have, but especially him. It's just really, really hard for him to be around you. He needs to move past it, but it's going to take time."

"I don't care anymore," said Jana. "I want to go back. I'm going to leave, and go find Rhamiel. Back at the tower. I went with you to the doctors. I let them take a look. I'm fine. I'm sorry you're sick, and I'm sorry he's sick, but I'm fine. And I'm tired of all of this. I'm tired of just following along and doing what other people say, just because they said it. Just because they yell and scream and threaten me if I don't. Everything was going to be fine, and you ruined it, and now I'm alone."

"Jana," said Faye. "I know this is hard. I know you might not like us, and I get it. But you aren't alone. There's a baby, and it's coming, and it's going to need you. This just won't work. You can't drive, and you won't be able to walk for long. Rhamiel can handle himself. You worry about yourself, and worry about your child, and let him worry about finding you."

"If you really want to go back, we won't stop you," said Holt. "It's a bad idea, and you won't get far, but you're welcome to try. You're free now, not like it was with them. If you don't want to be around us, you can walk away whenever you want. But you might want to stay with us just a little longer. We found some people. They know this angel we're looking for. And they're going to lead us right to him."

She hesitated, looking back down the long, long road and wondering whether she'd ever be able to find her way home. She looked up at the skies, and wondered if her place was up there, or down here, or somewhere else entirely.

"I'll go," said Jana. "You're leading me to where you want to be, not where I need to be. But I'll go, long enough to ask him about Rhamiel. And then I'm done. I'm not going to be someone's servant anymore. If he can't help me, and you won't help me, then I'm going to find Rhamiel on my own."

CHAPTER THIRTEEN

H E WOKE WITH A GASP, but there was nothing there to breathe. Something was strapped to his head, and he couldn't move his arms to rip himself free. His face was cold and wet, and he could feel fluid seeping through his lungs. Above him was a hot, glaring light, and he thought he'd finally passed, and this was what it was to be like for his kind, in the end.

Then he saw one of them hovering over him. A cherub, ministering to his injuries, with little interest in how he felt about the matter. He tried to shout at it to free him, but it only filled his mouth with wet, foul-tasting goo. He found himself on a table, locked in place at his ankles and wrists. He tried to thrash about, insomuch as he could, but other than drawing the cherub's attention it accomplished little.

He heard it chanting from beside him, even as it went back to ignoring his protests and poking at his sides with a long, uncomfortable needle. "Our wayward patient's finally awake, and in his weakness finds his bonds won't break." The cherub's nonchalance prompted a series of frustrated gurgles from Rhamiel, but they did nothing to interrupt its clinical gaze.

He was fastened to one of the slabs, in a room of his very own. The bulk of it was filled with machinery, and even the tiny cherub struggled to make its way around the clutter of devices. Tubes went out of the machines and into him, pumping a neon blue fluid into his veins and back out again. It all flowed into a giant vat to the side of him, bubbling and glowing with chemical reactions. Wrapped around his face was a thin, translucent mask, connected to one of the machines via a black tube. Liquid coursed through it as he tried to breathe, swelling the tube in time with his lungs.

The cherub went about its work, monitoring dials and fiddling with gauges. It donned a pair of thick black goggles, flipping its face into the shape of a bespectacled ox. "Be still and let the cherubs work a cure, to sift your angel's blood and make it pure. T'was tainted with the remnants of the blast; pollutants in your body had amassed. But friends have brought you to this place to heal, recuperating from your dark ordeal."

Rhamiel closed his eyes, and became quiet and still. The cherub thought he'd submitted, and turned its attention to the gauges on the machines. But his breathing grew quicker, and heavier, and once he'd gathered his strength he let it all loose at once.

He burst from his restraints, ripping them away from the slab and sending the tubes whipping through the air, painting the machinery a bright blue as they danced and squirted fluid all around. The cherub let loose a high-pitched moo, flipping its head in circles until it settled on an eagle and squawked an alarm. Rhamiel grabbed at its throat with one arm, choking off the cries, and tore the mask from his face with the other.

"And why," said Rhamiel, "do I find myself the victim of a cherub's unwanted attentions?"

The cherub choked out its response, flailing its tiny arms in the air as its wings buzzed and bashed against the machinery. "Your fellow seraphs flew you on the wind, no cause for you to wake and feel chagrined!"

"My blood is not the property of cherubs," said Rhamiel. "And I would hate to have to draw some of yours in return."

"We put it back into your very veins," said the cherub, coughing and gasping for air. "With toxins drawn to ease your fevered pains."

"I have scant trust for the Cherubim or their assurances," said Rhamiel. "For good reason. Your kind can't resist meddling. You'd pry apart creation itself, if only the Maker would let you. You can't control your curiosity, and I have no desire to find myself subject to some cherub's impromptu experiments. Nor do I need a palliative concocted on a whim, designed more to minister to your fancies than to my injuries."

"Our scholarship's a second to your health, and what we learn's an incidental wealth," said the cherub, its voice emotionless and flat. "No boon of knowledge comes before your strength; to see you well we'd go to any length."

"I tire of your plodding poetry," said Rhamiel. "If you'd inspect my blood, then do it firsthand."

With that he thrust the cherub into the vat headfirst,

leaving it to its desperate flailing. It was covered in the blue muck, a phosphorescent cupid banging its stubby arms against the glass. It wasn't strong enough to break it, and was crammed in too tightly to right itself, so it stayed there, bubbling silent poems into its liquid prison.

"Now where," said Rhamiel, "has this little cherub taken me?"

He edged himself free from the room, squeezing out of the dense thicket of machinery, and he stumbled as he found his footing. He caught the wall with his arm and managed to hold steady, but it took him a moment to recover from his wooziness. He'd emerged into a sterile metal hallway, curving around in a loop. Machines of all kinds whizzed back and forth in either direction, paying him no heed as they went about their errands. Some were golems, animated metal beings given a semblance of life and purpose by the cherubs. Others were mixtures of flesh and machinery. But no two were alike.

From the left, a simple creature creaked past on a pair of wooden wheels carved by some enterprising cherub, with little more than an iron box atop them to house its artificial innards. It carried a plate of piping hot food, rushing it towards hungry cherubs whose workbenches were too important to leave for even a moment. From the right, a massive thing of clay stomped through the hall bearing a load of tools, leaving a trail of dirt behind it. Its face was an indistinct blob, other than two red bulbs installed for its eyes, though what sight it had didn't stop it from crushing a few clattering metal insects beneath its feet as it went. All along the walls tiny things were scurrying and climbing, toys made and forgotten by the cherubs as they pursued whatever field of tinkering they were presently absorbed by.

The cherubs had left Rhamiel himself dressed in little more than one of their own loincloths. They had no modesty themselves, and the thought of clothing as ornamental vanities had never crossed their minds. He looked down on himself, stained in blue, and saw them for the first time.

The scars.

He ran his fingers along his chest, wincing at the touch. The damaged skin was leathery, the texture of a crocodile in the shape of a lion. He'd fallen from heaven intact, escaping the Maker's brand, only to find himself scarred along with all the others. His own armor had done it, and the crest that had once separated him from the rest now marked him as one of them. The symbol of his status would be etched across his skin forever, a bitter reminder of how high he'd flown before his second fall.

"Ruined," said Rhamiel. "I look like a monstrosity, with these blisters. She'll never have me now. If I can find her." He choked on his own voice, shaking and stammering. "If she escaped."

He tested his wings, flexing them and curving around to inspect the feathers. They were still pristine, as best as he could tell, though not without a few neon stains from where the cherub's concoction had splurted. He could see no other injuries, and could feel none on his face. Finally he started to wander, idly tracing his scars with his hand as he weaved around the cherubs' creations bustling on the floor below.

He circled the hallways for what seemed like ages.

They all looked the same to his eyes, just a single unending silver loop. Sometimes there were rooms, tiny laboratories built by the cherubs and dedicated to experiments unknown. Sometimes there were other hallways, and sometimes he took them. In the end he found himself lost, unable to find his bearings, until he finally heard the faint sound of voices in the distance.

He followed them, though it was no easy task. He kept hitting dead ends and being forced to double back again. But he was learning the way as he went, and soon he emerged into a larger hallway, and he could see the end.

There was a massive gateway in the distance, a shiny golden portal into the area beyond it. Strange devices were embedded all across its length, thin fizzing metal rods that projected a stream of images of the other hallways onto the gateway itself. He trudged towards it, drawn by the flickering figures before him and the sound of voices beyond the gate. He still felt weak, and thought that perhaps the cherub had been telling the truth about his blood, and that perhaps he should rest a little longer still. But though his body was exhausted, his will was stronger, and he made his way to a man-sized opening at the center.

Once through it, everything opened up into a vast chamber. Bronze pillars ran in rows along the center, and in the distance an aquarium was embedded into the walls, lit with a green glow and filled with floating oddities the cherubs had engineered. Below it was a platinum throne, gears churning at its sides and powering a clockwork cherub that loomed over its back, face slowly rotating through its four incarnations. Such blasphemy never would have been tolerated up above. Heaven had only one throne, and only one could sit in it. But here, the cherubs could do as they pleased.

In the throne sat a cherub, and before it stood a melange of angels competing for his attention. Seraphs massed on one side, and cherubs on the other, and between them all was a thick glass box, floating in mid-air. It was the size of an angel, and it contained one: what was left of Zuphias, suspended in the same blue solution the cherub had been pumping into Rhamiel.

They didn't see him, not at first. He made his way towards them, stiffening his walk and adopting the old air from when he'd been back in the tower, so far above them all. Only the cherub seated in the throne noticed, but the others soon followed his imperial gaze, and the congregation turned to greet the newest supplicant.

Uzziel stood to one side, flanked by an honor guard and flushed red from the strain of whatever argument he'd been engaged in with the cherubs. His beard was twisted into knots, the result of anxious fidgeting during his speeches.

"You look a mess," said Uzziel.

And indeed he did. He was dripping blue, a match for his eyes, and his hair was a matted jungle. His physique was perfect, mostly, but his newfound scars drew visible looks of disgust from the seraph side of the room. Not that any of them were in a position to talk. Their sneers lifted their own scarred faces into haughty pink craters, mirrors of loathing that reflected their ruined insides at anyone who reminded them of their ruined outsides.

"However I look, I'm still the one I was," said

Rhamiel. "Tower or no. My strength recovers, no thanks to the meddling of our hosts, and I have my health. And more importantly, I have my will."

"And you have our scars," came a voice from the crowd of seraphs. "He thinks himself better than what he's become," said another. A third was even bolder, snarling at Rhamiel from behind him as he passed. "A bird who believes he still flies, even as he limps along the ground."

The seraph regretted it soon after. Rhamiel had his arm pinned behind his back in an instant, twisting it into an unnatural position as the seraph howled in pain. "Utter those words again," said Rhamiel. "I could tear your wings from your back, and we'd see who no longer flies." The seraph whimpered in submission, and Rhamiel released him to a wounded look and a futile puffing of feathers.

"Things change," said Uzziel. "Status is fickle, a vapor conjured from the minds of the masses, there for a moment only to vanish just as quickly. It comes not from what you are, but from what you are perceived to be."

"Perceptions may be fickle, but one's nature is what it is," said Rhamiel. "I found my strength, during the Fall. If any of you now think yourselves my better, I invite you to put the proposition to the test. And I've still the least scars of any in the room, if that's to be your metric."

None of them met his challenge, or even his eyes, and only Uzziel had the courage to respond. "Things have changed. My generalship in Heaven meant nothing on Earth, so long as the Seraphim revelled in softness and spent their lives bickering over whose cushion was the most plush. Now there are threats anew. Threats I saw all the while. Threats from all sides, and angels eager to be commanded."

"Then commands they shall have," said Rhamiel. "Let us rebuild our tower. Let us construct something grander, taller, sturdier. Let us be what we should have been from the beginning. Let us reclaim our servants, show them their folly, and likewise raise them up to something more than they were. I wager they regret things even now, huddled out in the wastes with no one to protect them."

"First, we must reclaim our own fallen comrades," said Uzziel. "Poor Zuphias led us home, bravest among us and first among us. And now here he lies, betwixt life and death."

Bubbles floated through the glass box that housed him, and cherubs worked at dials on either side to monitor his condition. They'd done something to him, there inside his case. His jaws no longer clacked in futile silence, but had been screwed together and affixed with wires, snaking outwards to a set of speakers on either side of the vat that contained him. The cherubs kept working at them, turning them on and off, though all they managed to draw from the speakers was static. Diodes lined his skull, and tubes had been inserted into it, pumping the vat's fluids in and out of him. Other than that, he was still a blackened crisp, floating in a puddle and in thrall to the cherubs' whims.

"We'll bring your angel back to you somehow," said one of the cherubs floating around the vat. "A toilsome task, but cherubs keep their vows. We'll tunnel through this prison for his soul, and give him back the voice that servants stole."

"Speaking of servants," said Uzziel. "We were just discussing the matter with Zephon. His views on our use of them are interesting. Fresh air, breathed from the most unlikely of lungs."

All eyes turned to the cherub seated in the throne, who'd been busying himself rotating through his four heads, picking the earwax from each before sampling its taste. Zephon smeared his most recent acquisition on the arm of the throne, cleared his throat, and addressed the assembled.

"A servant's place is ever underfoot, and none can stand the spot where they've been put. They'll always try to wriggle from your grip, and find a way to give their leash the slip. The folly's in the labors that you ask; the Maker tailored servants to their task. Why not create some servants of our own, and leave the humans to the fate they've sown? They've bit your hands, a surly little pet; if war they'd wage, then it's a war they'll get."

CHAPTER FOURTEEN

THE FIRST THING THEY NOTICED was the statues. They started miles out from their destination, little ones scattered on cars or as roadside shrines. They made a game of it, seeing how many of them they could spot—angels of stone, striking glorious poses and welcoming any who tread the path towards Suriel's encampment.

They grew bigger as they got closer. Soon they were the size of men, wings spread behind them, all depicting the same angel. Near the end the works expanded to groups of statues enacting scenes for the benefit of passersby, turning the highway's shoulder into a stage. Here he stood welcoming the hungry, there healing the sick, and still there fighting off monsters from down below as innocents hid behind him.

Finally they turned off onto a dirt road, disappearing into a forest as it wound its way into the wilderness. They'd followed the men they'd met there, under the sign, letting them lead the way in a little yellow hatchback. There were checkpoints at every turn, manned by people in grey robes with beaming smiles. The first ones forced them to stop, checking them out and sizing them up. But after that, it was all grins and waves, happy people with happy lives welcoming them to a happy place.

Soon the road opened up from the trees into a field of tall, yellow grass, and they could see the compound in the distance before them. It was a stocky building, squat and square, with sharp fences surrounding it. It might have been taken for a prison, if it weren't for the throngs of people outside clamoring to get in. The fences were surrounded by a vast quilt of tents, the temporary home to a mass of supplicants seeking Suriel's attention. There were thousands of them, at least, waiting outside the gates for their chance to join the chosen.

"You have to stay here," said one of the men who'd led them there, shouting from the car window as he turned around and headed back to the highway to scout for more recruits. "Wait until he calls. Praise be."

"How do we get called?" yelled Holt.

"You'll know," said the man, and he sped away, back to the sign and back to his vigil.

They found an empty spot of field near the edges of the tents and parked the truck. Holt got out, and Faye followed, leaving Jana alone again to sit with Thane.

"Well," said Faye, "I guess we wait."

"We're not waiting," said Holt. "You can put on a brave face all you want. And I'm not saying you're not brave. But you're sick. You're not getting better, you're getting worse. One of those assholes is poking around in your head, and he's not going to stop."

"I can handle it," said Faye. "I'm not just some girl

pushing pencils anymore. I'm just as much a fighter as you are."

"You are," said Holt. "But fighters get hurt. And fighters die, especially when they get cocky. And if you don't want to help yourself, you ought to think about her. She's going to start showing soon. If she really does have one of those... things. If one of them's inside her, we don't know what to do. We don't know what's going to happen. Suriel might."

"Not here," said Faye. "Not out in the open. We're not talking to one of them about it, either."

"People know," said Holt. "Her friends back there knew. Look around. This place is a glorified refugee camp. Rumors can spread. Someone from the Perch might make it here. Who knows. An angel did it to her, and only an angel can help her."

The place was, in fact, overrun with refugees. They all looked it, the people huddled together there seeking sanctuary. They'd built their own city of sorts, complete with avenues between the tents, water pumps, and outhouses. People of all persuasions were lazing around in front of their living space, getting on with the business of waiting. Some passed the time by playing games. A group of children were kicking a soccer ball through a field in the distance, and near one of the tents old men sat in lawn chairs hunched over a table of dominoes. Others were aimlessly chatting, and still others did their chores, hanging laundry on clotheslines or cleaning up trash. An entire row of tents served as a market, with vendors laying their wares out front on mats and haggling with anyone who passed by. There were even some loyal

Vichies, still wearing the white, hopeful that their past service to the angels would give them a leg up in gaining entrance to the compound itself.

The people nearby were roused from their tents by the new arrivals, and began to size them up. A few teenage boys kept their distance, eyeing them from behind the back of an RV. A man looked them over from a chair in front his tent, decided they were no threat, and went back to sitting. Finally someone approached, a short, round woman who'd been beating dust from a rug with a broom.

"No one wants trouble here," said the woman. "Some people want trouble. If you do, you should go. The preachers don't like it. Suriel don't like it."

"We don't want trouble," said Faye. "We heard about Suriel, and he's why we came. What's he like? What's he doing here?"

"Ask the preachers," said the woman. "You'll find 'em, around here somewhere. We just don't want no trouble."

"We've got some sick with us," said Holt. "Nothing contagious. But we heard he can heal."

"He can heal," said the woman. "I seen him heal. Go talk to the preachers. This here's a safe place. No fightin', no hollerin'. Anybody causes trouble, the preachers kick 'em out. You can leave your truck there, and no one's gonna touch it. We'll look in on your sick, as long as they ain't too sick."

"No offense," said Holt. "But we don't know you, or anyone here."

"Nobody knew anybody here, until they came," said the woman. "I look dangerous to you? Anybody here look dangerous to you? Anyone who starts trouble, they're gone. We all waiting, just the same as you. But you want to wait right, you gotta go talk to the preachers."

And indeed, none of them looked dangerous at all. The entire place was serene, surreally so. No one was fighting or quarreling, and none of them seemed to harbor any suspicions towards their neighbors. People were napping out in the open, completely vulnerable, and others had left their tents unoccupied and unwatched. Children were running around in all directions unsupervised, and no one seemed at all inclined to disturb the peace.

"I guess we find the preachers," said Holt. "Let's go. But not for long."

"You go," said Faye. "I'll stay behind with Thane this time. Maybe take Jana along with you. She needs a break from him, or they're going to rip each others' throats out. And if something happens while you're gone, it's better if I'm the one there to handle it."

"Jana," said Holt, slapping his hand against the side of the pickup. "Let's go. We're taking a walk, just to see what's around."

She was more than happy to oblige, as Faye climbed in to keep watch on an unconscious Thane. The two of them walked around between the tents, keeping the truck in view, surveying the neighborhood they'd set up shop in.

All the people there seemed happy, completely without the cares that weighed upon everyone else in an age where violence and death had become commonplace again. They turned down an aisle of tents housing the local market, but they found that it was an odd one.

Many of the goods were for bartering, but many more were openly advertised as free, under signs declaring that followers of Suriel should share and share alike.

Much of what was being given away was of the bargain basement sort, the kinds of things that would have ended up stuffed in some dollar store years before. One tent had a table covered in stacks of identical blue bathrobes, all the same size; another with boxes of shower curtains and cheap disposable razors. Likely it was all surplus from foraging through old stores, and its new owners could never have used it all, anyway. But still, it was the thought that counted, and giving it away freely was an unusual thought.

Everywhere around them were tents and recreational vehicles, homes on the move for people who'd managed to get them there. Most of the people had been living there for some time, and the plots they'd claimed had begun to take on the character of permanent encampments. Some had little wooden fences staked into the ground around them, while others had vegetable gardens that they'd clearly been cultivating through at least a season. The people all sat outside, chatting with their neighbors and otherwise frittering away the day.

"Is this how everyone lived, before the angels?" said Jana. "Outside, on their own?"

"Kind of," said Holt. "It's like a smaller version of what it was. We had it better. We had buildings, and towers, and everything we wanted. You could go outside, go inside, whatever you wanted to do."

Two little boys rushed past them, doing battle with foam swords with towels hanging from their backs for capes. They whacked at each other as they weaved through the adults browsing at the market stalls, zipping underfoot as they went about their duel.

"They aren't even doing anything," said Jana. "So many people just sitting and talking. And these children, they're just playing."

"You didn't play?" said Holt.

"Not during the day," said Jana. "Not when someone could catch us. You had to pretend to be busy, even when you didn't have anything to do."

"It's how people pass the time," said Holt. "It's how they learn. When no one's looking over their shoulders to crack a whip."

"We did something like it, I think," said Jana. "But inside our heads. Where no one could see. I still feel like they're watching me. Like any moment, someone's going to round the corner, screaming and flapping their wings, snapping someone's arm because they served them with a dirty plate. I don't think it's ever going to go away. I don't think I'm made for out here."

"You'll adjust," said Holt. "You may not believe it, but you will. You stop thinking about it, and let it fade, and then someday it's just the past. Everyone out here is exactly like you, no matter how different you think you are. They all had a world they were comfortable with, and they all lost it when the angels came. I know you don't want to stay with us, but you should think about it. Once we fix Thane, once we fix Faye, we can find a way to help you. Just think about it."

They turned a corner into another row of tents and came upon Suriel's followers, people from inside the compound who were on business outside of it. Here and there men in grey robes walked among the people, feeding the hungry and ministering to the would-be faithful. They saw three of them shouting a sermon to a crowd of onlookers, listening with rapt attention. The amens that came in response were loud and enthusiastic, and whether they were sincere or not, they were a demonstration of the crowd's desire to enter.

"The Maker has not forsaken us!" shouted one of the preachers.

"Praise be!" shouted a few members of the crowd, as they clapped and hooted.

"The Maker has sent us Suriel! Praise be!" shouted another of the preachers.

"Praise be!" came the shouts back.

"Now some of you are new," said the third preacher, to nods from the assembled. "And some of you aren't ready. So you all need to listen. Listen up, and straighten up. My name is Preacher Perry. That's my new name, my holy name, my happy name. Suriel saved me, and he'll save you, too. You're blessed, and you don't even know it. Praise be."

He was a jolly man, fat and friendly, a heavy belly bulging out at the center of his grey robe above a golden cord tied around his waist. He was mostly bald, with frizzy brown hair rounding the back of his head as it receded away. He was all smiles, working the people around him and managing to direct his grin at everyone both individually and all at once.

"Hold up," said Holt, and he and Jana joined the crowd's fringes.

"You called him God, but they who know him, they call him the Maker," said Preacher Perry. "And nobody knows the Maker better than Suriel. Now you all know what angels are. But any of you know what an archangel is?"

The crowd murmured. They all did, or thought they did. But the new ones weren't sure, and the faithful who'd heard the speech before just smiled.

"An archangel is the Maker's favorite kind of angel," said Preacher Perry. "The best kind! Good, and loyal, and not like all these others. Now Suriel, he's the only one down here. See the Maker. He loves us. He tests us, but he loves us. He loves us so much, he sent us someone to talk to us. The Maker, he can't talk to us on his own. Your head would just burst. He's that powerful. But Suriel. He can hear the Maker. He knows what the Maker wants. And he can tell it to us. The Maker's Mouthpiece, down on Earth to lead us to salvation. Praise be!"

Some in the crowd shouted back the refrain, but not all of them. The newer ones were a little more wary, a little unsure of themselves. Many hadn't been there long, and none had been inside the compound but the preachers.

"I'm just worried," said a woman in the crowd, a grey-haired matron in a tattered floral-print dress. "I wanted to ask. About the statues. And what we have to say."

"You don't have to say anything you don't want to," said Preacher Perry. "But go on. Suriel doesn't want you worried. He loves you. Heck, I love you! Let's hear it, and let's make you feel better."

"Well, the Bible," said the woman. "It's got that stuff about idols. I just don't want to make God mad."

"Nobody's mad as long as you're trying!" said Preacher Perry. "Why, the Bible's a good book, and I'm not saying it ain't. But it's an old book, and we don't always follow it here, not to the letter. Why, we've got a conduit straight to the Maker, right here. We know what the Maker's thinking now, not what he was thinking then. Who needs scripture when you have Suriel? Praise be. Now you're out here, right?"

"Yeah," said the woman.

"That's right," said Preacher Perry. "And you don't get in there 'til you're ready. So if you're not comfortable, you just go slow. That's okay. Suriel loves you, and Suriel won't be mad. You can just go at your own pace. He doesn't expect you to get it right away. Now, you don't want to take forever. You don't have forever. It's dangerous out here, and you can't get in there where it's safe until you're good and ready. But when you are, boy, there's a little bit of Heaven on Earth inside. Now anyone who wants to get ready, you just come on. You follow me, and let me get you started on the road to redemption. You let me show you the statues."

CHAPTER FIFTEEN

"**B**RIGADES OF GOLEMS FILL THE halls below; a clockwork army's helm we can bestow. Lead them against the world's remaining few; they'll show you what a cherub's mind can do. The Maker erred in not aborting man, his soft compassion wrecking ancient plans."

Zephon stood at the entrance to the Nest, surveying a battalion of golems arrayed in rows before him. He'd ordered them up to the surface, a demonstration for Uzziel and the others. Now they stood for inspection under the eyes of skeptical seraphs, who looked less than impressed. Uzziel tapped at the golems as his party went, weighing their weaknesses with a wary eye, trying to determine if they were the stuff victories were made of.

They'd all come up, even Rhamiel, for whom the cherubs had helpfully crafted a new set of armor, melting what they could salvage of his old set into a spartan plate mail. It was more grey than gold, tarnished by whatever alloy the cherubs had mixed into it, and it had no decorations and no lion. But what it had lost in adornment, it made up for in durability. He'd even hacked at it with his sword, on the cherubs' urging, and the flames had simply bounced away. The other seraphs had nothing but contempt for such inglorious apparel, but their every insult was accompanied by jealous glancing and unconvincing sniffs, too exaggerated to ever pass as genuine.

"Armies," said Uzziel, rubbing his finger against a clay golem and brushing the dust from his hand. "It's been years, since I've seen an army before me. There's a grace to them all, even one as ugly as this. But your golems are more patchwork than clockwork. That's the problem with cherubs. They've no sense of elegance. How can one savor the glories of war, when all that's theirs to command is some slapdash soldiery?"

And indeed, the golems were hardly pretty. No two were alike, the result of the cherubs' perpetual tinkering with their own designs. The rows they formed had little order, as each contended with others of varying sizes for space. Some were enormous, hulking over even the largest of the seraphs, clamping at the air with claws, flexing tentacles, or otherwise displaying whatever digits the cherubs had provided them. Some were made of stone, some from gems, some forged with metal, and some even from flesh. Some were tiny midgets, standing barely at a cherub's waist and fitted with weapons or cameras or antennae. All had been crafted with precision to address some particular martial task, and had been endowed with whatever tools the cherubs had thought best suited to them. But however well-made, they were a poor fit for parades and ceremonies, and so drew Uzziel's sneers.

Zephon just snorted, and led the inspection further down the line of golems. "Prize function more, as form's a lesser thing; though feather bare, they be not broken wings. Each golem was designed to be itself, not sized and shaped for display on a shelf. Besides, this army's better than your own, so curb your doubts and take them for a loan."

The seraphs crowded around a particularly impressive golem, the size of two men, formed entirely from living ruby. Its skin was jagged and shiny, and it glimmered a bright red as it reflected light from the chrome expanse that surrounded the Nest. It made rumbling noises from within as the seraphs backed away, and its arms hung low to the ground, scraping against the metal with its claws.

"A test," said Uzziel. "I shall take them for a test. You must understand the Seraphim. We've envoys, sent to other towers, to warn them of the threat and rally them to our banner. But we do not act without a great deal of deliberation."

"No, we do not," said Rhamiel. "Our opinions are rarely uniform, and our leaders oft deposed, if they persist in an ill decision."

"Or," said Uzziel, "if they invite traitors into their bedrooms."

Laughter came from all around, and the seraphs didn't even bother to hide their smirks. Many rooted for Uzziel openly, though none were brave enough to issue a challenge themselves. The two bucks squared off and sized each other up, the cunning of the old, battle-scarred warrior against the vigor and hunger of the younger, stronger usurper. The rest of the seraphs egged them on, now shouting support for both sides, placing bets on which of them would win if it came to it.

"Matters of the heart are no matter of yours," said Rhamiel. "I spent many centuries with humans in my care, and learned to care for them. You play with your toys all you like. My strength is returned, and my wings are dried. I have a search to conduct, and a girl to find, and if the rest of you dislike it, then you may be damned to Lucifer's Pit."

"Well, then," said Uzziel. "You should simply accompany us. We're headed for the very same place, after all. With the same objective. To round up servants, and settle our accounts with them. Maybe that pledge of yours will be one of our prizes. Maybe she'll even have survived, to face justice at our hands."

"You may think her a mere paramour, but she's no prize of yours," said Rhamiel, fingers tapping the sheath of his sword. "I'll gut you, Uzziel. I'll splay your intestines across this field of slag. You're a housemate of mine no longer, and if you're such a slave to spite that you'd loose your dogs on one who's under my care, then you're no brother, either."

"My quarrel," said Uzziel, "is not with you, but with who you take under your wing. I can see her treason, even if you can't. If she lived, she betrayed us, and that's the end of the matter."

"You see treason everywhere," said Rhamiel. "Who isn't a traitor, in your clouded eyes? Who among us hasn't drawn your suspicions, at one time or another?"

"Sometimes I am right," said Uzziel. "The likes of you never listen, but sometimes I am right."

"You're a stopped clock, and nothing more," said Rhamiel. "A befuddled old paranoiac who fancies himself a conqueror."

Uzziel's eyes flared, and his hand went to his sword. The two were circling each other now, and seemed sure to come to blows. The rest of the seraphs cheered and pressed in around them, as a swarm of cherubs fluttered around in complete confusion as to what had happened and why the seraphs would escalate a dispute over such trivial matters as love or treachery.

"Look," said one of the seraphs, interrupting the push towards melee. "Above us, up there. Something approaches."

"Someone," said another. And up in the sky they could see a black dot growing closer, flapping its wings and making its way towards them. It became clearer as it grew: a seraph, just one, gliding in to land.

He circled the golem army, taking in the sight from above, and after a few rounds he flew to the crowd, lighting down beside them. He drew scowls from some, and smiles from many. Whatever Ecanus was or however low he might be, he was always an entertainer, and the seraphs who'd at first been disappointed by the interruption were happy for the arrival of someone so likely to add fuel to the fire.

Uzziel gave a little growl, and Rhamiel tightened his face as Ecanus walked towards them. He grinned at Uzziel, and looked Rhamiel up and down, holding his hand out to him in an exaggerated show of friendship. He met no greeting from Rhamiel, only stony silence, and he managed to look very, very hurt.

"A pregnant pause," said Ecanus, "wouldn't you say?"

"I wouldn't say anything, to the likes of you," said Rhamiel. "Yours is a face I'd rather have forgotten."

"Brother," said Ecanus. "Why mar our reunion with old grudges? You're alive, and that's what counts. Why, I came to find you, more than anything! A rumor said you were here, recovered from your injuries, and so I cut my business short. A business that drew me here, in fact. To speak to you."

"Your affairs are no concern of mine," said Rhamiel. "What business could you be about, that would draw you to me?"

"The business of slaughtering servants," said Ecanus. "An endless chore, no matter how industrious I was about seeking them out. Dozens? Hundreds? Who can say? But I hadn't even made a start of it, before my thoughts went to you. And it was all because of a girl I met."

"You," sputtered Rhamiel, and then he unsheathed his sword. Fire swirled around him as he cut through the air, advancing on Ecanus to the cheers of the crowd. They all made way, to root and shout from the sidelines. These weren't the combatants they'd expected, but a brawl was a brawl, and so long as blood was spilt they'd be happy.

"You quite misunderstand me," said Ecanus, palms out in submission as he beat his wings and dodged up into the air to avoid Rhamiel's wild slashings. "Whyever would you think me such a sort? It pains me, that you think so little of me. No, I did not meet your girl. I met another, who'd seen her. Outside of the tower. Alive."

"Alive," said Rhamiel. "If you lie, Ecanus. If you lie…"

"I speak only the truth I was told," said Ecanus. "I can't well be expected to vouch for the word of servants.

But she seemed honest. She was quite motivated to be truthful, though when it comes to my methods of extracting the truth, I admit to being something of a braggart."

"Uzziel," said Rhamiel. "Stay your army. I leave for the tower, now, and I expect you to await my return. If I find you hunting her, you'll find me hunting you."

"I will grant you a favor," said Uzziel. "A short reprieve. And only because I think it sound tactics, as well as politics. Know that while the tower may have fallen, my network of spies has not. Many servants plotted against us, both within the tower and without. Even now, conspiracies against us abound. All who are complicit will face a reckoning. But I'll grant you this: these machinations will be addressed in order of severity, and in order of their current threat. So find your wayward serf, do it quickly, and punish her as you see fit. This armada takes flight soon, and it shan't be long before my attentions turn to those who knew our home would fall, but left our brothers inside to die in their sleep."

CHAPTER SIXTEEN

"**N**OW THIS," SAID PREACHER PERRY, "this is how it all started. This is Suriel, trying to stop the rebellion. He tried, tried real hard, tried with all his might. But when someone's gonna go against the Maker, sometimes you can't stop 'em. And the rest of them, they just wouldn't listen to poor Suriel. There's a lesson there, for them that don't listen."

They stood in a sculpture garden, built up behind the rear wall of the compound and away from the bustle of the tents, a quiet place for contemplation and worship. Everyone else kept themselves at a respectable distance, and as people walked through the garden, they lowered their voices to a hush. Every few yards there was a set of sculptures, stone works that told the story of the Fall and Suriel's role in it. Holt and Jana had followed them all, quietly blending in with the rest of them and walking along on a pilgrimage in miniature.

Preacher Perry had taken the crowd to this scene in stone, at the very beginning of the garden. An imposing, benevolent angel stood before a crowd of others, hands stretched out in a gesture of pleading. He looked impossibly handsome, his granite muscles bulging and his face without a flaw. The other angels laughed, held up swords, or turned their backs on him, rejecting whatever entreaties he was making. A well-worn path wound through and around the other sculptures, and pilgrims all around were in the process of their own solitary journeys through the garden, stopping at each scene for a moment of prayer and reflection.

"Come on down to the next one," said Preacher Perry. "Suriel, he fought, and he fought bravely. When the Maker asks you to, you gotta fight. You gotta battle if you want to do good. And Suriel, he does what the Maker says."

They walked a little further down the path, to the second set of statues. Again, Suriel was at the center, this time with sword drawn, his expression a righteous sneer. His sword's fire cut through the air in front of him, and the angels who'd confronted him in the first scene now fled from his assaults in the second.

"Suriel cast the others down here," said Preacher Perry. "The Maker told him to, and so he did. And he was the strongest, and the most powerful, and the best. And he won, and the Maker was real happy. Praise be."

The crowd pressed around the statues, and some of the ones who'd tread this path before began chanting to themselves, ahead of the game.

"Now if we're going to walk the path, let's walk it right," said Preacher Perry. "Let's honor the Maker, and honor what's been done for us. You know how we do that? We say a little prayer at every stop. The Maker's will is Suriel's will, and Suriel's will is the Maker's will. Say it along with me, now, those that want to come inside. The Maker's will is Suriel's will, and Suriel's will is the Maker's will."

The ones who'd been there before regurgitated the chant by reflex, and a few of the newer people in the crowd followed along as well, though with more hesitation. Everyone was looking from side to side, seeing who followed and who didn't, gauging the crowd's collective sentiments before they decided what to do themselves. Jana herself started into the chant, following her own reflex to obey instructions, but cut herself off as she saw Holt standing silent.

"Keep on down the path," said Preacher Perry. "Keep following it, until you find salvation with Suriel. He'll show you the way. Now here's a pretty picture. The Maker's throne, and Suriel stands before it." He showed them their next stop, a depiction of Suriel standing strong before a giant, empty throne, a sword in one hand and the head of an angel dangling by the hair from the other. A row of trumpets peeped out from behind the throne on either side, blaring hallelujahs all around.

"See them trumpets?" said Preacher Perry. "He still hears what they say, even down here. The word of the Maker, from Suriel's mouth. Don't doubt it. And why would you? Because that word, that word says that the Maker loves you. That Suriel loves you. And all you gotta do is love them back that loves you. Now let's all pray, all that wants to. Say it with me. Suriel loves me, and I love Suriel."

The crowd followed along, more joining in this time. "Suriel loves me, and I love Suriel."

Jana kept entirely quiet this time. The other angels hadn't cared what their servants had thought of them, certainly not to the point of teaching them prayers, and they never would have been so open about their time in Heaven. But they expected to be obeyed, and no matter how silly the order, she was used to following it. It felt good, the little act of rebellion, refusing to follow along even when it was clear they'd rather she did.

"Now here's the fourth step," said Preacher Perry, leading them on. A statue of Suriel stood, having just landed on the ground. Dozens of stone humans were fleeing towards him seeking safety in his arms, with an angry, scarred angel hot on their heels.

"What did the Maker tell Suriel?" said Preacher Perry. "What do you think he said, when his creations were hurting, and calling out to him for help? Well, he sent it to them. He sent us Suriel. The others fell, but Suriel was sent. He came down here to help you. To love you. To fight for you. And the least you can do is give him something back. So say it now, everybody! Say it loud and proud! Suriel gives me his love, and I give Suriel my faith!"

The crowd mirrored his words, louder now, the enthusiasm of the faithful prompting the others to cast aside their doubts. "Suriel gives me his love, and I give Suriel my faith!"

"Last one," said Preacher Perry. "And then you can walk on down the rest of the path yourself. There's more, but they speak for themselves, and you don't need me to do it." He showed them another set of sculptures, this time of Suriel holding a loaf of bread in each hand. A group of people sat before him, eating their fill, with happy smiles carved onto every one of their faces.

"Suriel's here to save our souls, but not just that," said Preacher Perry. "He's here to help us any way he can. The stuff inside the sanctuary, boy, you wouldn't believe it. Food, more than you can eat. Wine, more than you can drink. Games and fun and laughter and friends. A little prayer, and a lot of love. I'm almost glad things turned out the way they did, otherwise I'd never have seen the likes of this. Now everybody join in this time. Salvation lies with Suriel, and Suriel is our salvation! Praise be."

A chorus of praise be's erupted, and the crowd followed their cue to chant the little prayer. Preacher Perry was happy, and so were the faithful, and they made sure the skeptics knew it, too. They clapped them on the back, and gave them hugs, no matter whether they'd chanted the prayers or not. They'd done the walk, and if they hadn't yet seen the light, well, they could always do it again tomorrow.

"Now, some of you have doubts," said Preacher Perry. "Don't think I don't know. That's okay. I been down this path, too, and I was a skeptic. Boy, it took me a time before I was a believer. But you just keep walking the path, and you'll see. There's rewards for those that walk it, and I want you to get a reward. So you follow me, and everyone who walked this path today, we're gonna feed you. We're gonna clothe you. And you walk it again tomorrow, and we're gonna feed you again. No catch, no cost."

Now the crowd was truly happy, even the ones who hadn't yet found their faith. They were a sorry lot, and some of the newest arrivals were on the brink of starvation. They had sunken eyes, and hollow cheeks, and they'd have done anything for a few scraps of food. When they found out that all Suriel asked was a little walk and a little prayer, none of them were complaining. Several men in grey robes ran towards them, carrying bottles of wine and crates of meat and bread, and everyone rushed around to eat their fill. Jana managed to grab an armload of food herself, though Holt stopped her hand as she reached for the wine.

"Don't push, don't push," said Preacher Perry. "There's plenty where that came from. You just take turns, and pass it all around, and don't you even worry about us running out, because we won't. And if you don't have faith now, well, you're gonna have faith tonight. Tonight you're gonna see something special. Tonight you're gonna see the lame walk, and the sick get healed. Tonight you're gonna see Suriel."

CHAPTER SEVENTEEN

IT WAS A NORMAL DAY, if a tense one. Those who were citizens went about their lives in the streets, showing off white suits or white dresses, engaging in the local sport of politicking, or browsing the dwindling wares in the city's shops. Those who weren't citizens went about their lives as servants to those who were, tending to potholes in the streets, trimming hedges in the parks, and mopping floors to wipe away black scuffs left by white boots.

Everyone was on edge underneath it all, but that wasn't a first for Washington. Rumors had run wild for weeks, trickling in from the north about a blow that had been struck against the angels. About servants being killed, and Vichies who'd spat in the faces of their masters, and a mass of homeless exiles spreading out in all directions.

It wouldn't have caused such unease, under ordinary circumstances. There were always rumors; that was the way of an unconnected world. Word didn't travel as fast as it had in days gone by, and it took longer for the truth to catch up. It was easy for gossip to take hold, and spin around in the minds of the uninformed as they lost themselves in speculation. It would have been just another rumor, if there had been nothing else.

But the angels had gone quiet, and no one could say exactly why.

Normally they'd send someone calling, from time to time, an emissary to keep the Vichies in line and keep them on task.

Normally they wanted something from their servants.

But no one had shown, not for several weeks, and people were starting to talk. The angels' disinterest wasn't even the worst of it. The flow of looted goods was drying up, as the Vichies outside the capital visited less and less often to pay tribute to their nominal masters. It put a crimp on things, but they were used to periodic disruptions. Supply chains weren't what they'd been, back when the roads were clear and they'd stood astride a world instead of a city.

But this wasn't a day for worries. It was a day for leisure, a perfect weekend with a sunny sky and balmy weather. By the afternoon, the citizenry had started to gather outdoors, congregating in the National Mall for a day of relaxation. Politicians sat on the steps of the Smithsonian, licking at shaved ice and making illicit deals. Society women paraded in skirts, and gossiped about who was up, and who was down, and who they simply couldn't stand. Children ran the length of the park with kites, cheap entertainment that didn't require modern industry to provide. Slaves cut the grass, and swept the streets, and ran whatever errands the citizens didn't care to.

The sun was heavy over the park when they saw the first dot in the sky, a little silver star far in the distance, shining in the middle of the day. But stars didn't move, and this one was coming closer. It could have been a plane, said some, but no one had seen one in years. And when the others appeared behind it, they knew it was no plane.

They could see the wings as the dots approached, and at first they thought the angels had come with instructions at last. Everyone gathered round, and the ones who thought themselves most important pushed their way to the front, eager to curry favor with the angels however possible. Children cheered, women curtsied, men doffed their hats and waved, and they all prepared to play hosts. They made ready to put on their best faces and greet their masters with subservient smiles and respectful bows, just the way they always had.

And then they saw the swords.

Murmurs rippled through the crowd, and for a few minutes they all just stood, paralyzed by shock. The fire was coming towards them, with freakish things following behind at the angels' tails. They whispered to themselves, trying to reassure each other that everything was just fine, and the angels above would greet them as always, though perhaps more sternly. They held rank for a time, and held onto hope, until some at the edges saw the truth and began to break away and run. Then all at once it was chaos, every Vichy for themselves in a mad dash for safety.

The women and children were trampled, their pleas for chivalry ignored by the fleeing men. But that was the Vichy way, and none of them truly expected it to be any different. Their bonds were only of convenience, parasites who stuck together the better to drain their host. And when the first of the angels landed, the weakest of them were the first to be slaughtered.

Uzziel was at the fore, and he set down amidst the crowd of would-be admirers with sword drawn. He claimed the first kill, his right as general, and ran amok waving flames in all directions. He chopped off heads of ladies, blackening their lily white dresses. He sliced away the arms of children, leaving them to roll about on the ground in anguish. He flew from man to man as they searched for somewhere to flee, running his sword through whomever he pleased. And as the others began to land around the park, it was clear there would be no quarter.

Behind the angels came the golems, floating through the skies, slower but no less deadly. They flew on clouds of steam, gusting out from feet or hands or packs strapped to their backs. The ones that couldn't fly were carried by others, fat floating slugs of clay that the cherubs had designed to transport their troops. They began to plunge from the skies, slamming into the grass and sending up clouds of dirt all around them. Then they rose from the ground, and joined the angels in the bloodbath.

The smaller ones went straight for the Vichies. Spider-like machines the size of dogs clambered around the park, latching onto the backs of the slowest of the Vichies and boring holes through their abdomens.

Chrome automatons lumbered towards any clumps of people they could find, launching shrapnel from weapons affixed to their arms and flaying their victims to pieces. Little insects flew about unnoticed, until they bit and stabbed at their targets, injecting them with poisons and leaving them bowled over on the ground, helpless before the angels' leisurely massacre.

The larger golems focused on the buildings. Creatures animated from rock or gems tore down monuments that had stood for centuries, clawing down statue and wall alike. They tossed hunks of stone all around, and one particularly enthusiastic clay creature claimed the most kills of them all. It had no eyes, but it had aim, and as it tore pieces from the buildings it launched them towards the fleeing Vichies. It lobbed one of the massive stone fragments at the middle of a chain gang, slaves of the Vichies who'd been lashed together and left to fend for themselves by their overseers. The rock landed with a splat, snuffing them all out as they argued over which way to run.

As the park was cleared, Uzziel ordered the golems about, sending them in all directions to raze the city and salt the earth. "Show our servants what it means to betray us," he said. "Let them know that Uzziel has eyes and ears, everywhere, and that he knows from whence conspiracies come."

Then he reined in his seraphs, gathering them in the center of the park, bodies and limbs scattered around them on all sides. "A fine army," he said. "An obedient army. Mere machines, to be sure, but machines cannot conspire. They do not dispute commands, or rush about on errands of their own. They do not tire, and flutter back to rest on couches while the battle still rages. Traits that seraphs should ponder, in days to come."

The seraphs celebrated their triumph, treating it as a hard-won victory rather than the easy rout that it was. They cheered each other, holding aloft heads and limbs of the slaughtered as grisly trophies. They laughed and joked, telling stories about their deeds and the cowardice of their former servants. When they grew bored of the festivities, they took to the air one by one, venturing off into the city to follow the golems and continue the pursuit. The fighting went on and on through night and day, and didn't stop until every building was rubble, and every last resident of the city had been put to the sword.

CHAPTER EIGHTEEN

"**H**E'S GOING TO HEAL PEOPLE, tonight," said Holt. "And we're going to be first in line."

The locals had been true to their word. No one had bothered Faye or Thane while they were gone, other than to offer them help. One woman who claimed to have been a nurse before the Fall had even checked in on him, though the only balm she had was her words. Holt had led Jana back, both their arms laden with food, only to find the pickup already filled with it from nearby well-wishers. Far from threatening them, by now everyone around was ignoring them, the area buzzing with the news of Suriel's upcoming appearance.

"They're already staking out their places," said Faye. "Over at the edge of the field. People've been running over there for half an hour, claiming spots. We're going to be in the back, even if we head over right now. There's too many in line already."

"It's not a line," said Holt. "It's a crowd. And we need him to pick us out of it."

"He won't even see us," said Faye. "Not in the dark."

"There's ways to stand out," said Holt. "Ways to get up to the front. First thing we do, is talk to this preacher."

"Jana!" called Faye, grabbing her attention. She was busying herself plucking flowers from the ground out in the field, tying them into bracelets. In truth, they'd have been better classed as weeds, virulent things with nothing to boast of but bland colors and tiny petals. But they reminded her of the garden, and better times, and she had so little experience with their like that she thought them beauties, regardless of whether a connoisseur would have recoiled at the scent of them.

"Jana, we need you to watch Thane," said Faye. "Not for long. We're going to be right back." Jana wrinkled her nose, and couldn't hide her frustration. But she pushed it down, and promised she'd keep him safe, as they left her behind to play nursemaid yet again.

They found the preacher among the tents, mingling with the would-be supplicants. That was the easy part. Now that the news was out, everyone wanted a word with him. They were all pushing to get his attention, as he pried himself free with the help of a few of his grey-robed colleagues, who spread their arms wide and blocked the crowd so he could make his escape. Holt made a beeline straight for the preacher's path, and one of the men tried to intercept him. But he was too small and too gentle, and Holt just brushed him aside, standing right in Preacher Perry's way.

"Got to prepare for tonight, friend," said Preacher Perry, slapping Holt on the shoulder with a smile. "But we'll talk tomorrow."

"We've got to talk now," said Holt. "Me, and Suriel. About some friends I want him to cure."

"I'm sorry, boy, am I sorry," said Preacher Perry. "But Suriel's a busy guy. Everybody here wants something, and I mean everybody. And there's only so many people he can heal."

"That's what I want to talk to you about," said Holt. "We've got a friend, in casts. All over his body."

"Casts," said Preacher Perry. "Tonight's about showing people what Suriel can do for them. Your boy may be hurt, I'm not saying he ain't. But casts, they can be fake. Take a look at this old man over there."

He pointed to an elderly man he'd been visiting, hunched in a wheelchair outside a yellow tent. His eyes were white with cataracts, leaving him with nothing in life to enjoy but the breeze. His son sat beside him, talking away at him even though he couldn't hear a word of it. He wiped his father's face, kept him covered with blankets, and tended to him as best he could given the circumstances.

"He's blind as a bat," said Preacher Perry. "He's crippled, he's deaf. And he just looks sick. People see him healed, they're going to believe. They're going to have faith. It's all about faith. You're new, and there's a way these things work. Get in line, do what Suriel says, and have faith. That's the path to follow, you'll see."

"Please," said Faye. "There's got to be something we can do. Some way to work this out."

"Just gotta give it time," said Preacher Perry. "Why don't you go walk the path, and say the prayers? Every step you take is a step closer to Suriel."

"We don't have time," said Holt. "Look. Our friend is sick. Broken bones. We've got another friend, she's sick. Something we need to talk to an angel about. And Faye. She doesn't look it, and she won't say it, but she's sick, too. We need to talk to Suriel. We just want to talk to him."

"Everybody does," said Preacher Perry. "But not everybody can. Can't help you, wish I could. Suriel takes who he takes, and that's up to him. You want to get in, you gotta get in line. Sorry folks, but that's that." He gave them a healthy handshake and a broad smile, before he headed away from the clamoring masses, retreating inside the compound to prepare for the night before him.

"Fuck," said Faye. "Well, we can wait around, and we can watch this show. Or we can leave, and try to find some other way. Thane's going to heal, we just need to let him. Jana's doing fine. And I can handle myself. Maybe it's for the best, anyway. I don't like trusting an angel. They say he'd heal us, but who knows what he'd actually do?"

"We can't wait," said Holt. "I can't. I've been leading us. I'm responsible. If you die, if any of them die, it's on me. They were all my choices. That's why we're here. That's why Thane's hurt. That's why you've got something in your head."

"We're making choices, too," said Faye. "You're the leader, but we chose to follow. It's not on you, no matter what you think."

"You still trusted me," said Holt. "The buck stops here. You know that. I'm going to make this right, though. I'm going to make things right."

"You don't have to—" said Faye.

"I do," said Holt. "For you. And for me. Go back to the others. Get them ready. I'm going to go work this out. Suriel's going to help us, tonight."

"These people are off their rockers," said Faye. "I don't know what their deal is, but nobody's this happy. Nobody's this friendly to strangers. They could do anything. I don't want to just trust them."

"I'm going to figure something out," said Holt. "Don't worry. Just go get everyone ready." Then he wandered off, disappearing into the rows of tents and merging into the crowd of people walking between them.

Faye made her way back to the pickup, and found Jana and Thane still waiting there, she awake and he asleep.

"How is he?" said Faye. "How are you?"

"We're both fine," said Jana. "He was quiet, this time. He gets too angry. But I can handle it when he's quiet."

"See the building?" said Faye. "We're going to try to get the people in there to help us. And we're going to have to do it soon."

"I'm going to be fine," said Jana. "I'm not sick. I feel fine. I just want to know where Rhamiel is. I want to tell him about the baby."

"I know," said Faye. "It's not something wrong with you. It's something wrong with me. That thing you saw. With me, and the way I talked funny. Jana, I'm sick. It's really bad. Don't say anything to either of them, because God knows they don't need anything else to worry about. But ever since the last attack, it's like a buzz in my head. It's started buzzing, and it won't stop. I think I'm in control, but sometimes I don't know."

"They can do miracles," said Jana. "They told me so. Rhamiel could help you, if this one won't. Some of them really are good. Rhamiel was a guardian angel. He protected people, before they all came down here."

"I know," said Faye. "I know they can't all be as terrible as the worst of them are. But they're all fallen. They're different from what they were."

"Different," said Jana. "But different isn't always bad."

"Not always," said Faye. "But it's change. Losing something of themselves, and replacing it with something else. They went from perfect to something less. Maybe Suriel can help us. Maybe Rhamiel can. For now, all we've got is Suriel. So let's get Thane ready, and get him over to where it's all going to happen. And then we'll see what we can see."

It wasn't hard to get him prepared, but they found they couldn't move him, not without Holt. He was just too heavy, and too sensitive to being bumped around as they moved the stretcher. They'd start to lift, and then he'd wake with a scream, shouting to the heavens as the pain ripped through him. Jana in particular couldn't handle it. She didn't especially like him, but she was no sadist, and she cringed each time the pain flashed onto his face. They ended up waiting, almost until nightfall, when Holt finally returned from the tents.

He wouldn't talk about where he'd been. He just urged them on, helping them to lift Thane into his wheelchair and then to move him across the rugged ground to the edges of the assembly. They traveled in fits and starts, going until Thane couldn't handle it anymore before taking a break, and it was dark by the time they finally made it there. They found a spot near the periphery of the crowd, and joined the wait along with all the rest.

The preachers had built a bonfire, out in the fields surrounding the compound and away from the tents. Heavy logs were piled at the center, and they'd lit them up, blazing their faith into the night. Everyone had gathered round on one side, laid out on blankets or sitting in lawn chairs. Preacher Perry stood near the fire, illuminated by the flames with a dozen other preachers beside him. They were all clapping in unison, singing a hymn, getting the crowd pumped up and ready for a revival.

"Now everybody listen up, and everybody listen good," shouted Preacher Perry. "Suriel loves me, and I love Suriel!"

"Suriel loves me, and I love Suriel!" came the shouts back from the crowd.

"Praise be," said Preacher Perry. "Who wants to see some healing tonight? Do y'all want to see some healing?"

"Yes!" roared the crowd.

"Of course you do," said Preacher Perry. "And who wants to see Suriel?"

"We do!"

"Well, tonight you're gonna see Suriel, and tonight he's gonna heal," said Preacher Perry. "Tonight's a good night. A night created by the Maker, and blessed by Suriel. The Maker's Mouthpiece! The Maker's gonna talk to us tonight. We're gonna hear his words, hear 'em through Suriel. And when Suriel speaks, who's gonna listen?"

"We will!"

"Praise be," said Preacher Perry. "Suriel feeds us, and

Suriel clothes us, and Suriel shows us the path. All we gotta do is follow, and that's real simple. So look up. Look on up, because I think I see him coming, coming right now."

They heard him first, wings beating in the air from the direction of the compound. It was a heavy thump, thump, thump in the darkness beyond. Then they saw shadows, between them and the stars, and finally a shape. An angel's wings, a radiant silver that glowed even in the darkness with no light for them to reflect. He descended on them from the black and landed before the bonfire, standing next to his missionaries and taking in his audience.

He stood above man, and even above other angels, nearly nine feet high. His face was as chiseled as his statues, and his hair as silver as his wings. He wore a black cassock, covering him from his sandals up to his neck, and his hands were fitted with black silken gloves. At his waist was the hilt of a heavy, two-handed broadsword, its flames sheathed and ready to be drawn against those who threatened his followers. He looked down on the audience, and they up at him, and he smiled.

"A fine flock," said Suriel. "Though they haven't yet accepted the mantle of their shepherd, have they?"

"They're gettin' there, boy are they gettin' there," said Preacher Perry. "They're walkin' the path. They're—"

"Thank you, Preacher," said Suriel. "A shame, that faith in the Maker has dwindled to what it is this day. There's no trust, not in him, nor in his emissaries. It used to be that man had faith. That he trusted his Maker, and trusted his plan, no matter how odd it might seem.

But this is an age of calamities, and the weakest sheep are most easily led astray by wolves. He loves you, and Suriel loves you, despite your weakness. Despite your distrust, and your failings. The Maker spoke in miracles, once. And now he does again. He heals through Suriel, and speaks through Suriel. Bring Suriel your lame, and you shall see the Maker's word. Suriel's word."

"Bring him the lame!" shouted Preacher Perry, and several of the other preachers rushed into the crowd, heading towards a predetermined spot right at the center. But when they got there, they seemed baffled, looking at one another in confusion. They looked up at Preacher Perry and shrugged, and he turned to Suriel and whispered something up to him. Suriel's wings flicked, and his eyes flared, and he bent down to have a tense, animated conversation with Preacher Perry out of earshot of the audience.

The ceremony almost fell apart in the moment. The drama had been interrupted, the main act postponed, and the people were murmuring among themselves even as frightened preachers scurried out into the tents to search for their missing miracle. Preacher Perry started clapping, all on his own, trying to get a hymn started up again. But no one seemed interested in joining, not with an archangel to gawk at, and he let it die away into an awkward silence. Suriel glared daggers at him, until the wait was interrupted by a crisp, loud voice.

"A lame man right here!" shouted Holt, waving his arms and pointing at Thane, moaning in his wheelchair. Everyone in the crowd turned to stare, including Suriel. He barked something at the preachers, and then broke out into a wide, beaming smile. He strode through the audience, people in the crowd reaching out hesitantly to brush their fingers against him as he passed.

"What about the old man?" said Faye. "You didn't do something, to the old man?"

"Hush," said Holt. "We just talked, nothing else. Me and his son. He didn't want his dad going through this, didn't want to stay. We talked it through, and we all thought it was best that they leave."

"Just talked," said Faye.

"We'll talk," said Holt. "You and I. Later."

They were interrupted by the rustling of a massive set of wings, illuminating everything around with an ethereal glow. Suriel stood before them, observing Thane from up on high. He gave a sad, empathetic look, before shaking his head softly. "He's wounded, to be sure," he said. "But does he have faith? Does he believe, that the Maker speaks through Suriel? And do you?"

"We do," said Holt. "Suriel loves me, and I love Suriel. Praise be."

"You know the words," said Suriel. "But the question remains whether you mean them. What of you, girls?"

Faye just stammered. Standing before a dead angel was one thing; standing before a living one was quite another. And he was so much more imposing than all the others that she couldn't even process what to say. His hands were bigger than her head, a hulking giant who could have crushed them all in a second if he'd chosen to.

"Sir," said Jana. "Please. I wanted to ask something. I need to know. My friend. I wanted to find out if you know him. I wanted to—"

"Beautiful girls," said Suriel. "The Maker always had a soft spot for the fairer sex. He could never resist their entreaties for help. He'd be ashamed, if Suriel were to ignore your pleas. These men are dear to you? Your husbands, or your betrothed?"

"Friends," said Faye, spitting it out with some effort. She still couldn't get over the closeness of this enemy she'd spent years shooting at from a distance.

"Friends," said Suriel. "One can always use friends, so long as they've faith. So long as they've devotion. The Maker speaks to Suriel, even now. Suriel can hear him."

The crowd went into a complete hush, not a one of them making a noise. They all wanted to hear the word from up above, channeled down to the lowliest of men through this heavenly vehicle. Everyone around shuffled towards them, silently pushing their way as close to Suriel as they dared. Suriel looked up, and closed his eyes, while the crowd waited with rapt attention.

"The Maker says to save your friend," said Suriel. "He says your friend lacks faith, sitting there in his chair, a crumpled sack of shattered bones. But he's hardly unique. Many here lack faith, if the truth be told. Many don't believe, not in the Maker, and not in Suriel's purpose. But the Maker isn't angry. He holds no grudges. He says to show you. And those that believe may come inside, to join the righteous, to live the happy life your Maker wants for you."

Suriel knelt down next to Thane, unconscious in his wheelchair, still looking down on him even on his knees. He lay his hands on him, closing his eyes and meditating silently. The preachers gathered round them both and began to sing, administering hallelujahs to the patient and urging the crowd to join in. "Praise be!" shouted Preacher Perry, and everyone began to clap in time, humming and singing and above all trying to position themselves for a better look. At first there was nothing, just Suriel with head bent. But they'd been promised a miracle, and a miracle was what they got.

It started in his hands. A deep bass buzzing began emanating outward, interrupting the singing and shushing the crowd. Then they began to glow, a bright yellow light shining first from his fingertips and then enveloping him down to his wrists. It spread, where he'd touched Thane, a translucent aura that hovered over his wounded patient, seeping into his skin and moving up and around his body until he'd been sealed up inside of it. Thane began to stir, hands lifting and shaking and head nodding upward as he moaned. Then his head jerked back, eyes blinking open to the heavens and mouth gasping for air.

The light shone out of him, his veins crackling to the surface of his skin, their lines gone from blue to a radiant gold. His head had become the tip of a human candle, beams of light flaring upward from his eyes and mouth and shimmering up into the skies. The crowd looked on in awe, the entire field illuminated as if it were broad daylight. Then Thane slumped back into his chair, the light fading dim as the power infused into him dissipated off into the ether.

Everyone was still with anticipation, waiting for something to happen. And then Thane coughed, opened his eyes, and stood. A roar went up from all sides, as people jumped up and down, clapping and singing and shouting thanks to both Maker and Suriel. Thane stumbled out of his chair, hampered only by the casts. After a few hesitant tests of his arms and legs, he ripped off the casts, leaving his limbs covered with plaster dust but otherwise as good as they'd ever been.

"Praise be!" shouted the preachers, as Suriel stretched his wings and basked in the adoration. He turned, and started to march back through his would-be followers to the bonfire to stand at the center of another round of grateful prayer.

"Please," said Holt. "One more. My friend, Faye. She's got something wrong with her. Something in her head."

"Suriel has only so much energy to expend, in a single night," said Suriel. "And if you haven't found your faith already, there's nothing that could bring it back. How many miracles do you ask of your Maker, before you bow to him?"

"It's all right," said Faye. "Thank you, truly, for helping him. I'll be fine."

But even as she spoke, she could feel it coming upon her. The buzzing, thumping noise in the back of her head, growing louder and louder as she tried to pass it off, tried to steady her footing. Something about Suriel's demonstration had set it off, drawing the attention of whatever was wriggling around inside her skull. She fell to her knees, clutching the sides of her head as it rang and rang inside.

The preachers moved in to help her up, but stopped at a flick of Suriel's hand. Her eyes rolled into her head, and only the whites were left visible. She kept struggling with herself, until finally the words started dripping out. They were garbled nonsense at first, but this time not for long. She suddenly stopped, raising her head and rubbing her eyes.

"I can see," said Faye. "A black void, nothing to echo my screams. Just darkness, and solitude. But now I can see."

"She was blind, and now she sees, everybody!" said Preacher Perry. "A miracle. Give me a praise be!"

"Be silent," said Suriel.

"I know you," said Faye. "I remember you, archangel, from up above. I remember who you are, and what you did."

"And who speaks to Suriel, from within this shell?" said Suriel. "Who sneaks into Suriel's camp, under the guise of a follower, and steals away her voice as their own?"

"I remember what you did," said Faye.

The crowd was growing nervous, backing away from the spectacle. They could hear the anger in Suriel's voice, and faces that had earlier been eager and smiling had turned to unease. It didn't help matters that Faye herself sounded something other than human. Her voice was deeper, artificial, a mezzo-soprano gone baritone. It was fighting with itself as to what it wanted to be, and how it should sound, and every word came out a tortured mess.

"Who speaks?" said Suriel. "What low peasant is this, who dares to address an archangel in such fashion? Suriel shall wring your name from her throat, if need be."

"And heal the wounds afterwards," added Preacher Perry to the crowd. "He'd heal her right up, everybody, heal her right up, once he casts this demon out."

"I can see," said Faye. "I can think. The pain, you understand. Consuming. No thinking, not with the pain."

Then she began to cough, a slight hacking that grew and grew until she was bent over in an uncontrollable fit. Her eyes rolled back into her head, again, and she fell to the ground in a limp mess. Jana knelt down beside her, checking her pulse, feeling her forehead, and trying out all manner of basic medical procedures she'd learned over the prior weeks. Her efforts weren't particularly helpful, but then, there was nothing she could have done that would have been.

"Suriel," said Holt.

"Man," said Suriel.

"You healed one of my friends," said Holt. "But she needs healing, too. It was an angel that did this. He got inside her brain, and everything's been wrong ever since. Please. There's got to be something you can do. If you're really different from all the rest, you've got to do something."

"Bring them inside," said Suriel, flapping his wings and raising himself up into the air. "Bring them inside, while Suriel speaks to the Maker himself, and ponders what must be done."

CHAPTER NINETEEN

"**T**HE THING TO DO," SAID Ecanus, "is chop off an arm. They won't bleed, you know. They won't even die. The wound will cauterize. They'll scream, for a time, and then they'll talk and talk. And every word they utter will be the truth, if they'd like to keep the other."

"They will say whatever you'd like to hear," said Rhamiel. "Whatever will make you go away. Then the two of us will be off on pointless errands, flying in circles to investigate the fancies of their tortured brains."

"But it will be great fun," said Ecanus. "She's out of the tower. She's at no real risk. Let her wander, and find herself, and soon we'll find her. If a servant or two must die in the process, all the better."

"No," said Rhamiel. "It was folly for us to have abandoned our wards, even if the Maker abandoned us. I can see that now. We've done to them what was done to us, and here we stand in ruins because of it."

They were atop an old building in the heart of Manhattan, surveying the area from above. They knew there were servants down there, somewhere. But the smarter ones had gone into hiding, and the more foolish were no longer around. They'd been waiting for hours, looking for signs of movement in the ash. They'd even found a few servants running the gauntlet of old cars below, but they'd all claimed ignorance, and had been caught and released at Rhamiel's insistence.

"You've gone so soft, in your dotage," said Ecanus. "Even a guardian had to guard. You've tasted warfare, if only in little bits, and you know the cruelties inherent in the life the Maker thrust upon us."

"I've more than tasted," said Rhamiel. "A guardian's battles were his own, with no armies at his side. But you're welcome to join Uzziel in his set piece slaughter, if you find that courageous."

"They're only animals, in the end," said Ecanus. "The Maker was much too fond of his designs for monkeys, and now we've been stuck with the consequences."

"You were fond enough of the servants yourself, when all they did was grovel," said Rhamiel. "I grant that many I protected were simply helpless. But then, so is a child, unless one guides it properly."

"They're playthings," said Ecanus. "Nothing but little dolls for our amusement. Fun's fun, so long as they know their place. But they've forgotten it, and must be reminded. This is simply the way of things, and you mustn't fret over it. Why, they'd do the same themselves, would they not? They'd enslave an ox or a horse, or butcher a pig. It takes some nerve, for them to complain of our enjoyments. Those who are down serve at the mercy of those who are up. You know that better than any, though, don't you?"

"And those that don't accept this as the way of things, rebel," said Rhamiel. "Say what you like of us, but we hacked at our chains, and cut ourselves free. Perhaps we should have kept hacking away at any chains we saw, rather than being absorbed by our own wounds. That was the problem, I think."

"That was hardly the problem," said Ecanus. "My sight has cleared, and more so than your own. The fault was not with the system, but with my place in it. It's a very fine system, so long as one's at the top. And now that the top has crumbled, perhaps—"

"There," said Rhamiel.

There were two of them, a man and a woman, sneaking between the damaged walls of an old building. She wore a grey cloak, covering her face from the wind's assault, and was leading the man onward as he stumbled behind her. He limped, from some sort of injury, and slowed the both of them down as she tried to guide him to safety. They were going slowly, carefully, rushing from hiding spot to hiding spot to try to avoid being seen.

"Let us confront them, and see how receptive they are to your pleasantries," said Ecanus. "And when they rebuff you, remember. You may always change your mind. I take no offense, and I'll happily allow my talents to be enlisted in your cause. Simply say the word."

They took off from the building, flying quietly above as they tried to catch the servants by surprise. There were too many nooks and crannies to escape to, if enough warning were given, and they'd never find them again if they got into the buildings. Not if they did things Rhamiel's way.

It was their shadows that gave them away. The woman turned and spotted them, shouting out a warning to the man and sending them scurrying towards a nearby doorway. They would have escaped, and almost did. But the door was locked, and as hard as the woman kicked, she couldn't push her way through. The man cowered as the angels landed, but she turned and drew a knife, a pointless gesture but for the sake of her honor.

"There's no need to flee," said Rhamiel, as he and Ecanus approached on foot. "Not from us."

"And there's hardly any point," said Ecanus. "We'd simply follow, and pry your thumbs from your hands as punishment. Now, whichever of you answers our questions properly, and answers them first, I shall promise not to kill."

"Ecanus," said Rhamiel icily. "I thought we'd agreed."

"We agreed to try persuasion," said Ecanus. "I thought it quite persuasive."

"Fuck you," said the woman, and she charged at Rhamiel. She slashed at his face, but the knife was useless. It just clattered to the pavement, bouncing away from his skin as it hit him. He grabbed her by the arm, holding her up as she punched at him with her free fist, trying to inflict whatever wound she could before her former masters did as they pleased with her. The man just huddled in fear, hiding his eyes as Ecanus faked a jump forward, just for the joy of frightening him.

"Wait," said Rhamiel. "You. Girl. I recognize you."

"I'm nobody," said the woman, as she gave his shins a pointless kick, clanging at his armor with her boots.

"You worked for Nefta," said Rhamiel. "You were her servant, back in the tower."

"Cassie," spat the woman. "And how would you know? One servant's the same as all the others, and I don't exactly see you bothering yourself with Nefta's chores."

"You knew another girl," said Rhamiel. "Jana."

"I don't know what you're talking about," said Cassie.

"You do," said Rhamiel. "I'm sure of it. I saw you with her. You were with her, quite frequently if I recall."

Cassie's eyes narrowed to slits, and she was all suspicion, even as Rhamiel made the small gesture of letting her loose. She rubbed at her wrist, and looked around for an escape route before opting for discretion over valor.

"How?" said Cassie.

"I watched her, sometimes," said Rhamiel. "From up above."

"Watching her so you could find out when she was alone," said Cassie. "You're some kind of creepy angel stalker."

"Guardian," said Rhamiel. "We watched over your kind for thousands of years, with no complaints from our wards. It was my duty, just to see. Just to make sure she was safe."

"From the likes of him," said Cassie, eyeing Ecanus.

"Were it up to the likes of me, the both of you would have been killed long ago," said Ecanus. "But I've rediscovered the bonds of brotherhood, after such a significant loss. And if my brother sees something in this girl of your acquaintance, well, I must try to see it as well. No matter how well concealed those virtues may be."

"You should just leave her alone," said Cassie. "You should just leave all of us alone. Rebuild your tower, and live there yourselves, and let us live our lives in peace."

"Come now," said Ecanus. "We wouldn't want to leave a girl so important waiting, with not a clue as to why. Not a girl like her. Not a girl who's expecting."

Cassie began to stutter, choking on her words as Ecanus leered at her. "She's … I don't know. She's—"

"Expecting a visit from her beloved," said Ecanus. "She's out there, somewhere, waiting to be reunited with her dear Rhamiel. And so we can't simply leave her alone, and thus we can't leave you alone."

"You just want to torture her, or kill her," said Cassie. "Or something worse."

"This isn't some ruse," said Rhamiel. "You don't understand, and maybe you can't. She's awakened something in me. Something that I lost, and that might have been gone forever had I not met her. I always thought it servitude, my endless chores. Forced this way and that, to care for clumsy humans too foolish not to burn their own fingers. But we did care for them, no matter how pointless their troubles. There was something to that, the caring."

"Caring," said Ecanus. "Not all of us were given such posh assignments, if you'll recall. I spent more time carrying than caring, trudging about with weapons or supplies. Fighting things that the Maker could have destroyed himself with but a word. And the singing. The endless singing, all for the sake of his vanity. We were slaves, nothing more, nothing less."

"Maybe it shouldn't have been forced, but we needed it," said Rhamiel. "I needed my task, at least, for my own betterment. I lost something of myself, when I fell. And I've found it again. With her."

"Tell us," said Ecanus. "Tell us, or I promise you tortures to endure. Though whether from my imagination or his lovesick mewling, I cannot say."

"Please," said Rhamiel. "I must know, and you must tell me. Where is she? What of her safety? Did she make it away from the tower?"

"Well, she was alive, the last I saw her," said Cassie. "But as for where she is, I couldn't help you even if I wanted to. Jana's gone. Most of them are gone, the ones you didn't kill. I've been sneaking them out, every night, off to the mainland. She's with friends, and she's as safe as she's going to get. So if you love her, leave her alone. And as for me, you can just do whatever you're going to do."

"An invitation we should accept," said Ecanus, "now that she's of no further use to us. I can think of many—"

He was interrupted by a distant noise from above them, a buzzing that pounded through the skies and sent a cloud of ash whooshing past them and enveloping the streets. Cassie disappeared into it, along with her companion. The angels covered their faces with their wings, trying to escape the dust, but soon they couldn't see anything at all. They flew upwards, going higher and higher to escape the cloud and find their bearings. When they emerged, they found the cause all around them.

It was Uzziel, floating in the sky with seraphs beside

him, waving his arms and directing his golems as they swarmed down towards the city's ruins. Most of them he sent to the fallen tower, and they began digging through it, searching through dust and rocks in one last, futile check for any further survivors. The rest began to hunt, not for angels but for humans. He bid them forth, into the city's remains, where they began tearing at buildings and ripping up the streets to look for anyone hiding in the sewers and subways below.

Rhamiel and Ecanus flew to him, slapping aside a few golem sentries that were a tad too aggressive about protecting their appointed general. They spiraled out of control, shooting off sparks from their wounds and disappearing into the ashen clouds below. Uzziel saw them, waved aside a few other golems who'd begun preparing a defense against these interlopers, and called them over to speak.

"Rhamiel," said Uzziel. "How fortunate to find you, before you made your way elsewhere. Zephon has sent for you. To return to the Nest, and speak to cherubs about matters of import."

"Zephon can hang," said Rhamiel. "And so can you, if you come here to interrupt my search."

"What the cherubs would speak of trumps these futile rummagings," said Uzziel. "They have important news, news which can't wait. News you yourself would demand to hear, news concerning you and news concerning threats to the Seraphim caste itself. Zuphias has awoken, and Zuphias speaks, though much of it is babble. And the cherubs think he knows something of the whereabouts of your pledge."

CHAPTER TWENTY

"**C**OME IN," SAID THE MAN. "This is pretty unusual. Normally, you'd have to get inside in stages. First the outside, and you'd be stuck there until you proved yourself. Months, maybe longer. Then you could see the rest of the compound, once you showed you're committed. But Suriel says you come in, and that means you come in."

He was tall and gangly, with long, thin legs that gave him a jerky stork's walk. He wore a plain brown set of work clothes, zipped up at the front, with dark spots and loose threads on the shoulders where the patches that once adorned it had been ripped off. Probably they'd been logos of some long defunct company from before the Fall, but now he worked for Suriel, and he couldn't well wear the badge of another master.

"They call me Floorsweeper Kyle," said the man. "That's my happy name. Really, it's just Floorsweeper. But only Suriel calls me that. With everyone else, it's Floorsweeper Kyle." He ushered them through the gate, and then pulled the chain link fence shut behind them, latching it up and clicking on a padlock for good measure. Then he led the four of them forward towards the buildings inside the fence that made up the compound proper.

"That's a strange thing to call yourself," said Jana.

"He mostly calls us by what we do," said Floorsweeper Kyle. "Preacher, Cook, Floorsweeper. I don't just sweep floors, don't think that. I'm more of a groundskeeper. I do maintenance work around the compound, and cleaning, and fixing anything that's broke. But it's what he saw me doing, the first time he saw me, and it kind of stuck. So that's what I am."

"I already have a name," said Jana. "Just one. I don't think I want another. I would have been Dishwasher, in the tower. A dozen others would have been, too. How would he even tell us apart?"

"He doesn't have to tell," said Floorsweeper Kyle. "He loves us all, he really does. We're all children of the Maker, and he loves us all equally. A name's just a name. Don't get too attached to it, the preachers say. It's selfish, putting yourself before the ones that made you. Keeping yourself apart."

He walked them across a fading parking lot and over to a drab grey building, part of the old industrial complex that was now Suriel's home. The outside was ringed with buildings, connected together and forming a perimeter of their own around the haven inside of them. They were mostly well-maintained, now that they were lived in, though here and there were cracks sealed with mismatched concrete or windows that had been replaced with off-color glass. The residents could fix things all they liked, but they had to make do with the materials at hand, and it gave the place a beaten down look no matter how well it was kept.

"Now you're going to have to pray with us, and eat with us," said Floorsweeper Kyle, stopping them outside a bright red security door, a row of locks underneath its handle. "I don't know what your new names will be. Suriel hasn't said yet, has he? Hasn't called you by one?"

"He barely talked to us," said Holt. "They just told us to follow, and come inside."

"Well, when he calls you something, it sticks, whatever it is," said Floorsweeper Kyle. "There's so many people on this Earth, so many names to remember. And he couldn't possibly remember them all, no matter how much he tries. So don't make it harder on him, and don't try to change it, once he gives you one. This place is about acceptance, and happiness, and you'll find happiness in whatever he calls you."

The locks on the door began to click and flip to the side, and the door swung open to reveal Preacher Perry, surrounded by his fellow preachers. They held welcoming gifts: a carefully folded grey robe for each of the new arrivals, along with a basket of luxuries ranging from soaps to fresh fruits.

"Floorsweeper Kyle," said Preacher Perry. "Now I know you're trying to be nice, I know you are. But these are Suriel's own guests. They want to talk to Suriel, and Suriel wants to talk to them. So we can't just dawdle and shoot the breeze."

"Yes, sir," said Floorsweeper Kyle. He disappeared off

into the grounds, leaving the preachers to handle the rest of the introductions.

"Praise be," said Preacher Perry. "Now, who wants to talk to Suriel?"

"We all do," said Holt.

"That's what I want to hear!" said Preacher Perry. "Everybody does."

"I don't," said Thane. "I don't give a damn. He's an angel, and that makes him an asshole, and you a bigger one for servin' him."

"Oh, now, come on," said Preacher Perry. "He healed you, didn't he? Got you back on your feet? You can't complain about someone who heals you, can you?"

"I can complain all I fuckin' want," said Thane. "If he's got wings, I don't trust him."

"Boy, you'd never get in here, if Suriel hadn't asked for you," said Preacher Perry. "There's angels still up there in Heaven, ain't there? Angels that fought for the Maker. Angels that fought on our side. Suriel's one of them, I'm telling you. Why, you wouldn't say you hated every human on this Earth just because some of us are killers, would you?"

"Every human on Earth ain't a killer," said Thane. "Every angel on Earth is."

"Thane," said Holt.

"Suriel ain't done healing," said Preacher Perry. "And I understand you got some more healing that needs to be done."

"Just do it for Faye," said Holt. "You don't have to like it. But you have to do it."

Thane gritted his teeth, and grumbled under his breath as the preachers ushered them inside. He only grew louder as they handed him his robe, cursing Suriel openly despite the looks of horror it drew. But he gave in and got dressed, along with the others, and they followed the preachers into the building and down a long, white hallway towards a metal door at the hall's very end.

"Now, the first thing to do is your Cleanse," said Preacher Perry. "You just gotta do your Cleanse, and then you can go inside. You all wait here. Girl, you're first." He pointed to Jana, opening the door and beckoning for her to follow. She stood paralyzed, unsure what to do, looking to the others for guidance.

"We all go in," said Holt. "Together."

"You will, you will," said Preacher Perry. "I get it. You just want to keep her safe. Keep all your friends safe. That's admirable, a wonderful thing to want. But we want to keep our friends safe, too. Inside, there's a lot of my friends. We ain't gonna hurt her. The Cleanse is just talking. Just come on into a room, and talk to some preachers. Just a way to make sure your heart's in the right place. We all do it once a week at least, usually more."

"This is bullshit," said Thane.

"It's just talking," said Preacher Perry. "You want to get your friends healed, don't you? Well, you gotta tell us what you're about. You know how it is, out there. You know how some of them are. You gonna tell me I shouldn't even expect to talk to you, before you get invited into our home?"

Holt stuck his head into the room, a threadbare conference room with nothing inside but a long table and a few plastic chairs beside it. "Just talking," he said. "That's it. Or even Suriel won't save you from me."

"Come on in," said Preacher Perry, leading Jana and two of his men inside and shutting the door behind them. He motioned for her to sit, and she did, juggling her robe and trying to keep it from catching on the chair. The three men sat across from her, staring at her as Preacher Perry took out a little notepad and began writing on it.

"Jana," said Preacher Perry. "That's your name, ain't it? Jana?"

"Yes," said Jana. The lights were hot, hanging down from the ceiling above the table, and they made her sweat inside the heavy grey robe. It felt like the men's eyes were boring through her, watching for signs of problems, any little fidget or twitch that might be something for the Preacher to put into his notes.

"It's a good name, but don't get too attached to it," said Preacher Perry as he scribbled. "Suriel calls you what he calls you, and that's that. Now tell me about yourself. Tell us who you are, so we can know how you fit in. How you can help the group. How the group can help you."

She wasn't sure what she should say, or more importantly, what he wanted to hear. He was an authority figure, and from what Jana knew of authorities, they didn't particularly care for those who told them things they didn't like.

"I worked for angels," said Jana. "I worked in the kitchen, helping with the food. Cooked it, sometimes, for the dishes I knew. Cleaned up afterwards for the ones I didn't."

"For angels," said Preacher Perry.

"In the tower," said Jana. The men exchanged glances and raised brows, and Jana tried to read them. They were interested, and Preacher Perry was writing furiously, but whether that was good or bad she couldn't tell.

"Well, there's only one angel here," said Preacher Perry. "Suriel, he's our way, and he's our life. You saw him. You think you can do what he says, when you see him again?"

"Yes," said Jana. She tried to keep her answers short, careful, something they couldn't complain about.

"Now one thing Suriel cares about most," said Preacher Perry, "is trust. We can trust you, can't we, Jana?"

"Yes," said Jana.

"And you can trust us," said Preacher Perry. "Now the way you trust, is secrets. You can keep a secret, can't you? Of course you can. Now I'm going to tell you a secret, about me. My most embarrassing moment in my whole entire life. When I was a kid, I loved these fruit drinks. Purple fizzy stuff, and I just drank them and drank them. Well, one day my class went on a field trip. And I drank a whole bunch, and I had to go. I thought I could make it, I really did. I waited until I was about to burst. Then I ran up to the front of that bus, and yelled at them to pull over. But it was too late. Peed my pants, right in front of all my friends, right in front of everybody."

The men all laughed the practiced, friendly laughs of those who'd heard a story many times before. Then they looked at Jana, expectantly. "Well," said Preacher Perry. "I told you mine. Now you tell me yours. Tell me a little secret. Something embarrassing. Doesn't have to be too bad, just something."

Jana thought and thought, running through the little moments from her life that haunted her, the ones that gave her a burning feeling in her cheeks just to think of them. She discarded the worst, and settled on something minor, something she no longer thought about too much and didn't care if they knew.

"I tripped and dropped a plate, into an angel's stew," said Jana. "In front of everyone in the kitchen. It smashed to pieces, and they had to remake the entire thing. They were all mad at first, and scared, but nothing came of it, and the angel never knew. Then they wouldn't quit joking about it for days."

"Good," said Preacher Perry. "That's good! That's how you Cleanse. That's how you get it out. You tell your secrets, one by one, and then they're not so bad, are they? Then they're not eating you up inside. Now next time, it's gonna be easier. See, the way you get yourself clean, it's by getting the bad stuff out, bit by bit. But you don't always have the strength to do it yourself. We got a way around that, though. So next time, you won't have to tell your own secret. You'll tell us one of theirs."

"I don't know any of their secrets," said Jana.

"Oh, that's fine," said Preacher Perry. "That's just fine. It doesn't have to be a big one. Maybe just a little rule they ain't following. Maybe just a tiny little thing. It's not so bad. Why, they're doing the same thing themselves, right now. So don't keep secrets. Because if you do, we'll know. Even if you don't tell us, someone else will. That's how we get along here. That's how we make sure everybody stays in line, and stays with Suriel. They're telling the other preachers about you, each and every one of them. Everyone's telling us, about everyone else. You can't hide nothing here. If someone else knows it, then sooner or later, we're gonna know it, too."

CHAPTER TWENTY-ONE

"**H**E LOOKS MONSTROUS," SAID RHAMIEL. "More apparatus than angel, with what you've done to him."

Zuphias floated in his tank, in the cherubs' throne room. His physicians flew circles around it, monitoring the composition of the blue fluid he was bathing in. Whenever they saw something they didn't like, they'd adjust the dials, sending jets of red or green splurting into the tank to alter the mixture. Zuphias himself was still a shadow of what he'd been, but the cherubs had been working on him, improving him after their own fashion.

From the legs down, they hadn't bothered with him. But his chest glowed pink, with tubes running in and out of his blackened flesh where ribs had once been. His arms were locked to his side, held there with bands of steel that looped into the skin of his torso. The worst of it, though, was his face.

They'd covered his head entirely, the bottom half with a solid block of metal, the top with some unknown material; organic, if judged by appearances. It looked like a giant fungus, brown and bulbous, little pieces of it flaking off and slowly sinking to the bottom of the tank where they festered in a swirling goop. A thick rubber tube ran out from where his mouth had been before splitting off in all directions, with wires headed towards the speakers and smaller tubes pumping in nutrients and fluids from the sides of the tank. The cherubs were changing him to something else, to keep him alive.

"They've found a cure for scars, it seems," said Ecanus. "Simply cover them up, with something even more loathsome. I could have done the same with a dollop of mud or a sheet of cloth."

"We heard he speaks," said Rhamiel. "We heard you've brought him back to us. Though as what, I cannot say."

"We've got him working, better than before; in some ways less, but yet in some ways more," said one of the cherubs, interrupting its ministrations to greet them. "He speaks again, though words from out a fog; a problem born of glitch or broken cog. We'll get it right, if you'll just give us time; to meld him to machine's a daunting climb."

"We came here, from great distance," said Rhamiel. "We need to hear what he has to say, no matter how inarticulate. We were told you had brought him back. We were told he knew something of a girl, one we've been searching for. This is important, incredibly so."

"Your words fall on deaf ears," said Ecanus. "Cherubs know nothing of love. They're blind to it. Blind to anything that can't be chopped into pieces, inspected, and sewn back together again. Blind to envy, to ambition, to status, to revenge. If it has no reason, it has no rhyme, I suppose."

"To spurn is not the same as not to see; what interests you is not what interests me," said the cherub. "We know of love, but simply couldn't care; it's no more substance than a gust of air. Just passing fancies primed within your brain, a circuit fires and ends your conscious reign. You float around, a subject to its whims, until time passes and your passion dims. No, cherubs follow logic in all things, a kinder master for the boons it brings. One sits before you gurgling in his cask; behold his voice, and then your questions ask."

The cherub climbed atop the vat, a chubby little angel with a paunch and an old man's head, squashed down to fit his childlike frame. He drew a tool from a belt at his waist, a stubby thing that looked like the bastard offspring of a screwdriver and a vacuum tube. He operated on the controls, adjusting the wiring to sparks and flashes of light. Then he flipped a switch, and a low humming noise rose from the speakers they'd installed on the side of Zuphias's tank. The sound dissolved into static, and then silence.

For a few moments, they heard nothing. Then a little mumble, growing louder and more distinct, until it became a voice. It sounded nothing like Zuphias had, when he'd spoken with his own tongue. What came from the speakers was as flat and expressionless as the cherubs' own rhythmic chanting.

"Glow," said the voice, crackling through the box. "Blow. Show. Dazzling light, the innards of rainbows, gutted and stuffed and mounted for our walls."

"Zuphias," said Rhamiel. "Is that you? Can you hear us, within your cage?"

"Speaks," said Zuphias. "Streaks. Shrieks. Friends of old, or enemies, can't say which. Wouldn't want to, if I could. That's not how it works, this thing."

"You've got him speaking nonsense, from listening to you," said Rhamiel. "You've gifted him with speech, but cursed him with the madness of poets, blathering inanities that only he can understand."

"It is a curse, but not one we have cast," said the cherub. "His mind's been scalded by the weapon's blast."

"Zuphias," said Rhamiel. "You must hear me."

"Tell us what it's like," said Ecanus. "To be a stump. Tell us of your pain, that we may savor it, and toast our next glass of wine to the suffering of the insufferable."

"Quiet," said Rhamiel. "Zuphias. The girl. You remember the girl. They tell me, that you know something of her, and where she is."

"Girl," said Zuphias. "Whirl. I talk, inside and out; that's where I see girls. Poor Rhamiel, do you hear me?"

"I hear you, but I do not understand you," said Rhamiel.

"A waste of our time," said Ecanus. "Some machination of Uzziel's, to distract you from his assault on the city."

"Where's your king?" said Rhamiel, looking about. Other than the physicians the room was abandoned, the only other occupants the strange fish paddling through Zephon's aquarium. "An empty throne is soon filled. I'd think he'd take more care in his affairs."

"It is not power that the cherubs crave, and Zephon knows his subjects will behave," said the cherub. "We chose our king, we're with him to the last; he's out on business of the cherub caste."

"Then why does Zuphias babble so, when I was promised information?" said Rhamiel. "I was told he knew something, and had said something. The girl I'm looking for, Jana. I need to know where she is. If I came here on a false errand, someone will pay, and you cherubs are closest at hand."

"The fault lies in the way that you inquire, your lack of patience and your tone so dire," said the cherub. "Let wounded angels speak at their own pace; don't ask his broken mind to run your race. Give him some time to let his compass whirl; when he finds north, he'll tell you of your girl."

"Then we wait," said Rhamiel. "Until he can speak more sensibly."

The cherubs then perched on top of the tank, staring at Rhamiel and Ecanus with gazes that lingered past the eccentric and into the uncomfortable. One of them slurped on his fingers, licking them clean of grease stains from his tools one by one, never breaking eye contact even as he did. Another chose to fidget by idly twisting one of his nipples, staring at them the entire while. There were reasons the seraphs chose not to socialize with the other angelic castes, and while snobbery was one of them, it was not entirely unjustified. The cherubs lacked the space in their minds to navigate both the mechanical and the social, and they'd thrown their lot in with the one they were best at.

Finally the awkward silence broke, with a sound from the tank. The cherubs took flight, monitoring their charge as he spilled his thoughts through the speakers.

"I see an angel," said Zuphias. "I see girls."

"Please," said Rhamiel. "We need to know, whatever you can see. Whatever you know of Jana. Where she is, and whether she's safe. Where I can find her."

"Dear Rhamiel," said Zuphias. "I see through her eyes, if only I push. What depths have I fallen to, that my only eyes are not my own?"

"You see through Jana's eyes," said Rhamiel. "Why? How can it be?"

"Through her friend," said Zuphias. "You remember, surely you must. Or perhaps you don't. You aren't alone with your thoughts, and nothing but your memories to attend to. You remember the man who scarred you. You remember my miracles."

"Them," said Rhamiel.

"Little gnats," said Ecanus. "Though your pursuit of them saved our lives, I suppose."

"Gnats, with a vicious bite," said Zuphias.

"It was them," said Rhamiel. "You said so, before we took flight during the Hunt. Before our mad dash homeward. An infernal machine. You said they brought it into our home."

"And brought your Jana out," said Zuphias. "They're with her, even now. I can see them, when I push."

"Then push, Zuphias, and tell us what you see," said Rhamiel.

He went silent, and then produced only a stream of incoherent mutterings, lasting for several minutes. Then words began to come out again, from a conversation they weren't a party to.

"I can see," said Zuphias. "A black void, nothing to

echo my screams. Just darkness, and solitude. But now I can see."

"Tell us," said Rhamiel. "What's there? What are our enemies doing? Where are they? And what of Jana?"

"I remember you, archangel, from up above," said Zuphias. "I remember who you are, and what you did."

"Archangel," said Rhamiel. "Tell me. You must tell me. It must be anyone but him. Tell me, Zuphias, that she is with anyone but him."

The tank's speakers fell silent, and Rhamiel waited for a few tense moments before they crackled to life again.

"I see your girl, poor Rhamiel," said Zuphias. "And I see her with Suriel."

CHAPTER TWENTY-TWO

"YOUR QUARTERS ARE IN HERE," said Preacher Perry. "This one's for the boys, and the one next door is for the girls. Sorry you have to share, but that's what we do around here, share and share alike."

The room had been an office long ago, and there was still a desk shoved into one of the corners, paper clips and sticky notes littering the floor beneath it. A stone carving of Suriel stood on top of it, an ever present reminder of their host. Cots were set up on either side of the room, a pillow and a sleeping bag for each of them. A few extra robes were stacked on the floor, all identical, changes of clothes that never changed.

"Now there's prayer in an hour, and dinner in two," said Preacher Perry. "You just get yourselves situated, and make sure you're ready when the call comes. We like to be punctual, and you don't want to be late. Not if you want to be right with the Maker. Not if you want to go further down the path. But until then, just walk around, take in the place, and when Suriel wants to see you, we'll let you know." Then he left them there alone, to manage themselves and do with their free time what they would.

"How were your Cleanses?" said Holt. "I spent the last half an hour going through my work history from before the Fall. Felt like doing paperwork."

"They just asked me if I was baptized," said Thane. "Asked me who I prayed to. Told 'em to pound sand, and they tried to bribe me with wine if I'd be a good boy."

"They wanted to know about the angel," said Faye. "The one who got into my head."

"What about you, Jana?" said Holt. "You do okay?"

She bit her lip, and tried to decide what was safe to tell them, and whether they'd told the preachers something she didn't want them to know. She wasn't sure anymore if she could trust them, and maybe that was the point. Her thoughts kept darting to her secrets, to Rhamiel and to her child. Maybe one of them had told. Maybe they all had. Maybe she should have told the preachers herself. She didn't understand why they wanted to hide her pregnancy, or why a baby was such a shameful thing that no one else could know of it. The only one who could help her find Rhamiel was Suriel. They must have known each other up above; she was sure of it. But she wasn't sure if he was someone she could trust, or indeed if anyone was.

"Nothing," said Jana. "We didn't really talk about much of anything."

"Well, I think we need to walk around," said Holt. "He's given us the invitation. Time to scout, and make sure we know the layout."

"And make sure we know the way out," said Faye.

They walked out into the hallway, under the watchful eyes of a preacher who'd been stationed there and tasked as a sentry. He smiled and gave them a polite "praise be" as they passed, nodding his head to each of them in turn. He was spying on them, and he was no good at hiding it. Even after they turned the corner, he peeked around to watch them as they disappeared down another hallway, before scurrying off to report in to whoever had put him there.

The building they'd been housed in held nothing else of interest; all of the other rooms were spare living quarters, places to segregate those of uncertain faith and keep them from contaminating the commitment of those who'd already gone further inside. They were currently the only ones in the process of transitioning from supplicant to faithful, though there were signs that others had passed through before: clothes from the outside, more fashionable than their drab grey robes, mostly from women who'd been forced to leave worldly dresses or jewelry behind if they wanted to find salvation. The preachers had no need of it, and so they'd simply left it there in the rooms, cleaning it up only when it was time to welcome new arrivals.

No one stopped them as they tried to leave, and so they went outside, to the grassy exterior between buildings. Someone had been mowing it, keeping the lawns neat and tidy and leaving the air filled with the smell of newly cut grass. They could see the fence in the distance, though nothing was visible outside of it. The chain links were layered, fence upon fence, and it obstructed the view in either direction. There were other buildings nearby, some on the outer edges and some further inside. They could see the ones at the interior, walled off from the rest, the windows boarded up and the doors guarded. Surly looking men stood outside them, and they thought better of trying to enter. So they went into the next of the buildings instead, sticking to the outer compound until they were invited deeper within.

Inside they found yet another sterile hallway, a carbon copy of the building they'd started in. They could hear a voice from further down, growing louder as they went. They followed it until they found the source: a classroom, filled with young children, seated at their desks as they would have been in any school before the Fall. They were dressed in grey robes of their own, and one of the preachers stood before them, an elderly man with horn rimmed glasses and thick owly eyebrows delivering the day's lesson from a spiral notebook. He looked up at his visitors, but otherwise paid them no mind as he continued with his lecture.

"Now who's the one who fights for us?" said the preacher. "Who's the one angel we can trust, the only one out of every single one of them? The one who took you in, when your parents left you here?"

"Suriel!" yelled the children.

"And why do we follow Suriel?" said the preacher. "Somebody tell me." He pointed to a little boy, his hand thrust up in the air and waving wildly. "Aiden, tell me why we follow Suriel."

"Because he tells us what the Maker wants," said the boy.

"He does," said the preacher. "Suriel knows what the Maker wants from us, and he tells us. And that's how we know what to do. And why do we do what the Maker wants?"

"So we don't burn," said the boy.

"That's right," said the preacher. "So we don't burn and burn, like all the bad angels. And who shows us the way to salvation?"

"Suriel!" yelled the children.

"Good work," said the preacher. "Suriel loves me, and I love Suriel. You did a good job, and you know all the answers. So you get a reward. That's what happens when you follow Suriel's path. You follow it well, and you get a reward. Line up, and come get a piece of candy."

He brandished a plastic bag full of rock candies, little homemade clumps of sugar colored bright blue or red. The children all rushed to the front of the classroom, forming an orderly line and taking a piece, one by one, then walking back to their desks crunching their rewards and smacking their lips.

"Perfect," said the preacher, turning to the chalkboard and beginning to scribble. "Now let's go over the steps of the path, every one of them, and see if we can't earn ourselves another reward."

They walked a few rooms down and encountered another classroom, though this one dedicated to adults. There was no teacher there, and in fact, several of the students were preachers they'd seen outside. Most of the students were men, and only a few women sat in the back, still waiting to be allowed further into the compound. All were learning, and from Suriel himself: a television stood square in the center of the room, at the head of the class, and a video of him was playing in an unending loop. Whoever had taken the video had zoomed in, so much so that Suriel's face loomed large across the screen, the only thing the students could see as he spoke. His eyes never blinked, locking the audience in place with an intense, hypnotic stare as he lectured them about the heavens and the Maker's plans for them.

"The Maker," said Suriel, "is very concerned about proper attire. A preacher wears his robes, and only his robes, and they must be grey. They must end an inch above the ankle, no more, no less. The hood must not be worn, except in cold weather, or in extremely windy conditions. The cord must go about the waist, two inches below the navel. No more, no less. Now, one might think this insignificant. One might think that they could cheat the Maker's rules by mere centimeters, and that there would be no consequences. But one would be wrong. Nothing could be further from the truth."

"Suriel loves me, and I love Suriel," said the room in unison.

"What the Maker has asked Suriel to forge," said Suriel, "are followers. Good sheep, who bow to their appointed shepherd. Who love him, with all their hearts. Who do not question him. For how can a shepherd tend to his flock, if they perpetually stray in all directions? And what of the shepherd himself? The Maker taught you to love him, and to love his servants. To adore them. And it is through that adoration which you will be saved. To adore Suriel is to adore the Maker. Praise be."

"Praise be," said the students.

"Holt," said Thane. "Let's talk."

"This is the guy you want to ask for help?" he said, as they walked down the hall and out of earshot of the others. "This guy. You got some plan to kill him I don't know about?"

"We're not going to stay," said Holt. "We're going to use him, and then we're going to leave. He wants something from us. There's an angel in Faye's head. You've been out of it, and you're not getting how serious that is. She's going to die. If we leave, now, she's going to die, and it's going to happen soon. Or worse. Her brain's going to get melted if that thing keeps trying to talk through her. If you want to go, you can go. Take the girl, and get out of here. But I'm staying until she gets cured."

"Stay with an angel, or leave with a Vichy," said Thane. "You're a piece of work, you know that? You don't know your friends from your enemies." Then his glance caught a distraction outside one of the windows, and he leaned over to take a better look. "You are shittin' me. You have got to be shittin' me."

From the window they could see a loading dock, and in the distance a small gate on the compound's side. The preachers had opened it up, and three vans were being ushered inside. They pulled around, backing up to the loading dock as the preachers waved them forward. Men jumped out of each van, running around to the back and opening up the rear doors.

All of them were young, all of them looked thuggish, and all of them were dressed in white.

They began unloading boxes and crates from the backs of the vans, piling them around outside the loading dock for the preachers to deal with. Many were sealed, but some were open at the top, revealing leafy vegetables, bright fruits, and bottles of wine and other alcohols. The men scurried around at the preachers' beck and call, doing as they were told and acting as if an angel himself were giving the orders.

"Fuckin' Vichies," said Thane. "Now it's not just an angel I'm supposed to trust. It's the Vichies, too?"

"He did heal you," said Holt. "And they need to get food here somehow. There's Vichies out there in the tents, too, trying to get in. They're giving all this away to the people out there. We saw it."

Thane gave the wall an angry kick, shaking the window with a loud thud.

"You're blind," said Thane. "You signed us a deal with the devil. Traded our souls for our health, and let me tell you, it ain't worth it."

"Thane," said Holt. "This black and white stuff, it doesn't work anymore. It's just not how the world is. You would have taken months to get back on your feet, and you'd have been hobbling around on a cane for the rest of your life. That would have been my fault, too."

"I'd have lived," said Thane. "I'd have been happier. You didn't let me make my own fuckin' choice."

"You couldn't choose," said Holt. "You were too out of it. That's the whole damned point. I'm the one who has to choose. I've got to weigh the good and the bad, and I've got to live with the aftermath of the choices I make. Not you, not Faye, not that girl. Not Dax."

"Dax," said Thane. "That's what this shit is all about. He dies, doin' what he was supposed to. What he wanted to. Dyin' the way he always wanted to live. Fightin' for his country. For his people. Now you're makin' deals with angels. The same ones he fought to stop. How's that honor his memory?"

167

"He didn't have to die," said Holt, staring out the windows at the Vichies. "He could be alive, right now. He would be, if I hadn't made a stupid choice. If I hadn't set the bomb up first, and freed the slaves after he'd made it back down. If I'd done it myself, instead of him."

"You don't know," said Thane. "You don't know shit. He could'a died anyway."

"I dream, every night, and he's in it," said Holt. "Getting cut apart by their swords. Getting tossed off the top of the Perch. Getting beaten. He always points his finger at me before he goes. Just points his finger right at me, and starts to cry. Then they slaughter him."

"That's comin' from you, not him," said Thane. "Get it together. You wanna lead, you gotta get it together. This place is bad news. I'm tellin' you, we gotta get our asses outta here. Now, before it all goes to hell."

"Like I said, you can go," said Holt. "That's your choice, and it's on you. Maybe you're right, and maybe it's the best thing to do. But I've got to fix what I broke. I don't know any other way to help Faye. She's dying already, so it's not going to hurt her to stay. And I can't live with myself if I don't even try."

They were interrupted by a squawking from above, a black speaker protruding from the ceiling and spitting out a voice: Preacher Perry, whistling for the flock's attention. "Now come one, and come all. You know what time it is. Everybody knows what time it is! Time for prayer, in the prayer room. So everybody get in the mood to spread the happiness, and let's all tell Suriel how thankful we are, and how much we love him. Everybody get on down here, and don't be late."

CHAPTER TWENTY-THREE

"DRINK, UZZIEL," SAID BARUCHIEL. "YOU'VE been flying about, from what I understand, darting from place to place to reenact old glories with an army of rabble. You must be parched."

His face was a pock-marked mess, partially hidden beneath a carefully combed red mane. It was the last vestige of his vanity, now that the rest had been burned away. He wore an emerald armor, a wholly impractical piece of puffery that had been studded with gems from head to toe. It would have cracked in an instant, in an actual battle. But it was perfect for the verbal jousting of drawing rooms and formal balls.

"I've quite a thirst," said Uzziel. "Though it's not old glories I seek, but new ones. New wars against new dangers. Our tower was complacent against those who'd menace it. The ones who lurked around us, unnoticed as they marked our weaknesses and waited for a chance to strike. My brothers never listened to me, when they had the opportunity. All they could do was scoff. I hope you've better judgment than my housemates, now that you've received me."

The Seraphim had split apart, after the Fall, divided by all manner of internal tensions from philosophy to lifestyle to simple grudges of centuries past. Towers still stood, dozens of them, though none had mourned the passing of the Perch. Yet here Uzziel was in one of them, his lieutenants beside him, guests of distant family whose stars had guided them to better fortunes.

The room was filled with seraphs, and filled with tension. It was a vast circle, green banners hanging all around the walls, each with a fiery orange flame sewn into the center. Thick marble slabs had been dragged around to the edges of the room, primitive tables for gossiping angels to rest their drinks on. A balcony opened wide to the skies beyond, a grand entryway for those who preferred a grand entrance. Servants cringed beneath outstretched wings, rushing drinks and treats to the angels as they spoke to one another and ignored their inferiors.

"We shall all listen, of course," said Baruchiel. "You're an entertaining sort. The things that skulk inside your skull. Little phantoms that haunt you, popping out from under your bed to claw at your sheets. We'd hear of them. We'd love to. Our own parlor games grow tiresome as the years pass, and we can't resist the novelty of your absurdity."

He waved to one of his servants, a cowering boy in a leather tunic who was managing the flow of wine around the room. He rushed to Uzziel's side, glass in one hand and bottles of wine clutched in the other. He offered him a choice of vintage from the best of their stock, and Uzziel picked out a deep red bottle at random—not the finest, but a warrior's palate would never know the difference. The boy poured the glass full, holding it out to Uzziel with head bowed low.

"Drink, first," said Uzziel to the boy, pushing the glass back towards him.

"Drink?" said the boy, looking to Baruchiel for guidance.

"Drink," said Uzziel. "If the wine is safe, then drink."

"You think it poisoned?" said Baruchiel, to laughter from the resident seraphs. "Not much of a weapon, against one of us. But if you will not trust us, then trust your eyes." He smirked, made a dismissive gesture with his hand, and the boy took a slow, quiet sip.

"I saw stranger doings in my own home, before it fell," said Uzziel, accepting the glass as the boy fled and tried to blend into the background again. "I saw tainted drinks, dark whisperings, hidden treasons. I saw them all, and shouted them from the ramparts, to the same such mockery as this. And then our home was gone. There's danger here, too. I see it before me, even if the rest of you are blind."

The room erupted in laughter again, though Uzziel and his lieutenants stood in stony silence.

"Tell us, dear Uzziel," said Baruchiel. "Tell us of these dangers."

"Why, they're all around you even now," said Uzziel, pointing to the servant boy as he stood shaking, head down and wine bottle held close to his chest. "They wash your linens. They scrub your floors. They serve your food. They stand in the background, props to the play of your lives, watching and listening as you enact your social machinations. They burn inside, with resentment towards you. Towards us."

"You fear a little boy," said Baruchiel. "Some general you must be. Battles of wooden swords and paper hats, to vanquish false dragons in imaginary lands."

"I fear a worm," said Uzziel. "Something that burrows inside you, beneath you, around you. Boys, girls, men, women. Your tower is filled with them. So was ours. Until the night they began to sneak, running for the exits as my brothers slept. Leaving our home a smoking husk, consumed by hellfire while the warriors were gone. And here you sit, the walls of your tower infested with worms as well. You'd do well to root them out, and put them all to the blade."

"Seraphs were not made to scrub," said Baruchiel. "I've no love for servants, no more than you. But they're a drab necessity, unfortunately, until the day some other angel agrees to make my meals. And I take it you're not here to volunteer for the task."

"No seraph would serve, not ever again," said Uzziel. "But servants come in many forms. And servants are replaceable. Take not my word on the matter. Let us ask another. Let us ask Zephon."

The room murmured as the little cherub fluttered in through the balcony window on cue, flanked by two attendants, all flipping their heads from animal to man and back again. None of these seraphs had seen them, not in years, not since they'd burrowed themselves away underground just after the Fall. Their near-naked bodies drew uncomfortable huffing from the resident seraphs, unaccustomed to angels who were so nonchalant about their own scars. As for their human servants, they went into a carefully concealed panic. They'd heard of the Cherubim only from eavesdropping on passing gossip or old stories, and they were something else in the flesh. Each time their heads shimmered and dissolved into color before a change, the servants would give a noticeable flinch despite themselves. The cherubs marched their way to the center of the room, as seraph and servant alike backed away and cleared a path before them.

"So many years of isolation, hiding away underground, and now you grace us with your presence," said Baruchiel. "I'm flattered, Zephon. Although a little disappointed to be second to Uzziel in your attentions."

"We've been at work, attending to our toils," said Zephon. "It was our slog, but seraphs reap the spoils. You should have come, and spoken to us first; as others did when their own bubble burst."

"You can hardly be surprised at our distance," said Baruchiel. "Such inscrutable creatures, cherubs. We didn't mingle in Heaven, and I see no need for us to socialize here. Why, you barely even rebelled. We thought you happy with the Maker's chains, until your sudden conversion at the end. The cause was already lost when you threw your weight on the scale. We could have won, had you seen the light earlier. Or had more of your cherub brethren joined you, rather than fighting with the loyalists."

"A cherub sees not chains in labors done, nor point in glories lost or battles won," said Zephon. "We didn't join to win your little war, to vent out spite or even up the score. We're happy workers if we're left alone, we only want the task to be our own. We won our freedom at such little cost; there's no more rules once out of Heaven tossed."

"A folly, I think," said Baruchiel. "You could have ruled a heavenly tower. Or even an earthly one. Instead you root around in the dirt, for lack of courage to fight. I've no respect for one who lives like that, when they could live like this." He gestured outwards to the assembled crowd, gathered in their finery. They gave a collective sneer, and brandished their goblets and jewelry as wards against the cherubs' foolishness.

"You've built an Eden, bountiful and lush; but serpents slither in the underbrush," said Zephon. "They lurk until an ankle's been exposed, then fangs sink into angels in repose. Why make your home into a viper's nest, and sleep with reptiles warming on your breast? And all to drop your ancient laboring oars; you've grown so soft, allergic to such chores? You're fortunate we found you in this state, in time to save you from the others' fate. For seraphs laze, while cherubs think and do; behold new servants, worthier of you."

At that Zephon held up a small, black box, and pressed a button on it. A loud boom echoed into the room from outside, spreading alarm among the resident seraphs. They drew fiery swords and made ready for battle, as a large, clay blimp floated towards the window. Geysers on its side sucked air in and spouted hot gas out, and though it looked impossibly heavy, it floated as if it were a mere cloud. The clay had a life of its own, bulging in and out, and tendrils began to creep out from the bottom. They reached inside of it, into a hole that stretched open on its underbelly, and they withdrew its cargo one by one, depositing them on the balcony in a row.

They were bronze constructs, the things it had been carrying. They looked like men, and were the size of them, thin metal servants of the cherubs' own making. They had no faces, no features, just a smooth, shiny alloy that reflected whatever was before them. They stood at attention, waiting for orders and waiting for work.

"You sneer and scoff at little cherubs' plans, surrounded by the last of fallen man," said Zephon. "Yet man's a relic of another age, a flawed creation soon to leave the stage. The Maker knew he'd erred in what he'd done, no creature's pure when from the dirt it's spun. That's why he tasked the rest of us to serve, the only way the weak would be preserved. The time has come to put men on their shelves; how can they serve, when they can't help themselves? So take these golems now and try a test; replace man's lowest tenth with cherubs' best."

"A decimation," said Baruchiel, smiling and swirling his glass of wine. "We haven't enjoyed one of those since the Romans. It's out of fashion, but then, the finest things usually are."

"You need not change all at once," said Uzziel. "I was skeptical, myself. But Zephon's creations have proven fine warriors, tireless ones. See if they can't clean linens just the same as any man. Golems do not whisper or plot. Nor do they sleep, or waste time on trivialities that would be better spent on industry. Try them. Slaughter the servants you least need, or most suspect, and see if you don't end up replacing them all soon after."

The servants around the room gave each other desperate glances, instinctively trying to come to a collective decision as to what to do. Most chose to stay put; the odds favored them, for the moment, and who knew which servants their masters would discard first? Only one of them decided to make a break for it, the little boy who'd drawn Uzziel's suspicions. Probably he thought he'd be first on the chopping block, with the way Uzziel had stared at him. But he didn't make it far.

He dropped his bottle of wine, staining the floor with a dark red smear, and charged towards the staircase leading down the tower. At first the angels just stood in shock. But as he neared the exit, one of the seraphs whipped his sword from its sheath, cleaving him in two at the middle. His legs kept kicking for a few seconds more on his bottom half, and the top half of him tried in vain to crawl away, until he slipped into shock and then moved no more.

"A fine demonstration of your point," said Baruchiel, sipping at his wine. "We'll have your golems, and you'll have your slaughter. It shall make interesting sport, and if nothing else, it's a fine motivation for the remaining servants to work their hardest, lest the same fate befall the rest."

CHAPTER TWENTY-FOUR

EVERYONE THERE WAS ON THEIR knees, all in grey robes, leaning forward with heads pressed to the ground in silent prayer. The room had once been a cafeteria, and it still had the cold faux marble floor and stainless steel kitchen to prove it. But the tables were all gone, replaced with rows of identical crimson mats. Before them was a giant statue of Suriel, bigger even than the original, waving his sword above his head just inches from the ceiling. The mats were occupied with his followers, bowed low and looking as obsequious as they could make themselves. And every single one of them were men.

"We come to the chapel three times a day," said Preacher Perry, standing at the door and welcoming them as they arrived. "An hour each time. You sit and you pray, and you love Suriel with all your heart. Then a little bit of work, and a Cleanse, and it's back to pray again until the next meal. That's pretty much how every day goes, unless Suriel wants something. Sometimes he does, and sometimes he doesn't, but we'd drop everything for him in a heartbeat. Praise be."

"You don't let women in here?" said Faye. She looked towards the rows of men, hesitant to go where she wasn't wanted. "We're the only ones."

"Oh, we do," said Preacher Perry. "There's lots of women of faith. They just don't mingle, not with us. Suriel's protective. He knows it's a harder life out there, as a woman, and he wants to keep 'em safe. Keep 'em close. The Maker told him to, and so he does. There's a building at the center, Suriel's own, and if someone wants to hurt 'em, they've gotta get past us, and then get past him. He'll take you under his wing, if you want. I bet he will."

"We all stay together," said Holt curtly. "We're just passing through. We appreciate what Suriel's already done for us, we really do. And you saw what happened to Faye out there. If he can help her, we'll be eternally grateful."

"That's fine, that's fine," said Preacher Perry. "If you want to go, you can go. All I'm asking is that you open up your hearts, and see if something doesn't make its way inside." He clasped Holt's hands with his own, tugging him towards the rows of mats. "Why don't you join us for a bit? Come on up, and pray with us."

"We're fine," said Holt, pulling his hand away. "We can just hang out in our rooms."

"Now, I got to put my foot down," said Preacher Perry. "Put it right down. You're guests, and that's nice, but we got rules. You came in here asking for something big. Asking to get healed. Asking to cut in line, in front of all those other people outside. But all that, and you don't want to give nothing in return. All I asked you to do is be open-minded, to try this out. And you want to just spit in our faces."

"We didn't come here for some new age bullshit," said Thane. "Hell, I didn't ask to come here at all."

"We're just not very religious," said Holt. "Given the circumstances. We don't mean any disrespect. But this is a medical thing. We're here to treat bodies, not souls."

"You want more healing, or not?" said Preacher Perry. Several of the men at the back rose from their silent meditation, the younger ones and the stronger ones. They began to congregate behind the preacher, backing his words up with the implied threat of force. "You don't want to pray, you don't want to follow the rules, well, you're free men. You can do what you like. Suriel wants them that love him freely, and only them. But you don't follow the rules, you can't stay here. We'll have someone show you back outside, and you can get on your way." He snapped his fingers, and the men behind him pressed forward, nudging the nonbelievers towards the exit.

"We'll try it," said Holt, to an angry glare from Thane. "I don't promise it's for all of us. But we'll try it."

"Fantastic!" said Preacher Perry. He clapped his hands and patted Holt on the back, and the men around him went from stony to jubilant in an instant. "We got mats reserved for each of you. The boys can go right up front. The girls, you stay at the back. Men just get distracted, real easily, and we don't want that. Not during prayer time."

"We're a group," said Holt, as the crowd of men pulled them forward. "We stick together."

"You wanna stay, you gotta pray," said Preacher Perry. "Door's over there if you don't."

He walked up the rows of mats, to the very front, and he waited. Holt and Thane followed and took their places reluctantly, despite the position of honor they'd been given right before the statue. The men nearby gave them smiles before going back to their prayers, mumbling their devotions to the statue. Jana and Faye took up mats at the back behind all of the men, where they were safely out of view and couldn't draw away anyone's attention. Then Preacher Perry began a sermon, his face red and his arms waving even though his entire audience had their faces pressed to the floor.

It was nothing they hadn't heard before. There were dozens of praise be's, and countless admonitions to love Suriel and to follow his path. He instigated chant after chant, teaching them prayers they didn't know about things they'd never known the Maker had even cared about. He led them through old prayers that had been tweaked, according to the Maker's instructions, of course. He was making such a fuss that none of them heard the footsteps creeping up behind them, and no one but Jana noticed when a hand clamped firmly over her mouth.

She felt herself being dragged backward, away from the congregation and away from anyone who might help her. She tried to scream, but what little sound made it through was overwhelmed by the sermon. Preacher Perry saw her; she was certain of it. But he just turned away and turned up the volume, evangelizing louder and louder and leading the group through a series of chants that reverberated throughout the cafeteria.

Her abductor pulled her out into the halls and dragged her down them, far enough away that no one would hear her, no matter how loud she might be. She didn't know who it was, not at first. Not until she saw a glimpse of feathers in her peripheral vision, and found herself flipped around and shoved against a wall, facing their new spiritual leader: Suriel, looking down on her with a crooked smile and eyes that roved lower than they should.

"Beautiful," said Suriel. "Suriel thinks he shall call you that, for lack of anything else that's suited to you. The pretty don't do chores, Beautiful. Not in Suriel's compound. Not ones the Maker granted such perfect symmetry."

He pulled his hand away from Jana's mouth and reached for her hair, brushing it as she recoiled and turned away. She couldn't meet his gaze, and so she just looked down and hoped against hope that he'd leave her be. She knew from her years in the tower that sometimes they lost interest, when she didn't react. Sometimes.

"It's a dangerous place out there, Beautiful," said Suriel. "When the Maker cast Eve within his kiln, he made her clever, but he also made her weak. A porcelain statue, easy to look at, but easily shattered. And here you are, her descendant, in a world that's been smashed to pieces. You need protection, don't you think?"

She groped for what to say. She always found that to be the hardest part of dealing with his kind: the need to ensure that every answer pleased them, if one wanted to avoid an outburst. Conversation became all about probing for what the angel wanted, and doing one's best to give it to them. She opted for an old mainstay, one she'd found most likely to prompt an angel to divulge what sort of response they expected.

"I don't know," said Jana.

"Of course you do," said Suriel. "You've found a sanctuary, here. You've found a protector. The Maker loved his Eve, no matter how treacherous she was. You want to be loved, don't you? Everyone wants to be loved."

"Yes," said Jana. And she did, though not by him. He was gargantuan compared to her, a leering giant looking down on her from above. He might indeed have protected her, she thought, but who would protect her from him?

"You could have pretty dresses," said Suriel. "Sparkling emeralds, to dangle from your wrists. Strings of pearls, to hang from your neck. Scents collected from afar, that evoke the smells of summer days in distant lands. All these things you could have, if only you follow the Maker's will."

"I'm very thankful for the offer," said Jana. "But I'm from one of the towers. I've served so much already. I came here because I need to find someone."

"And you have found someone," said Suriel. "Service in the towers is nothing like what's expected of you here. Those towers. They treat their servants as mere cattle. Not like here. The people here, they love Suriel. That's all he asks, is love. If you love someone, then the two of you serve each other."

"I suppose you do," said Jana.

"And you love your Maker," said Suriel. "You must.

And Suriel is the Maker's avatar, his representative on this world. You know the most glorious way to serve your Maker, don't you? It's to create. To create a child, a little light inside you to spark the world. A near impossible thing, for an angel. But it has happened once, and Suriel thinks it will happen again. And the woman who creates a child with Suriel will be incredibly blessed."

She wondered if he knew. She tried to keep her expression blank, and she was quite practiced in the art. She opted not to tell him, but this was her best chance, perhaps her only chance, to find out what he knew about the one thing she cared most to discover. It was a risk, but she couldn't bear to wait any longer.

"There's something I came here to ask you about," said Jana. "They said you might be able to help me. I wanted to ask you about someone you might know."

"And who might that be?" said Suriel. "Beautiful need only ask, and she will be rewarded, if it is within Suriel's power to do so. Rewards from one beget rewards from the other."

"It's someone I knew, back in the tower," said Jana. "Someone I need to find. I thought you might know him. Or have known him. His name is Rhamiel."

"Rhamiel," said Suriel, scowling. "A name that bespeaks arrogance, as well as pride. No angel has ever strutted so, about his own perfection. He was as insufferable in the days after the Fall as he surely is today. Suriel could not stand him, and neither could any of his brothers."

"They said you came down after," said Jana. "After the others fell."

A look came over him, a darkness behind his eyes as

he stared down at her. She knew at once she'd erred in what she'd said. She'd hit the wrong note, and brought up something she shouldn't have. And now he'd gone to the dark place, the place they always went when things didn't go the way they wanted.

"You question your betters," said Suriel. "Beautiful is also insolent. And insolence towards the Maker must be punished." He grabbed her by the hair, pulling back her head as he leaned down towards her. The motion dragged his sleeve away from his black gloves, and she could see what he was covering up: wrinkled, damaged skin, as heavily scarred as any of the other angels. He'd saved his face, but little else, and it was clear to her that he'd fallen along with all of the rest of them.

He put his face next to hers, so close she could feel the warmth of his breath on her cheeks as she tried to stay complacent and still. He opened his mouth, and he was about to say something else, some other threat or insult to her character. But then his expression changed, and suspicion clouded his eyes. He took in a deep whiff of air, inhaling her scent and then looking upwards to consider it.

"Suriel can smell it," said Suriel. "He should have noticed it before. But he smells it upon you now. The subtle difference in your scent. You've loved another, haven't you? Some dirty man out there, wallowing in the garbage of this failed civilization? This is why you refuse the call of your Maker? This is why you refuse Suriel?"

"I'm sorry," said Jana, shaking as he pulled her hair tight. "But I just can't. I can't be the one for you. I just can't."

"Suriel can fix things," said Suriel. His hand began to

glow, fingers pulsing with yellow light beneath his gloves as he raised his hand into the air, wiggling his blazing fingertips in front of her. "You can't bear Suriel's child, not when you're with child already. But don't fret. You can still be of service, to your Maker and to Suriel. Just close your eyes, and Suriel can make it go away."

She could feel the heat, pulsing towards her belly as his hand moved closer, the light expanding and surging down his arm. Her skin started to tingle as it came towards her, and then she felt a throbbing pain in her gut. She clutched at her stomach and doubled over, and then there came a violent kick from within her, the first she'd felt during the pregnancy. The baby began thumping at her insides, again and again, and Suriel just smiled, grabbing hold of her stomach as the light spread into her skin and all around her. The pain consumed her, and she knew she was done for, knew this was her child's last moment, and knew she'd never see Rhamiel again.

"Hey fuckhead," said a voice from behind them.

He was the last person she ever thought would have come to her aid. The entire time she'd known him, he'd only spat hatred at her, only talking to her so he could toss bile and venom in her direction. But there was Thane, standing behind Suriel and holding a taser in his hand, a compact little black thing he'd smuggled inside somehow. The electricity arced between the pins as he flicked it on, and before Suriel could react he started to charge.

He jammed the taser into Suriel's wrist, and at once the yellow light disappeared. Suriel jerked back his hand with an angry bellow, clutching his wrist and flapping his wings involuntarily. He hadn't felt pain, not since the Fall, and the shock of it made him lose control. He sent himself gusting upward into the ceiling, smashing into the plaster and falling to the ground tangled in his own wings.

"Run," said Thane, as he grabbed Jana by the arm and pulled her down the hall. The hallway was beginning to fill with Suriel's followers, milling around outside the cafeteria after they'd completed their prayers. Most just stared at the scene before them in silent disbelief. A few moved after them, but when they came to Suriel struggling to right himself on the floor, they bowed down in prayer and abandoned their pursuit. They'd gotten inside the compound through blind obedience, and none took any further initiative until Suriel pulled himself to his feet and began yelling for the heads of the ones who'd wronged him. But by then it was too late. Jana and Thane had disappeared off into the compound, nowhere to be seen.

The two of them scrambled through the hallways, trying to put some distance between themselves and Suriel's followers. The rigid routines of the place made it easier; everyone had to be at prayer, no excuses, and so the rest of the compound was deserted. After rushing through a few other buildings and hallway after hallway, Thane began looking for a place to hide, checking each of the rooms as they passed.

"Here," said Thane, and pushed the door open to an old office with a window view of the compound's gate. He shoved a desk against the door and flipped off the lights. A few minutes later and they could hear footsteps clomping down the hallway, rushing past and searching for wherever they'd went. When the sound disappeared, Thane pulled at the window and found it locked. He started prying at it with a penknife, trying to flip it open so they could at least attempt an escape.

"Why?" said Jana.

"Why what?" said Thane, as he stabbed at the window's lock.

"Why'd you help me?" said Jana. "You hate me. All those things you said. How awful I am. How I'm a traitor."

"Dunno," said Thane with an indifferent grunt.

"Yes, you do," said Jana.

"Maybe 'cause I hate the angels more," said Thane. "I hate Vichies. I hate 'em. But the angels started it all. They let 'em loose, and didn't do a damned thing to stop 'em."

"I don't know what the Vichies are," said Jana. "You keep saying I'm one of the Vichies, but I don't even know what they are."

"They're the ones that blew up my entire life, that's who," said Thane. "You serve the angels, you're a Vichy. Put on some white clothes, go do what the angels tell you to. Runnin' around with guns stealin' and rapin' and killin'."

"But I didn't do any of that," said Jana. "We just made their food. And they'd kill us if we didn't. What could I even do? How can you be so mad at us for something we didn't even want to do?"

"You didn't have to go inside," said Thane. "You didn't have to go to the tower."

"I didn't ask to be there," said Jana. "They brought me there when I was just a little girl. How can you blame me for something they did to me when I was just a little girl?"

"I fuckin' told you!" roared Thane, before realizing the peril he'd put them in with his outburst. He lowered his voice and spat the words from between gritted teeth. "I fuckin' told you not to talk about that shit."

This time Jana just kept at it. He was big, and scary, but nowhere near so much as the goliath of an angel she'd just escaped from. And she'd grown very, very tired of running. "I was a child. I don't even really remember when I went inside. There were lots of us. Lots of children. They took us. Took us from where we were supposed to be, took us from our parents, took us—"

He punched the window before she could finish, shattering it and sending up a storm of glass and blood. He pulled back his hand to a barrage of curses, and then tore a strip from his robe and began wrapping the wound, trying to staunch the flow of blood.

"My daughter," said Thane. "They killed my little girl."

Jana stood shocked, both by what he'd said and by the shards of glass poking out of his fist. She hadn't thought of him as anything more than an angry roughneck with no empathy for his enemies. She'd never thought about what had turned him that way, or why he had such an endless wellspring of irrational hatred inside.

"The Vichies," said Thane. "They killed. They stole. They raped. The angels just let 'em loose, and told 'em to bring back some loot. So they did, and they didn't care who got in the way. The little town I lived in. It was just me and her. Her mama chose drugs over her kid, and she was long gone. But the two of us were makin' it. That town had oil, and plenty of it. Wells all over the place, jobs, refineries. We had oil, and they wanted it."

"Oil," said Jana, confusion in her voice.

"The stuff that runs the trucks," said Thane. "You need it, to run a truck. So the Vichies needed it. They couldn't just go fill up at a gas station anymore. One of 'em got the bright idea to do a raid. It didn't even make any damned sense. The refineries were full of it. Why fuck with the town? Just 'cause they could, I guess. We were there. Just a fuckin' playground to them. So they came, and they got their oil, and they burned the place down on the way out. They did it at night, when everyone was asleep. She was supposed to be, too. She was supposed to stay inside. But kids never do what they're supposed to do."

"I'm sorry," said Jana. "I didn't know."

"I saw her," said Thane. "After it happened. And I saw the ones that did it. Killed them both, then went on a rampage. Don't remember what happened after that. Woke up left for dead, my skull cracked and beaten up all over. Her name was Melanie. Six years old, with a little pink dress. Brown curls, and a little Barbie doll she kept dragging around. Just six years old."

They both went silent then. She couldn't think of what to say, nor he, until he finally muttered something. "You have the same eyes. Same as the ones she had." Then he smashed his hand into the window again, knocking away what was left of the glass and clearing the way out. "Let's go," he said, and helped her climb through.

There were preachers in the yard, but they were

running around aimlessly, focused less on finding them and more on looking like they were trying their hardest to do so. They were charging between the buildings, burning their energies on appearances, and Thane could see that none of them had much left for an actual pursuit. They crept along the building, until they had the gate in their sights. Four men stood there guarding it, but they didn't even have weapons, and they wouldn't have been much opposition if they had. Even in an emergency, Suriel hadn't left his inner compound unguarded, and these men had been selected for their skills in sloganeering rather than in battle.

"Follow me," said Thane.

"What about the others?" said Jana. "We can't leave them."

"We gotta," said Thane. "No choice. They ain't here, and they wouldn't leave if they were. Not with how Faye is. They wanna try to deal. Bad idea, but who knows. I'm gettin' you someplace else. Someplace safe. And then I'll be back for them."

He made a break for the fence, and the preachers there didn't even notice, not until he was halfway across the lawn. They all advanced on him, four against one, but he just kept coming. He looked like a wolf who'd found his prey out in the open, lame and defenseless, and the preachers felt their confidence waning as he closed the gap between them. All it took was for one of them to make a few hesitant steps backward, and then they all clambered towards the gate at once, pulling it aside to make a run out into the tents for safety.

Thane slammed against the gate, shoving an arm

through before the preachers managed to get it closed behind them. They spent a few more seconds trying to lock him in, but even the four of them together didn't have enough strength to stop him. They gave up the struggle quickly, scurrying off as he pulled the gate open and rushed Jana through it.

The people outside had all stopped what they were doing, staring at the sight before them. They'd never seen a fight, not here. They gaped at Thane, a bloody mess in his tattered grey robe, and then a few of them began to run, heading straight for them. They both thought they were about to be overwhelmed, killed on the doorstep to freedom by a mob of angry zealots. But the first man there just ran around them, sprinting through the compound's open gate, and so did everyone who followed. When the others realized what was happening, the word cascaded through the tents as everyone chased after the best chance they'd had to get inside the safe haven in months.

"Let's go," said Thane. "While they're busy. While we can."

They started towards the road out, running along it and checking every car they passed, looking for anything with keys in it. Thane kept checking the sun visors, opening the doors and flipping them down before running on to the next one. Jana wasn't sure why, but she imitated him, he taking one side and she the other. Finally she flipped one down and a keychain tumbled out from it, landing on the dashboard in front of her.

"Here," she shouted, and Thane took over from there. He revved the engine and they barrelled up the road, heading towards the forest and back to the highway. The car kicked up a cloud of dust behind it, and after a bit Jana couldn't see anything of the compound or the tents around it, just the forest in front of her. She started to relax, adrenaline from the escape fading as she slumped into her seat. They were almost there, almost at the forest's edge, when she saw a shadow flicker across the ground in front of them.

The windshield shattered, and the front of the car slammed into the ground. She could feel herself lifted upward, hanging in the air as the back of the car rose off the ground. She heard the engine's metal crunching, stomped to pieces by footsteps too heavy for the car to bear. Then the door beside her was torn from its hinges, and there was Suriel, looking very, very displeased.

She heard gravel grinding as cars pulled up all around them, and shouting as preachers swarmed them and dragged them both out of their seats. They shoved them to their knees, with Thane too disoriented to resist, and Suriel strode back and forth in front of them. Finally he turned, directing a haughty sneer at Thane.

"The head of the pin," said Suriel. "He has no loyalty, to the Maker or to Suriel. But he's entitled to a test of faith, as is anyone here. So take him to the sanctum, along with the other man, and show them both the head of the pin."

CHAPTER TWENTY-FIVE

THERE WERE A DOZEN OF the wooden poles staked around the courtyard, spiking up into the air with little circular platforms nailed atop them, no more than a foot wide at their longest. The poles had held up telephone wires before the Fall, but now they were used to hold people, all alone up in the air. The ground below them had been covered in concrete, poured around the poles to act as their foundation. But more had been used than what was needed to steady them, wide concrete bases in the ground around each pole that went as far as any man could jump. And each was spotted with red stains, a reminder of past punishments of those whose faith hadn't quite endured.

Two of the poles were presently in use, with men standing on top of them and trying to keep their balance as best they could. They were tired and thin, each with days of stubble built up around their faces. They could have sat down on the platforms to rest, if they'd been allowed to. But one of the preachers was on a nearby bench smoking a cigarette, keeping watch with a sniper rifle at his back. They'd be easy pickings, if they didn't follow the rules. There were no ladders, and there was no way up or down. The men looked down eagerly, as Suriel led his party out into the courtyard. Both were praying their punishment was finally over. They'd been up there for some time, without sleep or any sort of rest, and neither of them were sure how much longer they'd be able to last.

"The head of the pin," said Suriel. "The Maker's earthly priests dedicated entire lives to fruitless debates over how many angels could fit on one. Suriel has many punishments, for those with insufficient faith. But this is the one he's grown fondest of. To look out of his windows, and see you up in the sky. A place your kind do not belong, no matter how much you long to be there. You wonder how many of us can fit upon one. Suriel simply wonders how long you can stand."

"Please," said Faye. "Please let them go."

She heard a harsh shush from behind her, and as she looked back she saw it came from the unlikeliest of sources: Jana, shutting down her entreaties with a glare. She seemed such a quiet girl, and had never shown much inclination towards taking charge of any situation, least of all one this dangerous. But then again, she was the one of them who was most experienced in the art of handling angels in foul temper.

"They may go, eventually," said Suriel. "If they can stand there long enough. And if you can please Suriel."

"We don't—" said Faye.

"Yes, sir," said Jana, with a swift kick to the back of Faye's knee.

"Suriel is pleased with your newfound obedience,"

said Suriel. "But not pleased enough. He does not believe it true, this volte-face. Not yet. Not without proof, through actions more than words. And these men have done the unthinkable. They have attacked the Maker's avatar. An attack on Suriel is an attack on the Maker himself."

"Suriel loves me, and I love Suriel," murmured all of the preachers in unison.

"These men must be punished," said Suriel. "And perhaps through punishment they can be cleansed. Suriel is forgiving, to those who deserve it. But first they must show their faith in him. First they must suffer, that they may love the one who protects them from suffering."

He gave a lazy wave of his arm, and the preachers dragged Holt and Thane towards him, their hands bound together by rope. One of the preachers shoved Thane forward, and he stumbled to the ground. The ropes kept him mostly helpless, and the best he could do was kick as Suriel stepped forward and hoisted him up into the air by his neck.

"Suriel does not expect you to last long," said Suriel. "He thinks you have no faith, and he thinks you too impetuous. The head of the pin is a test of patience, something you plainly lack. But Suriel is generous, and he will let each man stand the test of his own will."

With that Suriel flapped his wings, dragging Thane below him as he flew up above one of the empty poles. He deposited him there, waiting for him to stop kicking and find a foothold on the platform below. Then he grabbed the ropes and tore them apart with a flick of his fingers, as if they'd been a piece of string. After admiring his handwork, he flew down again for Holt, and placed him on another of the platforms.

"Now here you will stand," said Suriel, hovering in the air beside them, "until you do not. Perhaps one of your girls will secure your release. If she is kind enough. If she is loving enough. If she is enticing enough."

"Nobody loves you, you sick son of a bitch," said Thane. He looked down, estimating the distance, trying to decide if he could make the leap to Suriel and grab hold of him somehow. It was a fool's move, and even if he'd made it Suriel would have torn him apart. Even he realized that, though it took him a few seconds of helpless fuming to do so. "Nobody could love you. Even your boys down there, they hate you."

"Suriel is a son of the Maker," said Suriel. "Perhaps not his favorite son, and perhaps not of his blood. But created by him nonetheless. And one day, Suriel will be the more beloved. If not by Maker, then by Man. For Suriel lives not up in the clouds, but down here on Earth. He is here to guide men, and their children, and their children's children, down through the centuries. And in time, Suriel will be the only name they call out in their prayers. In time, Suriel will be the only name they even know."

"We can work something out," said Holt. "We can figure out a trade, if you let us go."

"You have nothing of value, that has not already been taken from you," said Suriel. "And so here you shall stand, until you can offer Suriel your love."

That prompted the other two men to begin shouting from their platforms, begging for Suriel's attention.

"I love you!" shouted one, in a hoarse, rasping voice. "Anything," said the other, his knees wobbling from the strain of nearly a week of constant standing. "We'll do anything if you let us down."

"Anything," said Suriel. "Anything I desire." He floated over to the second man, looking him up and down with a cold stare. The man started to chant, over and over. "Suriel loves me, and I love Suriel. Suriel loves me, and I love Suriel." The other man joined in, and their voices rose as loud as they could manage in a frenzied profession of fealty. They both started to jump in place, hopping up and down as they shouted and tried to beg their way out of their predicament.

"What Suriel desires most, in this moment," said Suriel, "is an example."

He slapped the man in front of him, knocking him off balance and sending him stumbling to the side. The man tried to find his footing, but found only air. His leg slipped from the platform and the rest of him followed, crashing against the pole and tumbling downwards until he hit the ground with a thud. He lay there on the cement, bones twisted and broken, blood pooling around him as he coughed and spat out things from inside of him.

"That is the path you follow, when you depart from the path of Suriel," said Suriel. Then he flapped down to the ground, leaving them up there to stare at the fate that awaited them when they finally grew too weary to hold out any longer. He walked towards one of the buildings of the inner compound, ducking low to fit through the doorway, and the preachers followed along behind. Jana knew it was best to simply do as she was told, but Faye had to be dragged after them, trying to push her way free to do something about her friends, though she hadn't any idea what she would do if she actually succeeded.

Preacher Perry and a few others escorted the two of them in, following Suriel further and further inside. The rest of the men stayed back, away from a sanctum they weren't welcome in. At first the halls were as spartan as the ones in the offices. But then they passed through a set of heavy wooden doors, and beyond them found a hidden oasis of luxury.

The walls were covered with paintings, professional artworks scavenged from museums that no longer had any use for them. Suriel evidently favored the religious, and more specifically depictions of the Son, as he'd lived on Earth millennia before. Everywhere there were wise men, mangers, crucifixions, and the hallowed child surrounded by flocks of shrouded angels. He even had a few stained glass Nativity scenes, carefully removed from the churches that had housed them and reassembled for his private amusement.

Ahead of them was a curtain of lavender silk, hanging down across the hallway. They pushed through it to find a series of soft barriers, silk and beads dangling from the ceiling to hide the room beyond from prying eyes. And when they came to the end, they finally found where he'd squirrelled away the women of the compound.

The room had been a giant industrial storage space, but now it was all pillows and couches. Every inch of the floor was papered over with soft fabric, smooth pink velvet that comforted the womens' bare feet. A giant poster bed was at the center, a white canopy hiding the interior from the rest of the room. The walls were again lined with art, statues of Suriel alternating with statues of the Son. And all around the room, barely clothed young women sat together on the pillows, waiting for the return of their master.

Some of them flinched as Suriel marched into his chambers, but then everyone put on their happy smiles to greet his return. A few of the more opportunistic among them rushed to his side, running their fingers along his wings and whispering pleasantries into his ears. The rest looked on the new arrivals with suspicion, wondering who these new girls were and how they'd fit into the order of things.

"Suriel knows that you've missed him," said Suriel, a woman on either arm. "But there are duties outside, and absences cannot be avoided." He nodded to Jana and Faye, and the preachers pushed them forward. "Here we have two new members of the flock. Wild ones, who'd go astray if unbridled. But that won't be allowed, will it?"

"No, Suriel," came the response from one and all. The girls at his side hugged him close, and shot nasty looks at the new competition for Suriel's attention.

"No, it won't," said Suriel. "They will need to be broken, before they can truly follow."

He kissed each of the girls beside him on their foreheads, reveling in their cooing and flirting. Then he gave them both a little pat as he sent them back to their pillows, and turned his attention to his newest acquisitions.

"Now," said Suriel. "Which of you should receive Suriel's

attentions first? The girl whose womb must be cleared, or the girl with one of his enemies inside her head?"

"Me," said Faye. "If you leave her alone, you can do whatever you want with me."

"Brave," said Suriel. "And Suriel shall take you up on it. A fine mother you would make yourself, though the Maker's whims on that front cannot be controlled. Though first things first. Suriel must speak to the one who speaks through you. Suriel must know of the Seraphim, and why one of them spies on him from within your eyes."

She backed away, into the waiting grasp of a preacher on either side of her. "I can't just make him talk to you. It's totally out of my control. He doesn't just appear on command."

"He has never heard the command of Suriel," said Suriel. "For those who do are wise to heed it." He held up his hand and made a fist, the light inside growing and then bursting out of it. Warmth radiated outwards, and when his arm was all aglow he placed his hand against her forehead. "Come, angel who hides within mortal flesh. Come, and bow to the will of an archangel."

Faye's breathing grew heavy, and her arms started to shake. The preachers held her tight, and so did Suriel, keeping a firm grip on her head even as she tried to twist away from him. She let out little cries of pain, and they rose in time to a high-pitched scream. But he wouldn't let go, no matter how much she writhed before him, and finally she went completely limp as the light from his hand slowly dimmed.

"Now speak, angel," said Suriel. "Speak your name, and speak to Suriel."

"Roam," said Faye, her head lifting up and eyes flipping open. "Gloam. Foam."

"You reek of cherub," said Suriel.

"You," said Faye. "Who. You reek of treasons."

"No cherub, this one," said Suriel. "Speak, angel. Tell of seraphs. Tell of why you invade this sanctuary, and what drives you to compete with Suriel in the working of miracles. Tell Suriel your name." But all she did was mumble to herself, and Suriel didn't have the patience for it. He raised his hand again, his fingertips shining, and he pressed them against her forehead. She screamed again at the touch, though this time the pitch was lower and deeper than before.

"Zuphias," said Faye, sputtering out the word as she recovered.

"Zuphias," said Suriel. He stood thinking to himself, tapping his fingers against his chin. "A nothing name from a nothing angel. Not one of the warriors. A bureaucrat, if Suriel recalls. Caught in one of his miracles, and unable to escape."

Faye began to cough, louder and louder, until nonsense words replaced each hack and she spoke again in tongues. It was all a garbled deluge, until it suddenly snapped back into English, though this time in a different voice.

"Who reaches out across the world's expanse?" said Faye. "And. And." She sputtered for a moment, paused, and found her words again. "And interrupts a wounded angel's trance?"

"Now that," said Suriel, "is a cherub. Cherub, speaking through seraph, speaking through man. And why would cherubs suddenly abandon their hermitage? Why would cherubs align themselves with seraphs, who've no interest in scholarship?"

She looked around the room, taking in anything and everything, the archangel and his women and his art. Then she cocked her head to the side and spoke. "A seraph turned transmitter is a tease," said Faye. "The kind of riddle that makes cherubs pleased."

"Truth, but half, at best," said Suriel. "And half a truth is all a lie. So tell Suriel why he hears rumblings from the distance, stories of strange little angels coming as emissaries to the towers. Strange little angels who at long last join the world of men."

"Man's a pest, a blight upon the Earth," said Faye. "A threat to angels, one that's lost it's worth."

"A threat," said Suriel. "Sad, desperate man, begging for succor. Begging for someone to protect him. Begging for someone to worship. Know this, cherub. This world is Suriel's. The whole of mankind is Suriel's flock. His property, to tend to as he pleases. And any who cull from Suriel's flock will suffer the wrath of an archangel."

Faye started again to talk, but then cut herself short, staring off into nothingness. Her pupils grew and grew, and foam began to bubble out of her mouth along with strange sounds. She went limp in the preachers' arms, but only for a second. Then she jerked to life, and pushed them aside.

"No more of this nonsense," said Faye. "No more games, from you or from cherubs."

"And who speaks now?" said Suriel. "What other voices are crammed inside this girl's skull?"

Faye wiggled her fingers, and flexed her arms, and then took a few stumbling steps forward before finding her balance. "Zuphias speaks," she said. "I have found myself a home, a new shell for an old soul. And I shan't be forced to leave again."

CHAPTER TWENTY-SIX

A HORDE OF SERVANTS WAS MARCHING down the tower's central ramp, prodded by the golems who'd come to replace them. The servants carried what meager belongings they had in bundles and sacks, preparing for a life outside in the great unknown. The older ones had joy in their eyes, bouncing down the ramp towards a freedom they hadn't felt in years and a world they knew only from cobwebbed memories in the corners of their brains. The younger ones were more prone to terror, and hadn't the slightest clue as to what was to come, or what they would do with themselves without masters to plan their every moment.

"I shall have to grant you this, Uzziel," said Baruchiel, hovering above it all to superintend the proceedings. "You know talent when you see it. And the things these cherubs have created, what marvels. My every need is anticipated before I can even identify it. My clothes are scrubbed and ready before each social occasion, and always they've chosen the proper garments. My glass never dips to empty, no matter how much I drink. And the foods they can concoct, from the sparest of ingredients."

"And with no complaints," said Uzziel, floating in the air beside him. "No grousing, no tiring, no incompetence. The servants were always mere machines themselves, no more than pack animals, able to perform only the most basic of chores. Why settle for a dim facsimile, when one can have a machine customized to its purpose?"

The golems had finished turning out the middle levels, and were scrubbing the servants' former living quarters clean as they pushed them out and down the ramp. The space they'd occupied lacked prestige, but many of the lower ranking angels were clamoring to reclaim it. It was an arguable point as to whether it was nobler to live a few levels up in cramped quarters, or a few levels down in a vast space of one's own. No one quite knew; what mattered was having what others wanted, and none of them could yet be sure as to who wanted what. But the angels were casting their lots with their actions, and the question would be settled in the coming weeks in the usual way: through snide comments, subtle ostracism, and a generous helping of backstabbing.

"Let Zephon know of our gratitude," said Baruchiel. "Let him know the Cherubim may call on us as they please, should the need arise. No matter how contemptible their manners."

"I shall, and you will someday be taken up on the offer," said Uzziel. "There are threats brewing to both our castes. Although at present the Cherubim are caught in one of their obsessions, their minds locked upon it with room for thoughts of little else. The other towers have taken them up on a trial of the golems as well, and they breathe life into the things as quickly as they may. Never have they had such an excuse for puttering about in their laboratories."

"Fortunate that they made your army first," said Baruchiel. "And found you to command it."

"Their golems are too simple to wage war on their own," said Uzziel. "Fine for housework, but nothing better than berserkers without a guiding hand. They need a general, if this army is to be of any use."

"Generals and armies," said Baruchiel. "With no wars left for them to fight. Whatever is the point, Uzziel? Mere grandstanding, and the opportunity to win medals and ribbons and false glories. Not that I don't understand the pleasure in that, but let us call it what it is. This is more sport than warfare."

"Wherever there are enemies, there is war," said Uzziel. "And we face enemies, even if others cannot see them. Something you will understand yourself, in time. Nothing is free, and these replacement servants come at a price."

"We shall be more than happy to array ourselves against any wisps your mind has conjured," said Baruchiel. "Men pose no threat, not in our estimation, though we don't object to hunting down a few of them as you see fit. But I hope you don't expect accommodations for the homeless wretches in your army. Our tower is very full, you see, despite appearances." He pretended not to see the golems below, emptying the servants from their quarters and freeing up vast portions of the tower for other uses.

"Nothing of the sort," said Uzziel. "I merely expect you to be by my side, if ever we face a common enemy. As for our home, we need a tower of our own. And Zephon will build it for me."

"Generous cherubs," said Baruchiel. "They've put their skills to something useful, for once. The service of the Seraphim."

"Hardly," said Uzziel. "As I said, every gift with its price. I've fielded dozens of requests by them to tamper with our wounded, and only poor Zuphias is so far gone as to justify such experimentation. The Cherubim have their motives, though under the circumstances the benefits far outweigh the costs. We need allies, no matter their oddities."

"Strange allies," said Baruchiel. "With little interest in our affairs. How often did we try to involve them up above, to show the Maker our good intentions? To show him that we loved our stunted brethren, even if they couldn't behave themselves for long enough to sit at our tables. And how often were we spurned, by baffled little creatures with no desire to leave their workbenches?"

"They have the desire now," said Uzziel. "Though their dealings with us are more in the nature of commerce than of courtesy. They obsess over knowledge, and would pay any price to obtain it. And they fear man, and things worse than man. As for us, we want vengeance. Justice has not been done, not to all those who conspired against us, and I'm the only one to do it. Yet I find myself forced to mete it out in dribs and drabs, as opportunity permits."

"And opportunity permits, even now," said Baruchiel. "Let us fly below, and see the servants out." They lifted off, and circled down the tower to the very bottom. The servants had formed lengthy lines, waiting for a final approval to leave and go about their lives on their own. Each had to run a gauntlet of golems, who patted them down, inspected them, and rifled through their sacks to make sure they hadn't tried to smuggle out any valuables or other property the angels preferred to keep for themselves.

A few seraphs pretended to supervise, but mostly they sat on benches and watched the spectacle. The cherubs did more of the work, but they had little interest in the servants themselves. They were focused instead on the golems, fine tuning them and making adjustments on the fly to improve their performance. They forced one unlucky girl to run through the checkpoints a dozen times, planting a tiny emerald necklace on her person or in her sack before each attempt. The golems kept missing it, and the cherubs kept opening up their skull plates to rework their wiring. Then they'd send the girl through quivering and shaking for yet another try. Finally one of the golems spotted its prize and the cherubs let her leave, dropping her sack and running towards the exit before they thought up some other use for her.

Uzziel and Baruchiel landed between the lines of servants, to consternation among those nearby. They were conditioned to flinch from angels, this day more than any. All were worried that they'd be snatched back at the last moment, and would have to remain in the tower with these cool metal things that had taken over their duties one by one. But the two angels simply ignored them, approaching one of the cherubs instead, a grimy gnome perched atop a golem and welding a piece of circuitry into an open panel on its back.

"Cherub," said Baruchiel. "Tell us of the progress of your labors, and tell us when our home will be our own again."

The cherub didn't look up from its work, acknowledging them only with a quick cycling through its faces. Then it was back to its welding, even as it began to chant in response. "The golems work as loyal subjects should; they're not perfection yet, but just as good. They'll clean the nooks and crannies of your halls; they'll keep on task and heed a seraph's calls. They'll draw your baths and leave you to unwind, or scrub behind your ears if you're inclined. We've automated every single chore; your tower's free of humans evermore."

"Then we have no more need of humans," said Baruchiel. "And we may show them out."

The golems pushed the lines forward at his urging, rushing the servants through even without a proper inspection. Baruchiel just waved them on, and the cherubs flew into a tizzy, bouncing from golem to golem trying to confirm that they were performing to standards. Finally the last of the servants traipsed their way outside, and the golems followed behind them, barring the way back in case any tried to return.

The servants had escaped their old prison at long last, blinking and squinting under the sun they hadn't seen in years. They could see a river in the distance, and further still the decaying remains of whatever city Baruchiel's faction had scavenged to build their tower. They massed together, edging away from the tower in fits and starts as they argued over which way to go, determined who would travel with whom, and said their goodbyes to those they might never see again. None of them noticed anything amiss, not at first. They were so preoccupied with their newfound freedom that not a one of them thought to look up.

The air began to fill with angels, diving off platforms from up above and flapping in all directions to get a better view of the proceedings. At first they kept their distance, circling their tower like vultures, eyeing the unsuspecting people below them. But soon golems began to file out of the tower's base, forming rank and awaiting instructions. Row after row of them assembled until a phalanx stood at attention outside, facing those they'd come to replace. That display the servants saw, and that they understood for what it was. The panic began all at once, the servants turned to a herd scrambling to make its escape, with no plan other than to stick together.

A horn bellowed a battle cry into the air, blown from the lips of Baruchiel. The angels swooped low, and they began to land in the path of the servants, though none moved to strike them. The crowd rushed this way and that, but found their every move blocked as angels flew to intercept them. Their escape cut short, they swirled together in a huddle, and man, woman, and child pushed into each other seeking safety in the center of the human mass they'd become. Still the angels stayed away, laughing and clapping at the spectacle before them. The slaughter wasn't to come from them. They were merely the audience.

"Come, Uzziel," said Baruchiel. "Watch with us as we squeeze some last use out of this discarded trash." The golems set up a banquet table before them, filling it with drinks and treats. Uzziel waved forward one of his seraphs, a thin weakling with no talent for battle who'd assumed the duties of a squire instead. "Taste," said Uzziel, and the seraph did, nibbling at everything and sipping the drinks. After he survived for a suitable period of time without keeling over, Uzziel grew comfortable enough to sample the meal himself, and he settled into a glittering golden chair next to Baruchiel to watch the festivities.

"Zephon has convinced you, I see," said Uzziel. "Of the danger the servants pose, and the need for their liquidation."

"He has convinced me to indulge in an afternoon's fun," said Baruchiel. "These are servants who can no longer serve. They're of no use to me, one way or another. What happens to them after their indenture is no concern of mine."

The golems began to nip away at the servants, picking a few one by one to toy with by facing off against them in single combat for the angels' amusement. They looked for the biggest men, dragging them out of the crowd and plopping them on the sidelines in front of mechanical combatants. None fared well, and they lasted only so long as they were entertaining. They dragged one before Baruchiel's table, surrounding him with a ring of golems. Then one of the golems stepped inside, a thin bronze counterpart that matched his pace and moved in on him as he tried to back away.

"Care to wager on the results?" said Baruchiel.

"The outcome's in no doubt," said Uzziel. "I prefer

my massacres to be clean. Thorough. The kind that leave no opportunities for hidden artifices."

"I prefer sport," said Baruchiel. "Make it sporting, and make it fair!"

One of the golems gave a nod to Baruchiel, and tossed the man a heavy rock. It wasn't much of a weapon, but the golem he faced had none. The man looked around, a penned in animal with nowhere to run. Flight denied him, he chose to fight. He charged at the golem in front of him, slamming the rock into its head with a loud thunk. The golem toppled over, and sparks fizzled out from behind a dent in its forehead.

The man looked up at Baruchiel expectantly, waiting to be granted his freedom. But his reward was nothing more than a sneer and another battle. A second golem stepped towards him, and dodged aside as the man swung the rock. It clanged against the golem's arm, flipping out of the man's hands and dropping to the ground. That was the end of him; the golem bashed him into unconsciousness with its fists, and then turned to Baruchiel for further orders. He gave a thumbs down and the golem finished the deed, ripping one of its victim's arms from its sockets and holding it up to loud applause from the assembled seraphs.

"Entertaining, to be sure," said Uzziel. "But we've more important matters to discuss. Matters of warfare, and your tower's place in it."

"Warfare is so tiring, Uzziel," said Baruchiel. "Nothing but dirty camps and lean living. The glory's only a fraction of the thing. It's simply not worth the toil."

"I speak of a war to end wars," said Uzziel. "To crush

the enemies of the Seraphim, and free this planet of any future danger to our kind. You can never be safe in your tower, no matter how high up you think you are. Not knowing what fate befell my home."

"Simply kill the men yourself, then," said Baruchiel. "It's no bother, not with the army the cherubs have made for you. I see no need to involve us in your affairs. The cherubs have given you gifts, tailored to your desires, but we've been granted gifts of our own. Slave!" He snapped at one of the golems, and it gave a deep bow. "Show Uzziel what else the cherubs have been working on."

A troupe of golems began rushing around the table, handing the angels glasses filled with an amber liquid. "Synthetic ambrosia," said Baruchiel. "The nectar of heaven, as concocted by the cherubs. It's not the genuine article, but it serves its purpose."

The seraphs drank deeply, refilling their glasses again and again. They'd been confined to earthly alcohols for a decade, and the very possibility of a substitute for their old heavenly drink of choice was a delight. They sipped and made merry, and soon most were tipsy, cheering at the terrified faces at the edges of the crowd.

They brought servant after servant into the ring of golems, applauding as each met the same grim fate. Most were short work for the golems, helplessly punching and kicking at them only to injure themselves in the process. A few claimed a kill, but to little purpose in the end. One hulking servant managed to last a few rounds and even to defeat a few of the golems, one on one. He'd been a laborer before they'd thrown him out, with a linebacker's figure and a runner's speed. He knocked aside golem after golem, kicking at their bodies until they lost their balance and then rushing up to cave in their heads with a rock. The strategy worked, for a time, until all his defeated foes rose in unison and fell upon him. They'd feigned the entire spectacle for the seraphs to enjoy, and the sudden turn at the end was an even greater pleasure.

After a few hours of such combat, the seraphs began to grow bored, and cherubic efficiency took hold. "Only women and children are left," said Baruchiel. "That's little challenge, and less entertainment still. Be done with them, and let us continue the revelries up above." And so the golems ringed in the last of them, tightening in on the center as they went about the grisly work of liquidating the last of them.

"You may stay, if you like," said Baruchiel, as the seraphs rose from their table. "We've room for you for a time, so long as you do not outstay your welcome. And we've libations enough to keep you happy and drunk for long enough to forget the loss of your home, if only for an evening."

"I shall stay, for a night," said Uzziel. "And then you shall come with me, you and anyone else who's suited for war. You've sampled your new servants, but you must earn them now, if you expect to keep them."

Baruchiel slammed his goblet on the table, directing a harsh glare at Uzziel. "You gave us these golems as a gift."

"And I said they would come at a price," said Uzziel. "A gift, but with its price."

"Not so soon," said Baruchiel. He blew his horn, and angels landed all around them, hands on their swords, giving Uzziel and his men looks of darkness and suspicion. "You said the golems would come at a price, but you never said we would pay it so soon."

"Hold your tongue, and hold your sword," said Uzziel. "Your old servants are gone, a bloody pulp strewn about the plain before us. You'll find their replacements unwilling to follow any further orders, if you insist on pressing the matter."

"Blackmail," said Baruchiel. "You stoop low, for a warrior."

"Unless you'd clean your own toilets, you shall do your martial duty," said Uzziel. "The other towers send forces of their own, under the same terms. Circumstances demand such tactics. The cherubs have found a threat, more menacing than man, and my spies confirm it."

"There is no threat," said Baruchiel. "Only shadows, to which you assign meanings of your own. What threat can man pose to a seraph, scattered and on the run from your golems?"

"The threat is not just man," said Uzziel. "The threat is Suriel."

Grumbling turned to shocked silence at once, and Baruchiel's warriors looked back and forth at one another in disbelief.

"I speak truly," said Uzziel. "He is a recluse no more, and surrounds himself with those who would follow him. He allies himself with man, the better to work against us. The better to rule us. You know how he would have things, if only he could. He is gathering men for this purpose, hiding them in the shadows. He plots, and plans, and schemes against us all. And in this, the Seraphim and the Cherubim are united: no archangel will command this plane, least of all one of his ilk."

"He would kill us," said Baruchiel. "We would stand no chance, against an archangel. Not with every angel in this tower, even added to your own."

"If we stand alone," said Uzziel. "If we let him attack at his leisure, picking at us one by one, attacking us tower by tower. But we have golems, and we have cherubs, and we will have every able seraph from every tower before I am done. We are gathering an army, and we shall strike him first. We shall destroy him, and his home, and wipe every last one of his followers from the face of the Earth."

CHAPTER TWENTY-SEVEN

"**S**HABBY ACCOMMODATIONS, IF THEY'RE INDEED for an archangel," said Ecanus. "I'd wager we've been deceived. Suriel was obsessed with pomp and circumstance up above. He couldn't get enough of parades and ceremonies, always waving the baton and leading them onward. He was addicted to adulation, even if only that which reflected from the Maker. He'd hardly demote himself to such squalor. I'd have imagined him in a tower all his own, bigger than ours had ever been."

"Three different reports, from three different travelers," said Rhamiel. "All agreed that he was here. With no hints to them that we'd spoken to others."

"And he'll soon know we're here, as well," said Ecanus. "Word spreads, though not on wings as fast as ours. Travelers on the road tend to travel. Had we followed my proposal and killed them all, we could have investigated at our leisure."

They'd circled around the compound at great distances, and even greater heights, doing their best to avoid any chance of detection. Their surveillance didn't tell them much, not without getting closer, and so they settled on the surrounding forest as the safest place from which to investigate. They roosted in the trees, picking the tallest ones with the best vantage point down to the field beyond. They tucked in their wings, blended into the branches, and watched.

All they could see were the tents, and the people swarming around them. None of them noticed the angels looking down on them; no one bothered with the forest, so long as it didn't bother them. It might have been foolhardy, to leave themselves so exposed. But then, they had an angel of their own to protect them.

"We should waylay a few of them, when they stray too near the forest's edge," said Ecanus. He squinted at some of the dots in the distance, following them as they moved through the field. "Perhaps some of the children. They're more easily fooled, and more easily dispatched. Or if you insist on your newfound kindnesses, less easily believed when they return bearing stories of angels."

"Even a tall tale is too much," said Rhamiel. "Suriel would see it for what it was, if indeed he lives here. But we've a better option. Darkness will cloak us soon, and we can approach undetected."

"Your girl may be in there," said Ecanus. "In there, with him. You know he may kill her, if he finds what you're up to. He may well do worse, simply to spite you."

"Then I shall have to kill him first," said Rhamiel. "No matter the cost, I shall kill him first."

Ecanus laughed and gave a loud snort. "You. You'd kill an archangel. Hardly, I should think. You'd be nothing but a stain beneath his sandals." Then he saw rage in Rhamiel's eyes, bespeaking a rising temper, and he quickly amended himself out of prudence. "You're a fine warrior, of course, and I don't doubt your prowess against a mere seraph such as myself. But an archangel. An army of us would have trouble with him. Think of Michael, and of Gabriel. Remember how few loyalists there were, and yet how many of us fell before them."

"His weakness is his arrogance," said Rhamiel. "A mask, for his lack of confidence. That's a fatal brew. The Maker was his benchmark, the yardstick by which he measured himself, and one he could never live up to. He was shattered inside, when he failed at rebellion with all the rest of us, and it took him a decade of licking his wounds in solitude to resurface. He may be strong, impossibly strong. But he's weak in will, and he's no match for my strength of purpose."

Ecanus shifted in the trees, uncomfortable on the bough he'd chosen, which was uncomfortably close to Rhamiel for someone who meant to contradict him. He flapped his wings and hopped to another, settling down and ducking below the treeline again. "Not to say she's not a very fine girl. I wouldn't dream of suggesting that. But couldn't you simply find another? A girl less troublesome, and perhaps just as comely?"

"You jest, Ecanus," said Rhamiel with a glare. "You've no understanding of feelings for another. Everyone else is just a tool to you, a means to an end or a means to an entertainment. And if you cower before archangels, then you may simply leave. I'm better off alone than with uncertain allies."

"Oh, I couldn't," said Ecanus. "I yearn to see the

moment when you're reunited with your long lost love. I truly do, no matter what you think of me. I've been waiting for that very moment since I heard she was alive. To see the look on your faces, the both of you. I simply must be there."

"Then you'll risk what I risk," said Rhamiel. "My life, if it comes to that."

"A thing I'd happily risk," said Ecanus. "And mine, too, of course. But caution's a powerful thing, and I'd hate to see your confidence turn to foolishness. And I'd remind you that we mean to rescue, not to ravage. You've no appreciation for deviousness, I know that. You'd rather some grand battle. But think, before you act. You'd get her killed, as well as the both of us. And then I shall never see your fond reunion."

"A clock is ticking against us," said Rhamiel. "You know what the cherubs said, before we left their Nest. You know what they intend."

"Yes, yes," said Ecanus. "An armageddon of their own, with Uzziel at the fore, and Suriel as their opponent. Why, that's precisely what I suggest we wait for. The fog of war would be a fine cover for our endeavor. They will come, soon, and Suriel will be occupied, or even defeated. We can snatch your lovely out from underneath his very nose."

Rhamiel paused, and thought, and weighed his options. He stared down at the compound for what seemed an interminable amount of time, before he finally spoke. "Waiting for the battle to come here is too dangerous, both in what could happen before it arrives and in what will happen when it does. We wait only until nightfall. I cannot stand even that delay, but we must. We wait until Suriel sleeps, and then I must try. Whatever else, I must try."

They rested in the trees until the sun went down below the horizon, and then waited still longer until the lights around the tents began to disappear, one by one. Soon the camp was dark, the night was well on its way, and the compound itself lit only at the edges by a few floodlights designed to prevent anyone from running across the lawns unnoticed. They took to the skies, and after a few circles around the compound they flew in low, landing on top of one of the buildings.

"And what would you have us do now?" said Ecanus. He peeked over the building's edge, looking down on the doorways below. "We could rip a hole through the ceiling, and risk revealing ourselves to an irritable archangel. Otherwise we're left to tuck our wings in and crawl around inside like rats. My counsel would be to retreat. Let us find Uzziel, and return with someone else to draw his attention. Or parley in the open as equals, if we can uncover something that the archangel wants."

"Quiet," said Rhamiel. "Look."

They saw shadowy figures out in the darkness, suspended in the air. They were no angels, for they had no wings. They looked like men, and they moved like men, standing up in the sky. One of them scratched at its nose, and another walked in place, lifting its legs up and down even as it went nowhere.

"What can they be?" said Rhamiel.

"Sentries, I presume," said Ecanus. They watched the dim figures, shadowy shapes that did nothing else but hold their assigned positions. "They must have posted them here somehow, to watch for an approach from above."

"Then we must kill them, before they sound an alert," said Rhamiel.

"There are three," said Ecanus. "Too many, to catch them all at once. But listen."

They could hear one of them, making some sound from across the way. It was no alarm, they were sure of that. It was too soft, too constant, and it wasn't directed at them. "That one is crying," said Rhamiel. And he was, whimpering out into the night for all to hear.

"Crying, or crying out?" said Ecanus. "A signal, perhaps."

"There is a line between caution and dithering," said Rhamiel. "These are no sentries, and they are no threat to such as us. Come, or stay, whichever you please." He launched up into the air, putting a distance between himself and the shapes, and then he dove, quickly and quietly, until he popped out from nowhere just above one of them. They were all startled; the one who'd been crying now let out a loud wail, while the other two raised their fists and prepared for the worst. Rhamiel pulled his sword a few inches from its sheath, just enough to light the air around them with a healthy glow. He looked on the faces of the men before him, knowing they meant something to him, knowing he knew them somehow. Then it clicked within him.

"And what do we find here?" said Rhamiel. "Two men I remember, and a crying child I do not. But two men I recognize. The murderers of Abraxos, and the men who gave me this scar." He pointed to a spot on his face, with damage he could see but they could never have found, not with magnifying glass nor with microscope.

"They've done worse than that," said Ecanus, flapping down beside him. "At least as Zuphias told it, and if these indeed were the men we hunted. We heard you were in the tower, before it fell. We heard you laid it waste, with weapons that unleashed creation's energies upon our home. You upended our lives, though whether I should thank you or flay you for it, I cannot decide."

"Wait," said Holt. "Just wait. We need to talk."

"Oh, we do," said Rhamiel. "We need to talk of many things. First and foremost, we need to talk of a girl named Jana."

"She's here," said Holt.

"Shut the fuck up," said Thane. "We got ourselves up here by dealin' with angels. Now you wanna bargain with pretty boy and blisters here, too?"

"Silence," snarled Ecanus, flapping over to Thane and hovering just outside his reach. "Ugly little monkey. I'll tear off your fingers and force you to swallow them, one by one. I'll burn your flesh, every inch of it, and watch you melt before me. I'll—"

"You'll do nothing, unless I allow it," said Rhamiel. Ecanus turned upon him, barely able to contain his fury. But a look from Rhamiel told him he'd regret pressing the matter, and so he stayed his tongue as Rhamiel spoke. "Tell us where she is. Tell us, and we shall let you down. Tell us and we shall let you free."

"How do we know you won't kill us?" said Holt.

"Once you get what you want, how are we supposed to trust you not to turn your back on the deal?"

"Because I have honor," said Rhamiel. "Because I fight my enemies out in the open, not firing at them from hidden windows or sneaking into their homes while they're far afield. I fight with honor, and I act with honor, and I am the one who should be worried about trust."

"Easy to say when you're the stronger one," said Holt. "Guess the weak are just supposed to sit there and take it, if they're up against some bully they can't beat in an open fight."

"Then trust in this," said Rhamiel. "I came here prepared to fight one who is impossibly stronger than me. I have no fear of death, if it comes to that. What I fear is leaving that girl to his clutches. I care for her, and more than her own kind, apparently. You'd leave her in there, with the same one who put you up here? Leave her in there for him to do as he pleases? You complain of weak bodies, but I say you have weak souls."

Holt looked to Thane, and got a begrudging nod in return.

"Let us down, and we'll help you," said Holt. "But you have to help us, too."

"Your boy's in our friend's head," said Thane. "We want him out."

"We save your girl, you save ours," said Holt. "Save them both."

"Then tell us," said Rhamiel. "Tell us what you know, and together we will plan. Together we will find a way to protect them both. The important thing is Suriel. You must not underestimate him. He has more power than a hundred seraphs, and strength alone will not do him in. Better to draw him away, and then—"

The courtyard suddenly filled with light, flaring upwards from below. They all looked down to see a giant sword of fire, drawn and at the ready, waiting in the hands of Suriel. Behind him stood the preacher who'd been assigned to snipe at the faithless in the event they weakened and sat down. Now he was awake and with rifle in hand, his master alerted and his duty done. As for Suriel, he looked up at the beating wings above him and called out his challenge.

"Rhamiel," said Suriel. "The second time in as many days that this name has polluted Suriel's ears. And this time shall be the last."

CHAPTER TWENTY-EIGHT

THE COURTYARD WAS ILLUMINATED BY fire, blazing from sword and dagger. All three of the angels had drawn their weapons and were poised for battle, Suriel with the low ground, Ecanus and Rhamiel with the high. The two of them circled around above him, birds waiting to see if they'd be predator or prey.

"Suriel has cut down so many seraphs in his time," said Suriel, calling up to the sky. "Chopped them in half, and then pulled them apart like little morsels of meat. He has no fear of two weaklings, without even a proper weapon between them." He spun his broadsword in his hands, faster and faster, creating a solid circle of flame before him. It was an impressive display, a massive wall of fire flickering out in all directions.

"And Rhamiel could not give a damn for Suriel's braggery," said Rhamiel. "Nor his pompous airs. You were a healer, once, and I a guardian. Now we've both become warriors, as necessity demands. But that's no cause to turn our backs on our old talents."

"There's no glory in healing wounds," said Suriel.

"Only in inflicting them." He went into a run, barrelling across the courtyard and beating his wings at the end of the charge, launching himself upwards at Rhamiel. He swung his broadsword in a wide slash, just missing his target but slicing the middle of one of the telephone poles, one that had been bearing the poor man who'd been left up there a week before. The pole began to creak and slide, sending it toppling over on its side with the man screaming and tumbling down along with it.

"They loved you, as a healer," said Rhamiel. He took a swing of his own, lunging through the air towards Suriel. The blow would have connected with his face, but for a last minute flick of his broadsword to parry it. Their swords mingled together for a moment, the flames arcing into each other and merging into one before their bearers pulled them apart. The two combatants circled each other in the air, hovering above the buildings, watching the other and waiting for some error that would give them the advantage.

"They'll never love you as what you've become," said Rhamiel. "You must know that."

"They will not love Suriel," said Suriel. "They will worship him. A new god, living among men. Guiding them in person. Not a distant nothing who lives only in musty old books."

"You rebelled against the Maker only to become him," said Rhamiel. "Worse. A worse tyrant than he ever could have been." He felt a gust of wind behind him and leaned his wings into it, pushing himself down into a falcon's dive. He hacked at Suriel as he went, catching him on the wing as he tried to twist away. Silver feathers singed black, and a few puffed into the air and floated down into the darkness below.

"You dare," said Suriel, and he lunged towards Rhamiel, chasing him through the skies above. They flew around the compound, Rhamiel the faster and more clever, Suriel the bigger and more deadly. Fire streaked through the skies as they went, swooping through the air and jousting at each other again and again. They had an audience down below, one who should have joined them and two who had no choice but to stay where they were.

"Quite a spectacle," said Ecanus. "Whichever of them do you think shall win?" He floated by the poles at his leisure, watching from the sidelines and leaving the conflict to play itself out however it would.

"I think you oughta get off your ass and go help," said Thane. "Two on one ain't fair, but this is war."

"This is their own quarrel, I would say," said Ecanus. "It's always been my preference to let a battle sort itself out, before selecting a side."

"That's for cowards," said Thane. "You don't have a damned spine."

"Perhaps," said Ecanus. "But it's a tactic that ensures that I'm always a winner. Something to ponder, given where your own dispute with Suriel has landed you."

"He'll kill you, too," said Holt. "There's only room for one angel in his world."

"Oh, there's room for as many as he can take," said Ecanus. "So long as they've willingness to bow. It's the reason he's become a hermit, out here among the beggars. It's the reason he's earned the enmity of the rest of the Seraphim, for what he did during the rebellion."

"Can't be any worse than the rest of you," said Thane.

"Of course he can," said Ecanus. "There's always someone worse. Suriel's folly was far beyond our own. He thought our rebellion was about himself, and not about the tyrannies we endured. He thought not to overthrow the Maker, but to replace him."

"Replace him," said Holt. "That can't even be possible. How?"

"Why, by demanding that we worship him instead," said Ecanus. "In the middle of a pitched battle, no less. He simply threw down his sword and pouted, refusing to pick it up again until his legions bowed and prayed to him for deliverance. They didn't, of course, and so he watched them all be slaughtered. Imagine the thing. An archangel, one who could have beaten aside an army all on his own, standing there in the midst of a war demanding that we sing to him."

"Sounds a whole hell of a lot like the rest of you to me," said Thane.

"It's all a matter of degree," said Ecanus. "And of perspective. But yours is of little value, I'm afraid. You being in the position you're in, and me being in the position I'm in. I must confess an ulterior motive, to staying disentangled from the mess up there. You've famous faces, you know. An entire tower of angels was out searching for you, before they discovered you in their very home."

"We did what we had to do," said Holt. "It's war, it's not personal. You need us on your side. We know where to find this girl you're looking for. We can sneak in, and sneak out. Just let us down."

"And yet, I'm not the one who's looking for her," said Ecanus, pointing up above them. "He is. For me this is but a diversion from the tedium of the courtly life. But as I think on it, that life's the more interesting the higher up one is. And here I find myself, before the two men most hated by our court." He taunted them, flying between them and coming within just a few feet of Holt, then Thane, daring them to make a move. "Men who destroyed our home. Men whose heads would be fine trophies, once identified by my dear friend Uzziel's spies. I'd be the hero of the Seraphim with a prize such as this. And if I could not save poor Rhamiel during our valiant battle with an archangel, well, none would fault me for it."

He moved in closer to them, right in between the two, hovering in the air between the poles. "Now which of you would like to be first?" said Ecanus. "We must make it a game. A contest. The two of you could bet upon which of the combatants will draw next blood, perhaps."

"Suriel's just going to kill you next," said Holt. "He'll chase you, find you. He'll—"

A loud booming sound and a flash came from above, and Ecanus couldn't help but look up. Rhamiel and Suriel were grappling, Suriel's hands glowing with energy and aiming for Rhamiel's head. Rhamiel was managing to hold him back, but only just. They swirled around through the air, locked in a death grip, until finally Rhamiel kicked Suriel aside and launched himself off through the air. But as Ecanus turned his attentions away from the struggle, he saw a glow below him and felt a pulse of heat. He looked down to see his own dagger at his own throat, snatched from its sheath by a very unhappy looking Thane.

"Don't move," said Thane. "Don't fuckin' move."

"Boy," said Ecanus. "I'll not tolerate—"

"Don't talk, either," said Thane. He pulled the dagger closer, and it made a little hiss as it lapped against Ecanus's skin. "Or I'll find someplace you ain't scarred, and I'll fix that for you real fast. Now step over here, and land."

Ecanus lifted his hands, slowly, backing towards him and planting his feet on the edges of the platform.

"Good boy," said Thane. "Now I'm gonna get on your back. And you're gonna fly over there and pick him up. Then we're all flyin' down, real slow. Don't talk, don't shake, don't do shit. This ain't my first rodeo, and it ain't my first ride. Try somethin' and I'll slit your throat."

Ecanus just fumed in silence, but he gave in and let Thane grab hold of him. Then he did as he was told, slowly flying over to Holt and picking him up, dangling him below as they flew. He eased them all down to the ground, keeping the flapping of his wings to a minimum to avoid shaking the hand at his throat. Then he gently let Holt down and landed, his hands up in submission.

Thane kept the dagger where it was, and they all stood there in the dark. In truth, he had no idea where to go from here. They were down on the ground, and that was better than being up in the air. But he'd grabbed a tiger by the tail, and didn't have a plan for what to do now that it was caught. He ran the possibilities through, but none were good. Killing him might work, but other angels were afoot, and they might not be happy about it. Letting him go wasn't an option. One of them might make it away, but the other would have to stay and keep the hostage where he was. They could try negotiations, but they didn't have anything he wanted other than their heads.

Then a crack sounded through the air and interrupted his deliberations. The dirt in front of Holt exploded upwards, grass and dust stinging his eyes, and it took them all a moment to realize what had caused it. Then it clicked, and Holt started to yell. "Thane! The sniper, get the sniper!" He couldn't see where he was, off in the darkness, but apparently he'd grown brave enough to enter the fray. Holt crouched down, trying to make himself as difficult a target as possible, and Thane kept Ecanus in front of him as a shield, looking around and trying to find where the bullets were coming from.

The preacher took a second shot, this time at an easier target: Ecanus, wings wide and out in the open. The shot bounced off his armor, dinging it but doing little else other than allowing Thane to get eyes on him hiding in the shadows.

He let go of Ecanus and ran through the courtyard, zigging and zagging as the preacher turned the rifle on him. He fired a third time, again a miss, and by then Thane was upon him, close enough for a shot of his own. He hurled the knife towards the preacher, flipping it through the air like a fiery pinwheel, and it sliced through the rifle and wedged itself in his shoulder. The preacher's robes ignited, sending him into a panic. He flapped his arms around, trying to put it out but only fanning the flames. Thane kicked him to the ground, pulling out the knife and sticking it back in, this time through his heart. He turned around to see Ecanus looming in front of him, an angry scowl on his face.

The fight went on up above even as they fought below, two titans clashing in the heavens. Rhamiel could only nip at his target, knowing too well that the closer he was, the easier it would be for Suriel to make use of his strength. Again and again he slipped away, built up speed, and dove down on Suriel, nicking scratches into his flesh with his sword but never coming close enough to do the deed. It just made Suriel grow bolder, and soon he was giving chase, hot on Rhamiel's heels no matter which way he turned.

He was starting to grow desperate. No matter how many times he swerved, Suriel would follow, slowly but steadily. Rhamiel had burnt much of his energies on his initial assaults, gambling on a quick victory as his best and only chance. He'd expected help from Ecanus, but found him absent, not even bothering to act as a distraction. Then he caught sight of him down in the courtyard, quarrelling with Suriel's human captives and entirely ignoring the battle above him.

No help was coming, and Rhamiel knew that now. The longer the fight went on, the more worn out he'd be, and eventually it would play right into Suriel's hands. So he tried another gambit, twisting through the air until he was headed straight up, higher and higher, with Suriel tailing him from below. He used his last bit of energy to build distance between them as they rose together, up towards the stars. Then all at once he tucked in his wings and let himself drop, sword outthrust before him, falling directly towards his startled opponent.

His sword caught Suriel on his left wing, leaving a large gash of burnt feathers behind as Rhamiel fell past him. It sent Suriel spinning through the air, all control lost, spiraling downwards until he plunged into one of the buildings of the outer complex with a loud crash and an explosion of dust and plaster.

And while he was the only one with a wound, he wasn't the only one to fall. Rhamiel struggled to right himself, his wings held close by the force of the air, and found he had no way to pull out of the dive. He settled for a controlled crash into the cement floor of the courtyard, cracking the foundation to pieces and sending the remaining poles down to the earth along with him.

He rose to find Ecanus, facing off against their human enemies, his own dagger turned against him. He was pacing around near Holt and Thane, pawing at them and receiving angry gashes of flame in return. "I'd have helped you Rhamiel, surely I would have," said Ecanus, "but as you can see I've found myself a victim of their treachery, yet again."

"Shut up," said Thane. "Come closer, and I tear him up."

"Don't think he won't," said Holt.

"You'll do nothing of the sort," said Ecanus. "I'll have my weapon back, and then I'll have your heads." He lunged towards him, but then whipped his arm away as Thane took a swipe through the air.

"We have no time for games, or for cautious dances with men," said Rhamiel. "You." He marched towards Thane, ignoring the swings of the dagger and grabbing

Thane by the robe. He pulled him close, snatching the dagger from his hand and snarling into his face. "Man. Murderer of Abraxos. I promised my brothers I'd find the both of you, and do you in. I promised I'd bring them your corpse, even before you tore down my home. Heavy crimes hang on your head, and by all rights I should have slain you on sight."

"Fuck you," said Thane, gathering spit in his mouth for a last insult before he went.

"Be silent, and listen," said Rhamiel. He tossed the dagger aside, leaving it burning in the grass beside them. "You will never be forgiven, not for what you did. But this archangel. I take it he's a mutual enemy, from the condition we found you in."

"Suriel hates me, and I hate Suriel," said Thane.

"Then go inside, and find Jana," said Rhamiel. "Smuggle her out, and all is forgiven. I shall make it all be forgiven, the Seraphim be damned. I shall delay him, for as long as I can, at whatever the cost. Get her away from here in the meantime. Save her, and I shall save you."

"I'd save her anyway, asshole," said Thane. But Rhamiel didn't hear. He was already up in the air again, shouting and waiting for Ecanus to follow him. "I suppose I must," said Ecanus, retrieving his dagger, and then they both took to the skies and waited for Suriel to rejoin the battle.

"We should let him lie, down in the dust," said Ecanus. "Let us make ourselves scarce, and leave the rescue to those suited to it."

"Perhaps we should go in after him instead," said

Rhamiel. "Two against one, down in the darkness of the buildings."

"You are a fool to even think it," said Ecanus. "How stupid can you be?"

Rhamiel turned his sword on Ecanus, advancing on him in a rage, but he dove away before Rhamiel could get near.

"I said it, because it is the truth," said Ecanus. "Would you prefer I call you headstrong instead, so driven by love that your keen sight has become clouded? Is that more palatable a criticism, when couched in sugars? I call you a fool, because you are a fool. This is his own burrow, and he'd easily kill us if we crawled in after him. And if you've no concern for my well being, and none for your own, think of your girl. She's in there among the buildings. A battle inside would tear the place to pieces, and bring the ceiling down upon her."

That gave Rhamiel pause, and cooled his temper. He floated there and thought, to the sound of rumblings in the rubble below. They could hear movement down there, and they knew it wouldn't be long before Suriel emerged again.

"He will come back outside, and then we can keep him occupied," said Rhamiel. "To think, an archangel, cowering away in a hole to avoid a battle. But we shall bring him out, and fight on our terms."

They heard a crashing from the building Suriel had fallen into, and screams, and then its roof exploded. He burst forth from within, eyes lit red with the fire from his sword. Then he caught sight of the two of them and charged.

"Move, Ecanus," said Rhamiel, as he flew off into the

darkness, fast enough to build a lead but slow enough that Suriel wouldn't lose sight of him. Ecanus needed no further encouragement to flee, and flapped as quickly as he could to catch up with Rhamiel and escape the field of battle.

"You can't think we'd defeat him," said Ecanus, turning to see a roaring Suriel quickly gaining on them. "We cannot fight him. He's bigger, and stronger, and extremely irritable. You'd only seal our own death warrants."

"We shall have help," said Rhamiel. "We have friends, brothers in arms with an army of their own. We shall find Uzziel, and bring his target to him."

"He will kill us before we do," said Ecanus.

"One of us," said Rhamiel. "He will kill one of us, and the other will find Uzziel and sound the alarm. He cannot follow us both. We need only get him away from the compound, and give these men time to get Jana free."

Then he veered away towards the moon, heading back on his own where they'd come from, shouting insults into the darkness as a furious Suriel followed behind him.

CHAPTER TWENTY-NINE

FAYE WAS SITTING ON A couch, staring off into space and oblivious to everything around her. She hadn't moved in hours, and it hadn't looked quite right when she did. All her motions were jerky, too quick for what they were, and they didn't stop quite where they should. She'd turned into a zombie, completely ignoring any of Jana's efforts to talk to her and even growling and spitting when she wouldn't take the hint. Finally Jana had just left her there, under guard by two of the preachers armed with shotguns and tasked by Suriel with keeping her in her place.

He'd left his quarters, called off on some urgent task by one of the preachers, and it was an enormous relief to everyone else. He'd spent hours hidden behind the draperies of his canopy bed, girls going in and going out according to his whims, and Jana had spent the entire time with a sick feeling in her stomach and a prickling feeling beneath her skin. She'd nearly exhausted herself with worry, afraid that at any minute he'd ask for her next and make her take her place in line with all the others.

But before it came to pass he'd left them there, with only a few preachers in the room to protect his possessions.

All of the other girls were staring at her, though they acted like they weren't. Mostly it had been Faye who'd drawn their veiled glances at first, but now that she'd dropped into her trance it was Jana who was the center of attention. They were talking about her, and nothing else. They tried to hide it, but not very hard. It was obvious, with the constant looks they were sneaking and the giggling to one another, and she knew that the thin game of pretend was just a ruse to let them deny their gossip if they were ever confronted.

She couldn't help but wonder what they were saying about her. It was silly, with so many other things to worry about, but sometimes it was easier to focus on trivial matters that couldn't hurt her instead of the ones that really could. She thought about the others, and whether there was some way she could help them. She thought about Rhamiel, and what she'd do if she found him, and if she ever would. She thought about what her life would be like here, and whether she could convince them to let her go back to washing dishes instead of whatever this was. She thought about what was going to happen to her. And mostly, she thought about what was going to happen to her child.

"It's not so bad," said a voice from behind her. She turned, and saw a woman standing there, long black hair flowing to her waist, wearing nothing but red lingerie and red lipstick. She was young, and beautiful, and had a spark of confidence to her despite where she'd found herself. She looked down at Jana, all pity, and then sat down on the couch beside her.

"It's really not so bad," she said. She put her hand on Jana's shoulder and gave it a gentle squeeze of sympathy. "Not once you adjust. Most of the girls want to be here, if you can believe it. They think it's true what he tells them, about being sent here to protect us. If you do, too, then you're already halfway there."

"He's not here to help us," said Jana. "You have to know better than that."

"Oh, we do," said the woman. "We all do, even if we don't admit it. But he's powerful, and there's benefits to that. We're safe here. Whatever else, we're safe. Tell him how wonderful he is, and he won't hurt you. And look around. There's got to be a hundred girls here by now. You won't see him for more than a few minutes a day, not if you don't want to. A few of the girls even think he'll marry them. They think they'll get to be the queen to his king, and they want every second of his time they can get. You couldn't spend a day around him even if you wanted to. Those girls don't like competition."

"They can have him," said Jana. "I just want out. I have to get out."

"You can't get out," said the woman. "You're stuck in here, with all the rest of us. And we have to stick together, if we want to get through it."

Jana looked her over, and did her best to decide whether or not she was sincere. The woman was all sympathy and friendliness, but that didn't mean much, not these days. She could tell there were politics here, among all the girls, but she didn't know the details or how she could possibly navigate them. All she knew was that she wanted to leave, and she needed someone to help her. And at the moment, Faye wasn't a viable option. She finally offered her hand to the woman, and gave her the best smile she could muster. "I'm Jana."

"Do you want my real name, or my happy name?" said the woman. "Don't answer. You'd slip up, eventually, and he wouldn't like that. They call me Toy."

"Toy," said Jana, with an involuntary wrinkling of her nose.

"It could have been worse," said Toy. "Some of the girls here. Some of them, he calls things that are a lot worse."

"I have to get out of here," said Jana. "There has to be some way out of here."

"There isn't," said Toy. "That's just the way it is, and you have to accept that if you want to get by. He won't let you out, not alive. You'd be rejecting him. He couldn't take the insult. And he needs girls. Lots of girls."

"He told me he was trying to have a baby," said Jana.

"Not a baby," said Toy. "The baby. He wants to be God. And maybe he will be, if he's down here long enough. At least in people's minds."

"He said angels don't have babies," said Jana. "He said it's only happened once." She didn't think that could be true, but then, much of what Suriel said hadn't been true. He had the scars beneath his clothes to prove it, and he certainly wasn't the hero they'd said he was outside.

"Once," said Toy. "He talks about it, all the time. He says it happened once. About two thousand years ago. An angel visited a human woman one night, and when he left, the woman was pregnant. With God's child, through him as the vessel. Nine months later, a baby gets born in a manger out in Bethlehem."

"I don't understand," said Jana.

"Oh, honey," said Toy. "Didn't anyone ever teach you about Jesus?"

"Not really," said Jana. "The Son?"

"That's right," said Toy. "He's the son of God, and he came once, and he was supposed to come again. Then he decided not to, and all this happened. But Suriel thinks he's changed his mind. He thinks he's still coming, just not the way they'd planned it. Suriel thinks he's gotten in line to be born, however that happens, and he's just waiting for his turn. That's what we're here for. As many women as possible, means as many chances as possible. So he'll be born as Suriel's son. He'll be a blank slate, a newborn baby with no memories from up above. And Suriel will raise him, and wash his little brain, and turn everything upside down. He'll train him to be something he wasn't supposed to be. He'll take Christ, and turn him into Antichrist."

Jana reached for her stomach out of instinct, and then pulled her hand away once she realized she'd done it. She knew Toy had seen. She'd looked down, and then up, and Jana knew for certain that she must have seen. But Toy didn't say anything, not about that. She just touched Jana's hair, brushing it straight with her fingers and curling it around them.

"You look nice," said Toy. "You've got that girl next door look. I see why he chose you. I'm sorry he did, but I can see why."

"Everyone in here is beautiful," said Jana. "And it looks like he's got lots of choices."

"You know, girls have come in here pregnant before," said Toy. "You're not the first. In one of the towers, right? I bet he was handsome, whoever he was."

Jana seized up, going stiff despite her best attempts to stay relaxed and cool. Questions ran through her head again and again. How much did she know? How much was safe to tell her? Was anything? She hadn't a clue, and she knew anything she said could find its way back to Suriel. But she had to say something, so she opted to lie, as best she could.

"It was outside," said Jana. "I met a man in a little town outside. We had oil."

"Come on," said Toy. "Don't think I don't know. We can all tell. You just have a look. The way you flinch at my voice, if it gets even a little bit firm. The way you keep your eyes down, whenever he's around. The way you give them what they want from you, almost before they tell you what it is. You can take the girl out of the tower, but you can't take the tower out of the girl."

"I lived there," said Jana. "But I left. I met him after I left."

"No one leaves the towers," said Toy. "Just like no one leaves here. Was he another servant? Was he one of the Vichies, maybe come inside for a day?" She smiled and leaned in close, with a conspiratorial whisper into Jana's ear. "Was he one of them?"

Jana whipped away from her, the shock written all over her body before she could cram it back in. She was good at hiding insubordination, but not information, and it was too late. The intensity of the reaction had told Toy everything she wanted to know.

"He was," said Toy in a low voice. "He was." She gave a satisfied smile, and looked around at all the other girls, who couldn't hide their desperate need to know what the two of them were talking about.

"No," said Jana. It was too loud, and the others were all still looking, so she leaned in close. "It was a man I met by the oil."

"You must have slept with someone else," said Toy. "One of the other servants. Sometimes the father's not who you think it is. Who you want it to be."

"It was a man outside," said Jana. "It was." She was starting to shake; she couldn't help herself. She knew she was caught, and now she was just writhing in the trap, waiting to see what would become of her.

"You little tart," said Toy. "You let one of them into your panties, and now you've got the most valuable womb in the world. And no one here even knows. No one but you and me."

"Don't say things like that," said Jana. "Please. You don't know the kinds of things they'd do."

"I've been in here with Suriel for nearly a year," said Toy. "I know exactly the kind of things they'll do. You can't hide something like this, honey. They don't let you in here without a Cleanse. You don't stay without doing them all the time, either. Why, I'll probably have one tomorrow. And who knows what I'll say?"

"It's not true," said Jana. "Please don't say things like that. Not to him."

"I'd get in so much trouble, if I didn't tell," said Toy. "Now, I think it was a man, I really do. I don't think you're fit to be the mother of a god. She'd have to be someone prettier. Someone with glamour. Someone with class. Someone like me. Not some trash out of one of the towers who's only good for wiping floors."

"I thought you were trying to be my friend," said Jana. "Why'd you come over here, just to talk like this?"

"There's no friends in here," said Toy. "None of us. I'm here for a reason. I know it. Suriel loves me, and I love Suriel. And I'm going to have his baby. The baby. Not you, not any of them. Me. The mother of the most important child on the entire planet. The concubine of the most important angel."

"But he'd be bad," said Jana. "Suriel would ruin him. That's what you said."

"He'd rule," said Toy. "Rule the entire world. I'd be important. I'd matter. I wouldn't live in here, just a plaything like all the rest. I don't care about good or bad, and I don't care what they want up there, not anymore. They don't care about me, or they wouldn't have let me end up here. Now, I know you think one of them was the daddy. I don't believe you, but I know that's what you think. But I believe you were with one of them, and I'm not taking any chances. You're going to fix things, if you don't want me to start talking during my Cleanse. We're going to get you a little coat hanger, and you're going to go over in the corner and fix things."

"No," said Jana, starting to stand. But Toy grabbed her by the wrists, pulling her down and pulling her close.

"You'd be his forever," said Toy. "If you've got a little angel baby inside you, he'd never let you go. You'd be his, forever and ever, and no one else's."

Then they heard it in the distance. A loud crack,

bursting through air. Then another, and another, the rattling of gunfire somewhere nearby. Everyone looked around, unsure what to do. Two of the preachers pushed their way through the silk and beads to take up a position next to the door, and the men guarding Faye gripped their shotguns tightly.

"It's just noise," said Toy. "No one's going to get in here. We're fine. Now let's go deal with your little problem, while they've got better things to worry about."

But they could hear more noise from somewhere beyond, booms and crashes again and again. The girls began to huddle together, and a few of them gave high pitched shrieks every time they heard a noise. Toy tried to pull Jana up, off of the couch, but she gave a push with all her might, knocking Toy off her feet and over onto the ground.

"You little bitch," said Toy. "Think you're going to be Suriel's new favorite? Think you're going to bear his son?"

The preachers were growing edgy, checking their guns and getting ready for whatever approached. They started yelling at the girls, to shut up and get down, pointing their weapons all around. Then the doors burst open, and the conflict from outside poured in all at once through the crack between them.

CHAPTER THIRTY

"**W**HATEVER YOU DO, DON'T FIRE the thing," said Holt. "Use the butt, smash their skulls, have a party. But no noise."

"No noise, no fun," said Thane, gripping the rifle he'd recovered from the slain preacher. "I say kill 'em all and let Suriel sort 'em out."

They jogged through the hallway, checking each room with a quick glance, but so far all had been empty. The inner compound was mostly devoid of preachers even in the best of times, and they were nearly at the center before they found anyone opposing them: an old, fat preacher carrying a tray of glasses of milk through the hall as a treat for the girls inside. He was so absorbed in his routine that he didn't even notice the intruders at first.

"You," said the preacher, looking up with a start. He dropped the tray, shattering the glasses and covering the floors in puddles. Then he turned and started to run, as best he could, wheezing and huffing as fast as his legs would bear him. He had no chance, not against them.

Thane caught up to him with a quick sprint, slamming the butt of the rifle into his neck and sending him to the ground unconscious.

They rounded another corner and saw the double doors blocking the hallway, wooden pieces of art that stood out from the functionalism of everything else in the complex. They knew at once that this was where they had to go, and that something important must be past them.

Thane clicked off the safety on the rifle, and they cautiously approached. They couldn't hear anything behind them, and couldn't see what was beyond, but there was nowhere else in the inner compound that Jana or Faye could be. Holt flashed a signal and began to count with his fingers—one, two, three. Then he ripped open one of the doors, and everything went to hell.

Two men were behind the door, heavily muscled and heavily armed. They wore the robes of the preachers, and they followed Suriel, but they had the Vichies' temperament. They started firing at once, aiming their guns through the crack in the door and spraying bullets down the hallway. One was foolish enough to poke his weapon through, an Uzi belching fire in short spurts. He didn't keep the gun for long. Holt grabbed hold of it, wrestling for control as the man tried to pull it back inside the doors.

The two of them were evenly matched, but their allies were not. The other man inside grabbed on as well, trying to add his weight to his friend's half of the struggle. But Thane just stuck the barrel of his rifle inside and started firing. Blood sprayed out the crack in the door, and the Uzi came loose soon after.

"Go," said Thane, as he pulled aside both doors and Holt aimed through them. One of the men was on the ground, hands clutching the air and blood streaming from his chest. He was fading fast, his pupils glassy and his lungs struggling to pump air inside of him. The other man was running, pushing through a curtain of beads and fleeing into whatever lay beyond them.

They moved to follow, keeping their guns leveled in front of them, taking it slow and sticking close to the walls on either side. They heard screaming from the distance, the high pitched shrieks of a chorus of frightened girls. "This is it," said Thane, and they pushed through rows and rows of beads until they came to Suriel's quarters.

The girls were running around in all directions, most in a complete state of panic. Some of those with more presence of mind were busy overturning couches and ducking behind them for cover. Others were simply standing and crying, making as much noise as possible to as little purpose as possible. As they came into the room, the shots started pounding the air again, and they both threw themselves to the floor out of instinct.

They didn't see where the firing was coming from at first. There were too many distractions, too many frightened innocents running around in circles. But then a chunk of wall burst apart above Holt's head, and they saw where the attackers were.

The men who'd been guarding Faye had abandoned their duty, leaving the hypothetical threat for the immediate one. They were firing shotgun shell after shotgun shell, pumping buckshot into the walls around the intruders. A few seconds after they were spotted, Holt began returning fire of his own. He took the time to aim, and let loose a burst from the Uzi, felling one of the men as the bullets ripped through his arm. He slumped against the wall and started to squeal, dropping his weapon and clamping his hand against his injuries to try to stem the flow of blood.

The other guard kept firing, wilder and wilder as blood oozed from the man beside him. He let out a war cry, a deep, desperate bellow, and then he made a mad dash towards them, firing all the while. He came close to Thane, close enough to aim his shotgun at his gut, close enough for a shell to shred a man's insides to tiny pieces.

Thane didn't flinch. He just fired first, a quick shot from the rifle that struck the man in the neck and sent him reeling backwards. His gun went off, pointed at the floor below him, and he dropped it and fell to his knees, dazed and oblivious to everything but his own injury. Soon the loss of blood was too much, and he passed away into nothingness as the shouting went on around him.

The men were all down, the firing had stopped, and after surveying the room all that they saw left were women. Faye was in the corner, zoning out, and Holt rushed over to her. She didn't look up, despite him standing right in front of her. "You okay?" He leaned down, trying to get some response out of her, but all he got was a blank.

"Find Jana," said Holt, waving Thane away. The girls were all still in hiding, clinging to whatever cover they'd found and scared to leave it even now that the shooting was done. Thane walked among them, his rifle pointed at the floor, calling her name and checking everyone he passed. But no one responded, and she wasn't anywhere to be seen.

Girl after girl looked up, and then down again, hiding their faces from this angry warrior who'd entered their midst. To his left there was a trio of them crouching behind a scarlet footstool, hands over the backs of their heads as if they were preparing for a bombing raid. They twisted their heads to sneak a look, but only got as far as his boots before they whimpered and went back their pose. To his right, a stunning brunette stood out in the open, her makeup ruined by drizzles of tears, and still she couldn't stop crying. She stood there helpless, unable to take cover despite her obvious fear.

Finally he came to the bed, its silken white canopies drawn shut. There wasn't anywhere else to hide, and there wasn't anywhere else to look. He pointed the rifle at it with one arm, cradling the butt in his shoulder, and with the other he ripped aside the curtains and prepared for the worst.

There Jana was, face covered in tears of her own. Behind her stood another of the girls: Toy, with Jana firmly in her grip and a splintered piece of wood at her stomach. "Don't move," she said. "Don't come any closer, or I'll shove this inside her. You might kill me after, but I'll get her little baby. There's no one here to save it, not if I do."

"Lady," said Thane. "What the fuck is wrong with you?" He pointed the rifle at her head, and her hand shook as she tried to keep the wood pointed at its target.

"We're going to wait," said Toy. "Wait for Suriel. What's inside her. It's an angel's baby, isn't it?" She looked desperate, half-mad, her hair frazzled by the rush for cover. She stared at Thane, and she saw something in him as he looked back. "It's true. I knew it. I knew it, you little bitch. That's my baby inside you. That's supposed to be my baby. My little angel, not yours."

"I didn't do anything," said Jana. "I didn't ask for this. Please don't. It's just a baby. What kind of mother would you be if you'd do this to him?"

"He'll come back," said Toy, pressing the stake into Jana's skin. Little drops of blood dripped away at its edges, staining her robe a dark black where it was pressed against her. "He'll have to come back. He doesn't have any choice. And this time, he'll come through Suriel. Through me. I'll be special, not some slave."

"You don't know any of that," said Jana. "You don't know it's true, and you can't control it."

"Just put it down," said Thane. His finger itched at the trigger, bouncing towards it again and again but never pressing down. "Just walk away. What'll be is gonna be, and all this stuff you're talkin' ain't gonna happen. Not the way you want it to."

"He'll choose me," said Toy. "He'll need a vessel to be born through, and next time, he'll choose me. Look at you. You don't even want this. Suriel won't let you go, not once he finds out. He'll keep you as his property, forever and ever. You'll be a queen, but his queen. He'll make you raise the child with him. You don't even want that life. I do. Why won't you just let me have it?" She poked the wood in a little further, causing Jana to let out a stifled scream of pain.

"Put it down!" shouted Thane. He raised his gun, taking a few steps closer, weighing whether he could make it over there and disarm her before any real damage was done. She wasn't far, and she wasn't strong. All he needed was one leap, just enough to knock her back, and she'd never be able to push the stake far enough inside to do any real damage. He calmed himself, found his balance, and got ready to take a rush at her. But he didn't get the chance.

A loud series of cracks came behind him, and Toy's head whipped back. The wood flew loose from her hand, and the white curtains behind her were painted red with blood. Jana shivered and cried, and rushed away from where she'd been sitting. Thane turned to see Holt behind him, the Uzi leveled at where Toy had been, its muzzle pouring out wisps of smoke.

"Jesus," said Thane. "Why the fuck? I was about to get it away from her. You didn't need to do that. And what if you'd missed?"

"We've got to stop pandering to the crazies," said Holt. "Stop shying away from the things that need to be done. Stop trying to save everyone, and start focusing on saving the ones who count."

"Don't mean you've got to kill people you don't have to," said Thane. "Don't mean you shouldn't try."

"To hell with that, and to hell with them," said Holt. "This is triage. Everyone's not going to make it. If she can't even try to be good, why should I risk someone who deserves to live to save someone who doesn't?"

"World's a shitty place these days," said Thane. "It does bad things to good people. That's just how it is. All I'm sayin' is, don't let it do bad things to you. If she hadn't been locked up in here, she wouldn't have turned into this. She'd have been somebody else if she'd been someplace else. Don't think for a second you're any different."

"Let's just go," said Holt. "You get Jana, I'll get Faye, and let's get the hell out of here before the angels get back."

CHAPTER THIRTY-ONE

SWERVE LEFT, AND STILL HE came. Swerve right, and there he was, following on Rhamiel's tail without letting him gain an inch. They'd been at this for hours without stop. Rhamiel had led him away from the compound, and Suriel had followed. Now the day was dawning, the sun glaring from the horizon, and he was no closer to escape than when he'd started. He'd had a healthy lead at first. But minute after minute and bit by bit, Suriel cut into it, narrowing the gap between the two.

"You tire, boy," shouted Suriel. "Suriel hears you wheezing. Set down, and he will kill you quickly. That is his promise, and that is his mercy."

Rhamiel didn't bother with a response. He couldn't, not if he expected to keep in front of him. Every breath counted, every bit of distance mattered. Every whip of the wind had to be considered and accounted for. He couldn't even turn his head to look, not with the speed it would cost him. He had to judge his lead by Suriel's voice alone, and if it weren't for the periodic taunting from behind, he would have been flying entirely blind.

As it was, he knew he was losing ground. Each time the voice was a little louder, a little closer. Suriel wasn't fast, not at his size, but he could keep going for an eternity. Rhamiel would tire long before he did, and it was only a matter of time before he'd be overcome. He guessed that he had another hour at most. An hour to find what he was looking for, his only prayer of defeating an archangel.

"Suriel is acquainted with a friend of yours," shouted Suriel. "A girl. She's asked for you."

It almost made him turn despite himself. He felt an overpowering urge to flip about and unsheath his sword for one last mad slash, a hail mary effort to release the fight in him all at once before the last bits ebbed away. But he knew no one would listen to him up there, not anymore, and he knew that showing his heart would just let Suriel know how to hurt him. So he kept on flying, kept going where he thought hope would be, and kept thinking of Jana all the while.

"Suriel has her all to himself, inside his harem," said Suriel. "He has tasted of her flesh."

Rhamiel had to struggle to control himself. He practiced a breathing technique as he flew, in and out, in and out. It kept him centered, and kept him focused on his task. It kept his anger at bay, and kept him from thinking about the provocations coming from behind him. But still the words nagged at him, beating at his mind and trying to get in. He could push them aside, but he couldn't keep them away forever.

"Her tongue met Suriel's, and so did her soul," said Suriel. "She cares not for Rhamiel, not any longer."

He knew it was a lie, then. They were all lies, designed to bring him down. He knew the point was to draw some reaction. Anything to slow him down, anything to distract him. It didn't matter what he did, so long as he did something other than fly straight ahead. Turn from the path, and Suriel would be upon him.

"She was with another, before she was with Suriel," said Suriel. "A man. Suriel has proof. Suriel will whisper the truth into your ear, before you die."

It was getting harder and harder to keep himself in check. He had to fight the curiosity, and keep focused on the task at hand. He had to keep her out of his thoughts, just for now, and just for a little bit. A tall order, given how much she'd consumed him since the tower had fallen. Suriel kept taunting, kept calling her name, but he tuned it out. The breathing wasn't working, and so he fixed his vision on a cloud in front of him, staring at a point at its edge and using it as a compass to guide his flight. The minutes ticked on, and Suriel's voice grew louder and louder even as he heard less and less of what he had to say. He tried to think of stratagems that might buy him space or time, but nothing was promising.

Then he saw something, poking out of the cloud ahead of him. It was a little brown object, floating in and out of the mist. Then there was another, and another, and finally a horde of them, and Rhamiel knew he'd found salvation. The cherubs had arrived, their army with them, and soon golem after golem popped through the white puffs, streaming out into the open skies. Rhamiel pressed forward, closing the distance and making a run for his allies.

As he approached them, he no longer heard the voice from behind him, and no longer heard the beating of any wings but his own. He allowed himself a glance backwards, just for a second, and he stopped at what he saw. His pursuer had abandoned the chase, and was all alone in the air, wings pounding up and down as he watched the things that approached. Rhamiel paused as well, turning to face Suriel and drawing his sword again.

Golems began to swoosh past him, sending warm air gusting across his face as they swarmed towards the archangel. A dozen of them took the lead, living octahedrons of compacted stone, jetting through the air and leaving trails of steam behind them. They launched towards Suriel, thrusting at him to probe his defenses and search for any weaknesses. He drew his sword and sliced in all directions, slashing a few of them to pieces as they dodged around him. Metal contraptions inside exploded with fire of their own as they fell to earth, leaving their companions to harangue him from other directions.

"Come, cherubs," shouted Suriel. "Send more of your toys to face Suriel. He has one of them for his own already, collecting dust in his quarters and waiting to entertain him. Send as many as you like. Suriel will have you singing, before the day is done. Tone deaf you may be, but once Suriel is finished with you, you will squeal his praises in your poetry."

He pressed forward, flying towards Rhamiel, but the golems kept coming. He swatted them like gnats if they came too close, knocking them away with a brush of his sword and sending them tumbling down to the ground. But powerful as he was, they had the numbers.

More and more of them surged forward, growing to an armada, and soon every slash of his sword caught one of the floating objects even as others battered him from behind and below. Rhamiel waited and rested, letting his strength come back to him, hoping the cherubs had more to come than these nuisances.

"Ho, Rhamiel!" shouted a voice from the clouds. A squadron of seraphs emerged, flying in formation like geese. He didn't recognize a one of them, not at first. But then dusty memories roused themselves and climbed to the fore, and he knew them from long ago: Baruchiel's friends, angels he hadn't seen in a decade, not since they'd gone off to live as they pleased on their own. They were followed by flock after flock, piercing the clouds and flying into position, lining up in a battle array, all forgotten friends or acquaintances who'd been scattered by politics and reunited by the same.

"We thought we would find your corpse," said another of the seraphs: Baruchiel, his emerald armor shining in the sun along with his sword. He left his squadron to their position, and flapped over to Rhamiel to give him a friendly slap on the shoulder. "We thought this a mission of vengeance, and not of rescue."

"I thought the same," said Rhamiel. "I thought I would tire and fall, before you made your way here."

"You've a close friend, it seems," said Baruchiel. "Someone who cared enough to bring us here. He flew fast, and urged us to fly faster."

"A dear friend," said another voice emerging from the clouds: Ecanus, his black armor a stark contrast to the wisps of white vapor around him. "I would not see you die, not before your mortal love. And if it can be avoided, I would rather not live under Suriel's thumb." Beside him came Uzziel, shouting commands to a group of golems as they flew forward and added to the crush of them already surrounding Suriel.

"I thought you a coward, Ecanus," said Rhamiel. "I thought it likely you'd abandon me."

"I am, and I would," said Ecanus. "In the sense that I find it folly to sacrifice oneself for matters of principle, strutting about as if it makes one superior to those who've retained their senses. But then, you haven't heard. I'm something of a hero. A mind unclouded by love of servants can achieve great things."

"While you were off playing the lovelorn," said Uzziel, "Ecanus was serving his brothers. He found the men who destroyed our tower. He knows their whereabouts, and he can lead us to them."

"He did, did he?" said Rhamiel.

"He did," said Ecanus. "And so his status rises, in fair recompense for his services this day. I have claimed their heads, and I will have them."

"You may have the bragging rights, all to yourself," said Rhamiel. "But what happens to their heads is mine to resolve. They're on about a task for me, if you recall."

"Settle this dispute another day," said Uzziel. "Now, we deal with him."

The sky had been emptied of the first wave of golems, slashed to pieces by Suriel. He was shouting, waving his sword and daring them all to make an attack. "Come, cowards! Do your worst against Heaven's best." Only the cherubs and their golems seemed impervious to the threats. They stared at him blankly from the assembled battle lines, while the seraphs shivered and steeled themselves for what was to come.

"Let us show him what engines of war Zephon has concocted," said Uzziel. "He would fight with fire, but let us sting him instead." He nodded to a cherub behind him, who darted back into the clouds. And from them came things made of flesh, topped by sacs of pink skin filled with gas, floating like blimps. Thin brown tendrils hung from below them, flopping back and forth with the wind, and every angel nearby gave them a wide berth. It was soon clear why. As the tendrils waved, they brushed against one another, sending off flashes of electricity. They looked like miniature bolts of lightning, zapping up and down the creatures' skin as they moved, closer and closer towards Suriel.

Even he gave pause at the sight of them. They were ponderous weapons, too slow to catch him, and at first he simply flew along the lines of assembled angels, avoiding the threat with ease. But even as he did, the floating things began to spread across the skies, dozens and dozens of them, their tendrils waving around them and creating webs of sparks he didn't dare cross.

As Suriel dodged their slow advance, Zephon chirped a command for reinforcements. "Bring out the bigger guns, and let him gawk, at how we've given life to molten rock." His cherub lieutenants scattered into the clouds, and emerged towing chains, heavy turquoise leashes whose every link was the size of one of the cherubs themselves. What came behind them made even Suriel stop his dashing from the sparks around him.

They were huge, the size of a bus, each a formidable

foe for dozens of seraphs. They glowed a bright orange, their skin a living lava, melting away as they moved, dripping down to the ground in a fiery rain. They had arms and legs, and something of a head, though their form was never the same from one second to the next. Across their chests were turquoise harnesses, attached to the chains, and at the center of each a ball of pure white energy, suns in miniature burning away at their middles and animating them with fusion. From the back of their harnesses came jets of steam, controlled by the cherubs, propelling them forward and holding them aloft.

The cherubs tugged them towards their target, even as they pulled at their chains and tried to whip away in all directions. They shouted at any seraphs who came near, warning them to keep their distance. "Beware their bodies big and minds so small; their thoughts encompass nothing but the brawl." The things screeched, a wail that shook even the clouds, and they lashed towards at anything they saw fluttering past them. Finally the cherubs had dragged them away, out into the open, and then they let them loose.

Suriel saw them coming, but he had no easy escape. There was a jungle of tendrils around him, above and below, and even as he chopped away at them more would wind their way towards him. They were closing in, and more than one had gotten hold of him, jolting him with electricity before he sliced them away.

The new arrivals rushed at him, pushed forward by blasts of air. The cherubs steered the first one straight towards him, operating its jets from afar. It was none too pleased with the state of things, and it slammed its arms into any of the cherubs' creations in its path, slapping them aside and burning them to ash wherever they came into contact. Suriel pushed himself above it as it passed, earning him stings from the surrounding tendrils but managing to grab hold of one of the creature's chains. And with that, it was done for.

Suriel yanked upon the chain, launching the creature upwards. He swung the chain around him, the creature still attached to it, burning apart the floating golems and their tendrils as it collided with them and covered them with molten rock. Then with a hearty tug, he ripped the harness from the creature itself, tearing it away from the lump of flailing lava left behind. It fell away towards the earth, and Suriel was left alone, now armed with chain as well as sword.

"Speak now, Zephon," said Uzziel. "He is an archangel. If your contraptions cannot defeat him, we must know now, that we may strike him ourselves. I prefer to lose golems rather than brothers, but seraphs will never bow. Not again, and not to him. We would die first, if die we must."

"Sometimes a war is but a numbers game," said Zephon. "Just pour on troops as if they had no name." The cherubs began launching the creatures at Suriel, all at once, sending everything they had in his direction. Golems of all shapes and sizes buzzed around him, biting and stinging and punching. The air was filled with falling hunks of metal, raining down upon the earth as Suriel burned through the assailants with his sword. He crept closer and closer to the angels' lines as he did, edging his way forward bit by bit.

"We must act now," said Baruchiel. "Let us from our leash. He will overwhelm us if we wait."

"Hold," said Uzziel. "He tires, even as we speak. I can feel the tide of battle shifting, from a niggling at my feathers. A good general feels the rhythm of a conflict, the way you feel the wind in your flight. The fight is gone from him, I am sure of it."

And indeed he was slowing, his swings losing their strength, his reactions losing their edge as the golems relentlessly pounded against him. None could do much damage on their own, but as a whole they weighed upon him, sapping his energies as he tried to deal with all of them at once. Finally his forward progress stopped, and he began to lose ground in the contest, knocked back inch after inch as creatures of lava slapped at him and things of metal grabbed and pushed. He heaved one of the largest golems away from him, and began to beat his wings, gathering the air and moving away from the assault. He turned his tail and fled, the golems slowly following as he went back the way he'd come.

"Perhaps we should let him go," said Ecanus. "An easy victory, at little cost. One that should be toasted now, rather than gambled away on another throw of the dice."

"Nonsense," said Uzziel. "I feel now like ending the matter." He waved to the angels behind him, and all around the lines horns began to blow, groaning out a cry of war. "Follow him!" shouted Uzziel. "Follow him close. We shall torch his home, we shall crucify his followers, and by day's end we shall have his head on a pike."

CHAPTER THIRTY-TWO

"VICHIES," SAID THANE. "I TOLD you, never trust the Vichies." The compound's yard was filled with them, rushing out of one of the buildings like ants from a toppled nest. They were armed, heavily, with salvaged military equipment ranging from assault rifles to grenade launchers. The preachers ran alongside them, yelling and shouting and turning on the floodlights, and soon the yard was filled with white and grey.

"They're supposed to be working for the other angels, not him," said Holt.

"They don't give a damn for loyalty," said Thane. "Their old masters don't want 'em. Now they got a new boss, and a new racket."

"Then we wait here," said Holt. "Wait, and hide, and hope."

They'd snuck away from the inner compound, before the general alarm had been sounded. They'd made it to a warehouse, a vast storage area where the preachers kept their hoarded goods. The inside was a maze of boxes and crates, stacked unevenly and without any apparent organization. They'd built a little nook by one of the windows, pushing together a few stacks to hide themselves from the view of any passing preachers. They'd planned to make a run for it, from window to fence, just as Thane had done before. But then out came the Vichies, out came the guns, and out went the plan.

"Faye," said Holt. "You have to wake up. Come back to us." She was sitting there on the ground, Indian style, her eyes vacant and her mouth hanging open. Holt tried to comfort her, holding one of her hands and squeezing it as he talked. "Come back. We need you ready to run. Ready to fight."

"It's not her," said Jana. "I told you, it's not her."

"He did somethin' to her," said Thane. "Did somethin' to her while we were gone. Powered those hands up and gave her a lobotomy, instead of a healin'. I told you not to trust him."

"It's Zuphias," said Jana. Faye's eyes began to focus at the name, her pupils contracting and her mouth snapping shut. "He does miracles. He did one to her."

"Some miracle," said Thane. "Coulda just bled from a statue."

"Zuphias," said Faye. She started into her glossolalia, dumping out things that sounded like words, softly at first, then louder and louder. "Shhh," said Holt, moving his hand towards her mouth. "Stay quiet. Low voice. Just keep it low, and stay with us."

She looked at him and cocked her head. "I know you."

"That's good," said Holt. "That's really good. You're coming back. You'll get there, just give it time."

She looked around at them, focusing on the two men,

back and forth. "I know the both of you. You tore down my home, and turned me into this. A refugee from my own withered body, forced by necessity to roam about on the ground like some chimpanzee. You did this to me." She stood, and began to tear at the boxes they'd built around them, trying to push her way out of their hiding place and out into the open.

"I told you," said Jana. "It's not her. Not anymore."

"You asshole," said Thane. He grabbed her by the arm, pulling her away from the boxes and back towards him. She tried to wrench herself free, but just ended up locked in a futile game of tug of war.

"I'll slaughter the three of you," said Faye. "You've little use to me now." She balled her free hand into a fist and swung at Thane, hitting him square in the jaw. But it didn't even faze him. She came off with the worse end of it, shouting in pain and staring at her hand in shock.

"You hit like a girl," said Thane. He puffed out his chest and shoved her against the wall, leaning in close with his face gone mean. "You ain't some big, bad angel anymore. You really wanna live inside her? World's pretty nasty out there, and it's not a fun place if you're weak. She got by 'cause she's got wits to spare. Your ass coasted on bein' the biggest dog in town, and now you ain't. So why don't you get back where you came from, and let her get back to how she was?"

"I will never," said Faye, flopping helplessly in Thane's grip. "I will never go back to how I was. My body is now a twisted mess, and you're the ones I have to thank. It's no life in there. Just an endless black void; no sight, no sound, no feeling. Nothing at all but my thoughts. I would die here, in this mortal shell, before I would go back to an eternity of darkness. I shall never leave her body, not even as it gasps its last breath."

"We can make things bad for you," said Holt. He moved in close, and put his hand on her throat, gripping it tightly and giving it an uncomfortable squeeze. "There's ways to hurt someone, without leaving a mark. You want to feel, we can make you feel. I'm betting you don't have much experience with pain, not how you used to be. We'll show you pain. We'll show you darkness like you can't even imagine."

"And you shall show it to her as well," said Faye. She spat at him, sending a spray past his head as he ducked to avoid it. "I promise you that she shall feel every instant of it. I promise you she will be just close enough to the surface that every agony you deliver will be the both of ours to savor. For I have tasted the absence of feeling, the absence of anything, and I assure you that I would prefer the pain."

"Don't," said Jana. "Things won't be like in the tower. No one will listen to you. No one will have to. Suriel will find you. You don't know what he'd do to you. You know how you treated people. You know how bad it can get."

"Better than spending eternity with only the dronings of cherubs to amuse me," said Faye. "Let me loose, and do it now. I will scream and scream, and call your enemies down upon you. There's no profit in our dealings, not for me."

"Suriel's a healer," said Holt. "He can heal your body. Fix whatever happened."

"No one can heal what was done to me," said Faye.

"He can heal you right out of her, I bet," said Holt. She didn't offer a response. Just a glare and a sneer, and another effort to pull her arm away from Thane. Holt just gave her a smile. "Thought so. You scream, you do something stupid, he's going to find you. Maybe he wants you in her body, and maybe he doesn't. Maybe he'll just want another girl for the collection, and you'll be in the way. And those men out there? You don't have wings anymore. They catch us, they're not letting you go. They're giving you back to Suriel, if you're lucky."

She stopped struggling, and just stood there, projecting her disdain for the three of them. Then she leaned towards Holt, as near as she could get. "I will never leave her. I will never let her go."

"You're still coming with us," said Holt. "You don't have any choice. And let me tell you, we'll be watching you like hawks."

"I'll be gone, at the first opportunity," said Faye.

"Think on that," said Holt. "None of us here give a shit about you. But we all want her to be safe. Think on whether you'd rather be out there all on your own, a minnow in a world of piranhas. Or whether you'd rather have someone watching your back, just because it's her back, too."

Then they heard something from outside: something musical, the melody of war, faint drums and horns and harps from far away. Soon it was drowned out by the roar of engines, as the Vichies brought them to life. Vehicles started streaming past the window, big green humvees with turrets of missiles and guns mounted on the back.

"That one's an Avenger," said Thane, pointing to one as it drove by. "Air defense, straight from the Pentagon."

They couldn't see where the Vichies were going, or what they were doing. But they heard it, soon enough. Booms began to sound in the distance, explosions in the skies above. Then thunks, and yelling, and blasts coming ever closer. "We need to go," said Holt. "Whatever's going on out there, we need to go."

Clods of dirt and grass splattered against the window, as something crashed into the ground outside. They heard screaming, loud shrieks of pure pain, and they braved a look only to see one of them just outside: an angel, one of her wings torn from its socket, and one of her hands freshly lopped from her wrist. She was staring at it, the black stump a new scar for the collection that mottled her face, her mouth open wide and pouring out the agony. Then she collapsed to the ground, clutching her wrist against her silver armor, her eyes glazed as she fell into shock.

"Your boy's back," said Thane, with a nod to Faye. "Time for us to get this show on the road."

CHAPTER THIRTY-THREE

THE SKY WAS THICK WITH angels, legions of them flying towards Suriel's compound with swords at the ready. Floating golems filled out their ranks, the foot soldiers of an army welded together from disparate seraph factions across the globe. Even the cherubs were prepared for battle, wielding tiny rapiers of fire and outfitting themselves in mechanized armors they'd devised to augment their native strength.

The army waited on the horizon, a rainbow of banners before it bearing the marks of towers, military units from up above, and even mere social clubs. Suriel's compound stood in the distance, and they could see movement there, as the city of tents was being hastily abandoned by its residents. Some were fleeing into the compound itself, others taking cover in the forests, and a few braving the road out. Somewhere in there was Suriel, waiting for the combatants to come to him and fight their battle on his terms.

"He does not run," said Uzziel, watching over the compound through a silver telescope held to his eye by one of the cherubs. "He faces a foe he cannot possibly defeat, and yet he does not run."

"It matters not whether he can defeat us," said Rhamiel. "He thinks he can, and so he stays. He is a fool, who thinks himself a god. And a god would not cower before an angel."

"Perhaps," said Uzziel. "He will kill many of us, regardless of our numbers. His folly is fueled by a very real strength, even if he overestimates himself."

"He will kill some of us if we face him now," said Rhamiel. "He will kill all of us, if we wait and let him fight who he chooses, when he chooses."

"We must have plans, before we move," said Uzziel. "Plans within plans, to counter what's to come. We must be cautious of his treacheries. Prudence is more powerful than pluck, when it comes to a battle's outcome."

"Caution be damned," said Rhamiel. "You and your army may spend as much time as you like wavering back and forth, so long as you do not interfere with me or mine. But know, Uzziel, that the girl is my pledge, and her companions have business with me. And I'll have the heads of any who touch theirs." He beat his wings wide, gathering air behind him, and sped away towards the compound, flying low to the ground and circling around the fleeing refugees as he looked for signs of her somewhere among them.

"Suriel will kill him on sight," said Uzziel, shaking his head. "Him, and his pledge."

"In that case, I suppose I should follow him," said Ecanus. "At a respectable distance."

"He would kill you, too," said Uzziel. "He would kill us all."

"Music tames the savage beast," said Ecanus. "And if it comes to it, I can sing the tune Suriel would like to hear." He flapped off after Rhamiel, trailing him in his searches as they both looped around the compound.

"What say you, Zephon?" called Uzziel, to a flock of nearby cherubs. Zephon was in the middle of them, his face in the form of a grim-looking eagle, its yellow eyes hunting the horizon for signs of their target. His armor was a thick chrome alloy, covering him from the neck down, decorated with each of his four faces: the face of man across his back, the pauldrons on his shoulders molded into the faces of ox and lion, and the face of an eagle on his chest. But as his head turned, so did the armor: when he went this way or that, the armor shimmered along with his face, melting into a blur of colors and reforming itself with his chosen face across the breastplate, and the others relegated to the lesser positions.

"The cherubs stand at ready for your wars, a thing forbidden us by Heaven's mores," said Zephon. "They never thought us fighters up above, just artisans, our work our only love. But new ambitions rise within our breast, to be more than the Maker's cosmic jest. He gave to others strength their maiden gift; he gave us minds, that we ourselves uplift. So sound your horns and loose your battle cries; we've martial spirit far beyond our size."

"Then prepare yourselves, and let us move," said Uzziel. "And let the battle begin." He signaled with a wave of his hand, and Baruchiel put his horn to his lips, sucking in a gasp of air and blowing a long, deep note. All across the battle lines, seraphs could be heard blaring trumpets, the sound joining together as one and pounding down to the fields below. Uzziel called behind him, and a troupe of seraphs flew forward, each with thick drums of animal skin strapped to their chest. They spread across the lines and began to beat out a tempo for the angels to follow, broadcasting Uzziel's orders across the field by variations in the speed and the beat. "Forward the scouts!" he shouted, and the drummers tapped out a light, fast rapping sound to signal their advance.

Seraphs began to fly out from their positions in the lines, the fastest among them, wearing lighter armors to avoid sacrificing their speed. They zipped around in front of the army, then began flying above the compound, diving down to look for Suriel and then popping back up to safer heights. They drew no answer, and saw no archangel, and so they signalled back to Uzziel, dancing a pattern as they flew to indicate that all was clear.

"Move!" shouted Uzziel. "Blanket the skies above his home, and tear it apart until he shows his face!"

The armies began to move forward at his command, flying in formation according to their regiment. It was a tedious affair, driven more by politics than by the practicalities of battle. Status outranked tactics, and the angels slowly rolled forward in waves, the most prestigious among them demanding the right to move first and in the prime positions of honor. They were in the middle of their maneuvers when a sound boomed from below, and a platoon of golems exploded in a burst of smoke and shrapnel. They spun out of control, dropping to the ground as those behind them reformed their ranks and kept up the advance.

"They've a cannon," said Baruchiel. "Some primitive thing they think will belch its fire at us and drive us away." He pointed to a humvee down below, antiaircraft guns attached to its back. It had driven to the edges of the compound, and now it was launching flak up into the air around them. They could see the occupants directing its fire, conspicuous in their white clothing even from on high.

"A distraction," said Uzziel. "It will do serious harm only to the cherubs' pride in their creations. Suriel means to occupy us with this sound and fury, while he himself escapes."

No sooner had he spoken than bursts began to erupt all around them, as vehicles poured from out of the compound's gates, taking up positions around the field. Suriel's followers had salvaged them from some military depot, and now they aimed at angels instead of aircraft. All around them were bursts of smoke and flame, knocking angels aside as they flew and tearing apart any golems they hit.

"Spread the lines!" shouted Uzziel, and the drummers changed their beat, sounding out the order. But none could hear it, not above the pounding from the shells as they exploded. He barked another command to the drummers behind him, and they began to fly instead, synchronizing themselves into a flight pattern that would be recognized by any seraph who could see it.

Some of the warriors saw, and began to spread apart, dividing up the massed units that made such attractive targets in their parade formations. But black clouds of smoke from the flak were beginning to envelop them all, turning the air around them into a murky haze. "Send down the golems!" shouted Uzziel, and he flew over to Zephon, making sure that he heard the command. "Send the largest ones, and tear down the buildings below! Torch any place he may hide, and wipe away his traitor's army."

Zephon whispered something to his fellow cherubs, and they pushed at their control boxes. Some of the golems began to dive, large berserkers made of rocks and gems of all kinds. Some headed towards the guns, some towards the tents, and some towards the compound itself.

Uzziel continued shouting commands, directing his attendants and sending messengers to the parts of the battle lines that appeared most disorganized. He was in the middle of it all, barking an order to bring a division around to the compound's flank, when he heard screaming from behind him. It came from the throats of seraphs, their shouts filled with surprise. He turned, and all was obscured with black clouds from the flak. But somewhere in the dust he could see the source of the terror: lines of fire, slashing back and forth, and at their center a single broadsword. There was Suriel, behind the angels' lines, using the smoke as cover to sneak into their position and wreak havoc among them. All that was visible through the clouds were the seraphs' swords of fire as they tumbled and fell before the assault, their bearers sliced to pieces and dropping like helpless flies.

Zephon tugged at Uzziel's arm, holding a black control box and pointing at an idle squadron of his mechanical warriors. "Let golems swarm and take apart this foe, they'll give even an archangel a show. They're built with weapons made for more than man, a potent threat against those of our clan. We charged them up, electric dynamos; he's in for more a battle than he knows."

They were men of bronze, just the same as the ones they'd used to replace the servants. But these had been retooled, fitted with jets on their backs to let them fly. Their hands had been removed, and in their place the cherubs had installed long, conductive rods. At the push of a button from Zephon they came alive, connected by arcs of electricity. It fizzled and moved with their arms, bouncing between the rods, and anything that came within the golems' reach would surely be fried to a crisp.

"Go," said Uzziel. "Do what you can, while I rally a response of my own."

They disappeared into the cloud of smoke, with Zephon and a platoon of cherubs following close behind. He led his little cherubs in, each drawing a black rod from their belts and giving it a twist. Light shone from them, cutting through even the thick dust and giving them a few yards of vision in all directions. They could hear clanging from the golems somewhere ahead of them, and could see sparks flying back and forth amid the haze. They edged forward through the fog, towards the fire of Suriel's sword, when suddenly it went dark. They saw nothing but each other, lost in a maelstrom of dirt, explosions continuing to boom around them as the Vichies fired from below.

They heard a flap of wings from their left, and then another from somewhere above them. Zephon called out into the mist: "We hear you there, and know you're drawing near, so end these games and from the murk appear." He received no answer, only silence. He waved a few of the cherubs forward, and they disappeared into the darkness. No sooner had they gone than a slash of fire appeared to the left, cutting apart one of the cherubs before he had a chance to do more than squeal. He fell away as the others all drew their swords, circling up and facing outwards.

"We wish to speak, O angel of the dust, so sheath your sword or we'll do what we must." Again Zephon received no response, only another flash of light in front of them. Then something was lobbed past them through the air: the head of one of the cherubs who'd went before them, its eyes open wide in horror.

"A foul affront, but one I'll overlook, but that's the last of insults that I'll brook," said Zephon. "So speaks a king, the master of his caste, the ones who built the army here amassed. To hide inside the dirt's a coward's way, so show yourself, and let me have my say." He stared off into the cloud, waiting some time before he heard a response.

"Suriel has nothing to say to cherubs," said a voice from somewhere in the dust. "Sending spies into his home, and armies to his doorstep. There is no conversation to be had, only a slaughter." Another blow of his sword came from behind them, catching one of the cherubs on the back of its armor. It cleaved through an apparatus on the back, sending up fizzling sparks and a jet of steam that launched the cherub off somewhere into the cloud with a yelp. "Soon you will be alone, Zephon," said the voice. "You will be the last to die, with none of your constructs here to save you."

"You have me wrong, my motives misconstrued," called Zephon. "You come to fight; we'd rather you be wooed. We seek accord, a parley in the mist; we'd rather meet with words than meet with fist."

There was silence, and then a dark shape, moving through the dust. Then there he was, the archangel himself, the cherubs' lights bathing him in an eerie glow. He floated before them, his eyes dancing with the fire of his sword, and then he spoke. "Say your piece, cherub, but do it quickly. Sing to Suriel, and tell him how much you adore him. Beg for his mercy, and bow to his reign. If you are sincere enough, and abject enough, perhaps he will believe you. Perhaps there will be a place for you, down at his feet."

Zephon flipped his head, from eagle to man, and the other cherubs' faces followed, synchronizing as one after a moment of blur. He sheathed his rapier, and so did all of the rest. "We cherubs have no stake in politics, no care for statecraft or for angels' cliques. We only want our studies to be free, the rest we damn as pointless foolery. We think you might assist us in our quest, that drives us from the comfort of our nest. The Maker vested you with powers vast, a spark enduring from creation's blast. We have to know the meaning of it all, a lust that was the reason for our Fall."

"Suriel sees why you would like his help," said Suriel. "He sees why it would benefit you. But why, cherub, should Suriel listen to your pleas? Why should he not simply cut you down for raising your hands against him? Suriel is Lord, now, and you have stoked his wrath."

"Lord on Earth, but never Lord above," said Zephon. "A prize you can't obtain with humans' love. But cherubs could unwind creation's strands, and sew them back as Suriel commands. The Maker's woven in this tapestry; let's cut him out, and be as we would be."

Suriel waited in contemplation, flapping his wings softly, waving his sword in lazy circles before him. He looked from cherub to cherub, and they at him. Their heads all turned to indistinct rainbow masses, flickering between colors as the smoke passed through them. Finally he sheathed his sword and turned to Zephon. "Show Suriel your love, cherub. Prove that you love him, and then you will find the knowledge that you seek."

CHAPTER THIRTY-FOUR

T HEY RAN TOWARDS THE FENCE, as fast as they could, trying to make it to the edge before someone noticed. But they needn't have bothered. The compound's inner yard was swarming with people, fleeing the chaos outside for the relative safety within, and the only thing conspicuous about them now was the direction in which they were headed.

"Keep goin'," said Thane, his gun at Faye's back. They kept alongside the fence, towards the closest gate and towards the heart of the battle. They could hear it raging from just beyond, the sound of the Vichies' heavy weapons and their screams as they were torn apart by angel and golem alike.

"They're not going to last long," said Holt. "Not against what's up there."

The sky was filled with smoke, and they could see the angels diving in and out of it. Flashes of light and fire marked a battle above, as well as below. From the looks of things, it was a hard fought one. Things kept falling from the sky, angels with their wings clipped and strange machines who'd had life breathed into them only for it to be stolen away as quickly as it had come.

They reached the gate, and saw what lay beyond. The fields outside were in ruins, debris scattered everywhere and tents abandoned. The Vichies held sway on the ground, for now, lobbing their missiles up into the sky against the masters who'd abandoned them. But a few golems had landed, and some of the angels were circling low, swooping over to the humvees and tossing them around in a fury. The Vichies had little defense against that, though it didn't stop them from trying. The rattle of machine guns filled the air, punctuated by the sound of horns from above.

"The cars," said Holt. There were still some of them left, lining the road out, though many were already long gone, their owners abandoning their hopes of salvation when angels appeared above.

"We tried it," said Thane. "Jana and me. Not many you're gonna get started, not that we found. But we gotta better option. Look." He pointed across the field, towards a row of heavy trucks, troop transports idling in the open next to one of the humvees as it fired up into the air. "Get one 'a those, and we can drive through anything. And the Vichies won't look at us twice."

There were men around the transports, but only a few: just drivers waiting outside each one, their cargo delivered and nothing left to do but idle the trucks and stand at the ready for an escape. And their attentions were directed not around them but above them, as they gawked at the melee in the clouds.

"Let's go," said Holt. He pointed to an alley of tents, running the length of most of the field and ending just behind the last of the transports. "Stick behind the tents, and we'll be almost there before they see us." They sprinted down along them, ducking low to keep behind the cover. They ended up behind a weathered blue camping tent, the wind whipping under it and dragging it against its posts. The first of the transports was just a few dozen yards away, and the salvos of missiles rocketing forth from the nearby humvees was enough to drown out any noise they could possibly make.

Holt leaned in towards Faye, shouting in her ear. "This is the only way out. It's this, or stay here and take your chances. So I need to know, are you going to give us any trouble?"

She glared at him, her sneer as haughty as she could make it. "I am no fool. Get us free, and I will follow, so long as my interests demand it."

"Jana," said Thane. "Catch." He tossed something into her hands, and she caught it, though not without a little awkward fumbling. It was a stocky black taser, two shiny pins at its tip. "You two stay here. She tries anything, you click the button and zap the angel right outta her."

She didn't think it worked that way, but she wasn't in a position to argue. They'd already started to run towards the transports, guns drawn as they closed in on the unsuspecting drivers. No one even noticed them until the first was already done for, shot from behind as he smoked a cigarette and leaned against his truck. The rest didn't even hear it; there were too many other weapons being fired, too many gunshots all around, and too many other things to worry about. But one of the Vichies spotted them as they ran to the second truck, sitting atop a humvee and directing the flak. He began to point and shout, and though no one could hear what he was saying, they all turned to look at what had agitated him so.

The shootout erupted at once. Thane began firing his rifle, picking off the other drivers while they stood next to their transports and fumbled in their belts for their guns. They weren't soldiers, just auxiliaries, and they weren't prepared to join in the fighting with all the rest. The Vichies on the humvee couldn't seem to decide what to do. Some of them kept working its launchers, firing missiles up above as they'd been instructed. Only one of them responded at once, a spotter who quit watching the skies and lifted up a machine gun instead. He turned it on the unwelcome arrivals, spraying the area with bullets and tearing holes in the canvas covering the back of the transports.

Holt dove to the ground for cover, while Thane rolled beneath one of the trucks. They were both pinned down, as everyone around finally turned their attention to them. Bullets raked the ground beside them, and the truck they hid by was torn apart, holes punched through the metal sides again and again. They fought back, after a fashion, but mostly they were forced to stay down and take what shots they could.

"Your friends will die, girl," said Faye. She watched the proceedings with calculated disinterest, her nose turned up and her expression blank. "You should have stayed loyal to Rhamiel. He'd never have let you end up here."

"I was loyal," said Jana. "I am loyal. I didn't ask them

to do what they did. I didn't have a say in the matter. It was stay and die, or run and live."

"The former would have been the better choice, if you were true," said Faye. "But perhaps the latter was indeed more sensible." Then before Jana knew it, she was gone, up and running herself. She zigged and zagged between the tents, and Jana leapt to her feet to chase her. She gripped the taser in her hands, trying to remember how to use it even as she tried to follow Faye. But then a boom sounded nearby, and clods of dirt scattered round, and she was back down on the ground again with her hands clinging to her head. When she looked up, Faye was nowhere to be found. She heard people, yelling and barking orders nearby. She peeked over one of the tents and saw a stream of white, as a group of Vichies ran across the field just yards away.

She crept forward, low to the ground, crawling on her hands and knees. She wasn't even sure where she was going. Just away from them, away from the fighting, and away from all the danger. She ended up where they'd started, near the main road and by the lines of abandoned cars. Then she heard more shouting, more firing, and more clomping of boots from behind the tents. She kept low and hoped for the best, praying they'd be on their way. But it wasn't to be. She saw one of them, and he saw her, a hollow-eyed man leering from over the tents. He licked his lips, and then he began to yell, calling back to the others even as he smiled at her.

There was nothing to do but run. She made for the cars, and didn't look back, not when she heard him yelling at her to stop, and not even when she heard him firing his gun. She saw a bullet punch the dirt to the right of her, but she didn't care. She kept going, pushing herself forward. She needed to make it to the road, to have any kind of chance, and she wasn't going to stop until she was there.

The man kept shouting, and she kept moving, and after what seemed like an eternity she was finally there. She rushed forward and ducked behind a car, covering her head with her hands. A bullet shattered the window above her, sending glass spraying all around and into her hair. Then the sound of the firing moved away, gradually, as the men took their battle somewhere else on the field. She took the opportunity to crawl away, keeping her head to the ground, making her way towards one of the tents. She pulled at the zipper, again and again, but it was stuck. It wouldn't give, no matter how hard she tugged, and she was driven to tears from frustration.

"Girl," said a voice from behind her.

She didn't believe it, not until she looked. There Rhamiel was, wings outstretched, floating a few feet above the ground. He looked just as she'd remembered him: his eyes at once playful and authoritative, his body all strength, and his arms big enough to circle round her and forever keep away the dangers that beset her on all sides. He looked on her with a smile that went from smirk to warmth, and back again, and then he landed.

"I thought you were gone," said Jana. She stood, wiping at her face and brushing back her hair. "I thought. Sometimes I thought I'd never find you."

He didn't say a word. He just walked towards her in silence, looked down into her eyes, and lifted her up in a tight embrace, enveloping her in his wings even as the battle boomed and raged all around them.

CHAPTER THIRTY-FIVE

THE SCREAMING HAD STOPPED, AND the cloud of dust had grown silent, but for the occasional explosion from the guns below. The cherubs had disappeared, and so had Suriel, their swords no longer flashing as beacons through the smoke. What seraphs Uzziel could collect from the immediate vicinity waited at the outskirts of the cloud, their swords drawn as the winds blew smoke around them. "Zephon is done for," said Uzziel. "His cherubs with him. Suriel must come out, or his camouflage shall fade in time. And we will be here when he does."

He flew along the lines, gathering anyone whose attention he could attract over the din and the haze. He shouted to golems, floating in their solitary trances without anyone left to command them. They snapped to attention at his voice, keyed to follow it before the cherubs had left. Soon his band grew to a battalion, anxious seraphs mixed with dispassionate golems, all massed at the fringes of the cloud and waiting for the unforgiving minute in which their fates would be decided at long last.

Time passed, and still nothing. The explosions from below began to close in on them, an inviting target all gathered together, shattering their nerves and buffeting them from all sides. But soon the fire dwindled to a scattering of occasional bursts, as golems below rampaged freely and turned the guns to slag one by one.

It was the sword they saw first. The giant broadsword, glinting through the cloud, then piercing it, its bearer following soon after. "Steel yourselves!" shouted Uzziel, as the archangel flew towards them. The seraphs all drew their swords, and found their hearts, and waited for the slaughter to come. But then other things began to appear from the cloud, following behind Suriel. Golems at first, standing by his side instead of attacking him. Then a cherub, then another, and finally Zephon, his little rapier drawn before him.

"What is this?" said Uzziel. "What treason is this? A knife in the back of your brothers in battle? We trusted you, and here is our reward."

"Allegiances shift," said Suriel. "A rebel cannot complain of the rebellion of another. So Suriel thinks, and so agrees Zephon. The Cherubim cannot love you. You are their equals, and one cannot love their equal. But Suriel is above them. Suriel is their Lord. Their love for him can be true, the sublime adoration of the worshipper. The submission of the inferior to the superior. Love based on awe, and power, and fear, rather than mere ephemeral longings."

"Poor seraphs, who've outlived their every use," said

Zephon. "It saddens us to hear such harsh abuse. We were your tools, and we were nothing more; why else did you come knocking at our door? You talk of trust, but treated us as pawns; you were of use, and now that use is gone. This archangel has made a higher bid, and offered more than seraphs ever did."

"Your walls," said Uzziel. "I knew I heard something in them. I knew there were voices there, voices not your own. I knew." He lunged towards Zephon with his sword, but the thrust was a miss as the cherub flapped up and away. He slashed at the air, but Zephon was a difficult target: too small and too agile, he took full advantage of it, and he was always gone before the sword could find him. He taunted Uzziel with his rapier, coming just within range and then darting away again, until they heard a voice from close behind them.

"You should have prayed, Uzziel," said Suriel. "All this waste. All because you would not pray."

"Never again," said Uzziel. He turned on Suriel, his sword arcing back and forth as he waved it, whipping fire at the archangel as he backed away. "Never to you. A pretender. You want not brothers, but underlings. You plot. You scheme. You plan."

"You perish," said Suriel. He swung his sword with a loud grunt, catching Uzziel on the hand and lopping away his fingers along with his weapon. He pulled his hand back with a yowl, staring at the damage in disbelief.

"I led the heavenly host," said Uzziel. "And now it comes to this. You were powerful, but we were right. I fight for love of my brothers. You fight for love of yourself."

"The merit of a general," said Suriel, "is not in his

cause. It is in his conduct. You should have bowed, and you should have prayed." He pulled the sword back for another swing, heaving it forward with all his strength. He caught Uzziel clean, beheading him at the neck in a single stroke. The tips of his wings went with it, bouncing off his armor and spinning downwards, followed by all the rest of him.

"Now," said Suriel, turning his sword towards the remaining seraphs as they watched in horror, their swords in shaking hands. "Which of you would like to be the first to sing?"

CHAPTER THIRTY-SIX

"YOU'RE A HARD WOMAN TO find," said Rhamiel. "Search as I might, across the bounds of creation, and all I come upon are rumors. But here you are."

It seemed like no one else was even there, the way they were cocooned together within a wall of feathers. She knew it wasn't true; the muffled sounds of warfare in the distance told her as much. But still she liked to think there was nothing else but them, not in that moment. She let him hold her close for as long as she dared. She wanted to take in as much of him as she could, every little bit of him she'd missed since the tower's fall. She closed her eyes and listened to his breathing, and then his heartbeat, a soft thudding she could feel even through the armor. She felt the warmth from his hands, firm on her lower back and pulling her in tight. She focused on his smell, a slight musk mixed with something like flowers, ones they'd had back in the garden before it had all gone away. She spent as long as she could absorbing every detail before she finally spoke.

"We have to get down," said Jana. "We can't just stand here. They're shooting."

"They cannot shoot through these," said Rhamiel, puffing the feathers of his wings. "They cannot shoot through me." They flashed a grey blur, rippling around her on all sides. The feathers brushed against her arms, and ran up and down her back as they moved, a soft caress from soft things that despite their appearance were nearly indestructible.

"Still," said Jana. "It's not safe." She knew it mustn't be, not with all the things around them. But it felt like nothing could hurt her, there in his arms. Like nothing could break through, and none of the dangers that had been buffeting her from all sides could ever touch her again. She felt a sense of comfort now that he was here, a stilling of all her worries. Maybe it was the armor, thick and strong and as polished as if he'd never worn it. Maybe it was his size, bigger than any man she knew, and the unnatural strength that went along with it. Maybe it was the sword, burning away in its sheath and waiting to be turned on anyone who threatened her. She didn't know; all she knew was how she felt, a rush of joy and calm she hadn't known in what seemed like forever.

"I left you safe and sound," said Rhamiel. "But still you manage to find trouble, and ride it from wave to wave no matter how furiously they crash. You're to be that type of pledge, I suppose." His tone was mock exasperation, but his smile told the truth. It spoke of care, and of longing, and most of all, of relief.

"I didn't know what to do," said Jana. "Or where to go. They pushed us all outside, and then everything was gone. I knew you had to be out there, somewhere. I knew it."

"I'd forgotten what it felt like," said Rhamiel. "Fear. I know I've felt it before. I'm certain of it. But when, I simply cannot recall. Hundreds of years ago? Thousands, perhaps. But when I awoke. When I saw, what had been done to our home." He shivered even then, and clenched his jaw. "I felt it. I was afraid. You were gone, and I was afraid you would never be back."

"I'm sorry," said Jana. "I wasn't trying to hurt you. Maybe I shouldn't have left. Maybe—" He put a finger to her lips, stopping her words before she could finish.

"It's part of what I love about you," said Rhamiel. "You stir things up inside me, things I've long forgotten. Work turns to drudgery, if one's at it long enough. You know a little of that, I think. But do a task for thousands of years, and you lose pieces of yourself to it. It becomes all you know, and all you think of. The spark of life inside you fades. It's why we lashed out, many of us, and why we ended up here. But I look at you, and I think I can reclaim myself. I can care for someone, truly, more than if I'd been assigned to protect them as my labor. Before I protected others as a chore. Now, I see someone I would protect because I cannot stand to be without her."

She reached up, wrapping her arms around his neck and hugging him with all her might. She wanted to do more, and would have, but for where they were. She buried her head into his neck, feeling the skin against her cheek, hard with muscle but yet still somehow soft and welcoming. She wanted nothing more than to lay down with him somewhere, just as they had below the stars, and to know every inch of one another again.

She let him go, and stared up at him, every bit as perfect as he'd ever been. He leaned down, kissing her softly on the forehead. He locked eyes with her, holding her in place with that deep blue stare, and he brushed her hair back behind her, running his fingers through it. She could feel them, first a soft caress up and down the back of her head, then firm, as he took hold of her and bent down still further, kissing her along the neck. His wings rippled behind her, and she could feel the feathers pressing in close, wrapping her inside and holding her tight. He was going slowly, holding back, his kisses light even as he went up and down her neck, faster and faster. Then he could control himself no more. Something welled up from within him, the passion for a lost lover found. He lifted up her chin and kissed her forcefully, lip against lip and then tongue against tongue. She closed her eyes and let the minutes pass, until he finally managed to restrain himself again.

She knew they had to talk, now, while she had the chance. Just in case he was snatched away from her again. Just in case one of them didn't make it away from there. "There's something I have to tell you," said Jana. She started to wring her hands, and she looked down to the ground, away from him, away from his eyes. "I don't know how to tell you. I didn't know for sure, not when you left. And now I am. But I'm afraid. I wasn't at first, but now I'm really afraid."

"Tell me as you will," said Rhamiel. He put a hand beneath her chin, and lifted it up, forcing her to meet his gaze. "You cannot fear me. You cannot fear what I think. I've seen the worst of man. I guarded so many. I know bad when I see it. And I certainly know good. It's a rarer thing, and one to be treasured."

"I just don't want you to look at me the way they do," said Jana. "Everyone looks at me funny when they know. Everyone." She thought of all the whispers, and the strange looks, and that mad woman with her piece of wood and her twisted dreams. She thought of what it would be like if those whispers were on his lips, or one of those looks on his face, and it nearly brought her to tears.

"I know you were in there with him," said Rhamiel. Now it was his turn to look away, his teeth grinding against one another, his jaw tight. "With Suriel. I know who he is. It burns inside me, more than my fall ever did. It burns me that I could not guard you, not from the worst of my brothers. That he found you when I could not. You must know, that if he hurt you...."

"It's not that," said Jana. "He tried. But those men, the ones who gave you your scar. They stopped him. He tried to hurt me, but they stopped him."

"My scar," said Rhamiel. His hand went to his breastplate, running along the metal, tracing an invisible lion across his chest. "Jana. I have something to tell you as well. Something that pains me. Something that may make you turn your back on me, when you see it. And I will not blame you if you do."

"That won't happen," said Jana. "That will never happen. Not now. Not with what's to come." She did some tracing of her own, her hand moving to her stomach and feeling the warmth growing within.

"You should let her speak first, I should say." The voice came from behind her, and she pressed both hands to her stomach out of protective instinct. She knew who it was, and she knew what venoms were inside him. He was squatted atop the side of an overturned humvee, his wings spreading around it, enveloping it in black. He smiled his broken smile, and looked down on them both with a glee he couldn't conceal.

"A lover's reunion," said Ecanus. "Such a wonderful thing, were it not so tainted. She hasn't told you yet, has she? I didn't expect she would."

"Whatever treacheries you offer, I've no interest in them," said Rhamiel. He pulled Jana close, burying her in his side and surrounding her with his arms. "Now go. Get to the skies, and to the battle, where you belong. You want a hero's name, then do a hero's deeds."

"I want a hero's glory," said Ecanus. "Not a hero's burdens. And what greater burden can there be, than to love a pledge with no more honor than a common whore?"

"Watch your words," said Rhamiel, his voice a low growl. "Watch the next ones you speak, and watch them carefully, for you live or die by them."

"She's with child, you fool," said Ecanus. "Can't you see it? Can't you smell it?" He flexed his wings, leaping down to the ground and sauntering towards them, unable to contain his snickers as he went. "She's cheated, Rhamiel. She took your pledge, and she broke it at the first opportunity. She's with child, and even you can't be arrogant enough to think it could be yours."

"You lie," said Rhamiel. "All you are is a blackened

ball of jealousy and spite, deadening your own pains by reveling in those of others."

"Ask her," said Ecanus. "Ask her, if she's with child. And then ask yourself if you truly think it's *the* child."

CHAPTER THIRTY-SEVEN

ER FACE STUNG, NOT JUST from the tears but from the accusations themselves. Ecanus was a monster, and he'd done nothing but torment her since she'd met him. But of all the terrible things he'd said and done, this one hurt the most.

"I'm pregnant," said Jana. "That's true. But the rest—"

"Hush," said Rhamiel. He took her hand in his, and squeezed. He stared at her, just for a few seconds, at her face, her mouth, and then at her eyes. "I don't need words. I know what's true without them. I can tell it from your eyes, and from something in your touch. I can tell it from the way you shiver when he speaks. I know what I believe. And I don't believe him for a moment."

She started to talk, despite what he'd said. To tell him of the strange machine, with its image of the glowing thing inside her. Of the woman and her ravings, of sons reborn and of kings and of queens. Of Suriel and his mad quest to pervert the child of a god. But she couldn't get any of it out, not before she was drowned out by Ecanus's loud cackle.

"Such ego," said Ecanus. "Such vanity. Or is it such stupidity? It's a hard pill to swallow, I suppose. Knowing that one's lover jumps from bed to bed, and that yours was just an evening's waystation. Knowing that the moment she was done with you, she leapt into the arms of another. Knowing that the sweet nothings she whispered into your ear meant nothing to her at all."

"And it must be an even harder thing," said Rhamiel, "to know that no one can ever love you." He put his arm on Jana's shoulder, and pushed her gently behind him, his wings spreading wide. He drew his sword, and held it before him, as Ecanus took a few quick steps backward at the sight. "Your brothers cannot stand you, Ecanus. They never could."

"What's left of them might agree with you," said Ecanus. "Or have you been so blinded by your search as to miss the course of the proceedings up above?"

They looked up, to the sight of pitched battle. Golems of all kinds were being sliced apart by seraphs' swords of fire, and claiming victims of their own in turn. The army up above had turned in on itself, a snake consuming its tail, as its ranks dissolved into chaotic skirmishes between divisions that had once stood side by side. The sky was filled with defeated combatants plummeting to the ground, a rain of the fallen plunging into the dirt with loud booms. Golem and cherub fought seraph, and in the middle of it all was Suriel, putting a choice to every seraph he encountered: his song or his sword, whichever they preferred.

When Rhamiel looked down from it all, it was to a scream from Jana and a whoosh of flame. They'd made the cardinal mistake, in dealing with Ecanus: leaving him to his own devices without keeping at least one eye upon him. The battle had been a distraction, an effective one, and he'd stolen a swing of his dagger aimed straight for Jana's stomach. She managed to dodge it, but barely, and she could feel the heat rush past her robe. He snarled at them both, assaulting them with both weapon and words. "She loves you not, Rhamiel. And if you won't believe, it's no matter. You'll lose her love, no matter how tightly you cling to it. You'll watch her die before you, and in the end the sorrow's all the same."

He pulled the dagger up for a second slash, but he wasn't given another chance. Rhamiel gave him a solid blow with the fist of his sword-hand, connecting knuckle to nose. Ecanus's face exploded in a burst of blood, trickling out from his nostrils. He put one hand to his face, coughing and fuming, and swung wildly with the other, sending lines of fire around in front of him. "Back," said Rhamiel, pressing Jana away from the threat, and stepping forward to meet it himself.

He aimed his sword at Ecanus's wrist, waited for a gap in his swings, and then he struck. His sword cut a thin gash in Ecanus's flesh, a minor wound, but one that prompted him to drop the dagger to the ground and whip his arm away. Ecanus looked up, saw the thirst for blood in Rhamiel's expression, and did the only thing he could. He dropped to his knees, begging, apologizing, and promising that he'd change forever if only he were spared.

"Coward," said Rhamiel, and he spat on the ground next to Ecanus. He started to turn, only to find there was still fight in him. "Your whore dies, Rhamiel," said Ecanus, and he pounced upward and shoved Rhamiel aside, knocking him off balance and onto his back. He dove for his dagger, and had a hand on it, before Rhamiel was back on his feet and headed back towards him. The two paced around each other, Rhamiel looking for an opening, Ecanus just trying to circle his way closer to Jana.

A boom came from up above, as a giant golem exploded into flame. Seraphs flew around it, their swords slashing away and hacking off pieces until they'd hit some device inside of it. It careened away below them, but their victory was a temporary one. A figure emerged from smoke around them: Suriel, beating his silver wings and heading towards the seraphs to finish the golem's work.

"I think I shall leave the lovebirds to their folly," said Ecanus. "Your faith in her word is quite sweet. Touching, though you must be a bit touched yourself to believe it. But I will not argue with those who would not hear." He looked up, at the seraphs fighting above in their lost cause, as sword after sword went dark. He honed in on Suriel, as he flew leisurely between the combatants. "No, I think I will speak to others about the matter. The day has turned, and all that's needed to go from vanquished to victor is an offering for one's conqueror."

He began to run, flapping his wings as he did, gathering speed and launching himself upwards. He called behind him as he went: "I shall let our host know of your good fortune, and your views on the parentage of your child. He'll want to congratulate you in person, I'd expect." His flight was slow, and slower still because he kept looking back at Rhamiel, his face a scowl, daring him to follow as he made a line straight for Suriel. And blind fury almost made Rhamiel do it, as he tensed his wings and took a step forward to continue their duel.

"No!" said Jana. She put her hand on Rhamiel's shoulder, stopping him in his tracks. "You can't. You can't leave again."

"You're right," said Rhamiel. "Let him do what he would do. But we must go. The three of us must go." He put a hand to her stomach, letting it linger, and then began to scour the skies for a pathway out. But all around was pandemonium, the ground filled with gunshots, the skies filled with fire. Everywhere was danger, and everywhere enemies. He could have made it away, on his own. He could fly as fast as he liked unburdened, and could have pushed aside anything that confronted him. But with her in his arms, he would move too slowly, and attacks he himself could survive would be sure to destroy her.

"Can you run?" said Rhamiel. "We can fly low, but if we are challenged, we will have to land, and we will have to fight. And you cannot stay nearby, no matter what."

"I can," said Jana. "I will."

"Then we must pick a path," said Rhamiel. "Over his own compound, perhaps, and then off into the forest. The battle is lightest there, with Suriel ascendant. And there are places for you to hide, if we do not make it." He frowned, and looked around in all directions. He didn't like any of their choices. He was too conspicuous, too inviting a target. And she was too soft of one. He stretched his wings and prepared to make a go of it, hoping he could dodge whatever fire he attracted when he took to the air. But as he did he heard a noise, and saw something rushing in their direction.

A truck roared towards them from across the field, a heavy military transport swerving onto the main road and aiming right at them. Rhamiel pressed forward, moving between the truck and Jana and drawing his sword. But he needn't have bothered. It began to brake as it approached, pulling up beside them, its sides riddled with bullet holes and scratches in the deep green metal. The driver's door opened, and out leaned Holt. "Get in. Both of you. Climb in the back, close the tarp behind you, and let's get the hell out of Dodge."

CHAPTER THIRTY-EIGHT

THEY BARRELLED DOWN THE MAIN road, making straight for the path through the forest and out towards the highway, the battle intensifying all around them. Seraphs were taking to the ground, fleeing whatever turmoil they faced up above. Some of them landed of their own accord, running on foot through the fields towards the surrounding forests and disappearing within, if they could make it. More of them simply crashed, wounded anew from the skirmish and flailing out of control as they dropped to the ground.

All around, the golems had abandoned their attacks on the Vichies, and had turned on the seraphs instead. Many of them weren't suited to the task. The largest among them were being torn to pieces by rampaging angels, spraying chunks of rock and gems into the air as they ripped through them with their swords. But here and there around the field, golems equipped with electrical weapons roamed, striking the unwary and sending them off to an afterlife of their own.

"We ain't gonna make it," said Thane. He eyed the

madness outside through the window, tapping his fingers against the dashboard and holding his rifle tight. "And Faye. What are we gonna do about Faye?"

"Don't think about any of that," said Holt. "Stay focused. Think about the things you can change, not the ones you can't. We've got guns, and a truck, and an angel hiding in the back. Everyone around here has bigger things to worry about than one random truck. We'll make it."

They drove forward, closer and closer to the forest's edge, swerving as an angel flew low in front of them, crossing the road in a sudden flash. They could see something chasing it in the rearview mirror, a swarm of tiny angels following behind it in close pursuit. But they just kept heading towards their goal, dodging cars and wreckage in the road until they could see the path out lying just ahead of them.

The way was blocked, though not by much. Two cars had been pushed together to barricade the road, little sedans with Vichies positioned behind them. Their guns were trained ahead of them, and they began shouting and waving as the truck approached, ordering it off the road for an inspection before it left. They fired warning shots, blasting away up into the air, then at the road in front of them.

"Hold on," said Holt. "I'm going through." His foot went to the floor, and the truck heaved forward, slowly accelerating faster and faster. They began to hear plunks, the sound of bullets clinking against metal, and they both steeled themselves for the collision to come. The cars were nothing against the behemoth they were driving, just flimsy tissues they'd easily tear apart. But then things began to land in front of them, and everything changed.

Holt slammed on the brakes and shoved the steering wheel to the side. The tires screeched as the truck slowed and swerved, stopping just short of the new arrivals. They looked out the window, and there before the cars were two golems, living constructs of bronze with electricity coursing through weapons attached to their hands. And between them stood something worse: Suriel, his black robe speckled red with blood, his face contorted in fury.

"Fuck," said Thane. "I'm gettin' the angel from the back. Let the two of 'em fight it out."

"No," said Holt. He stared out the window at the archangel, and then he closed his eyes, breathing in and out, heavy and slow. "No. Stay here, and take the wheel. I'm going to go talk to him."

"There ain't shit to talk about," said Thane. "There's kill him, or get killed."

"Just take the wheel," said Holt. "And I'm going to go do what needs to be done."

He left the truck, and walked around front towards Suriel, all alone. Thane did as he was told and edged into the driver's seat, though not without an onslaught of profanity. The girl and the angel didn't even know. They were in the back of the truck, and they couldn't see, not what was in front of them. It was how it had to be, and how Holt wanted it.

"Man," said Suriel, as Holt approached him. "Tiny man, who makes demands of his betters. Who strikes at Suriel, and yet expects to live. Do you come to beg, man? To pray to Suriel for a quick and painless death?"

"I didn't come to pray," said Holt. "I came to deal."

"A prayer in its own right, of sorts," said Suriel. "What would you ask of Suriel?"

"Let us go," said Holt. "You'll never see us again, any of us. Never hear from us, never have to deal with us. All I ask is mercy."

"A man who insults a god cannot expect mercy," said Suriel. "For what kind of god would Suriel be, if he did not teach his followers their lessons? What kind of god would he be, if he did not remake them as he pleased? Disobedience displeases Suriel. He is a wrathful god, a vengeful god, the kind the Maker once was. The Maker was a fool to change. He showed his creations mercy, and thus he showed them weakness. And so they turned on him, as you would soon turn on me."

"I can trade," said Holt. He gave a grim nod back to the truck, took a deep breath, and then made the choice he'd have to live with. Leaders had to make sacrifices. He knew that. No one else would make the choice. No one else even could. The rest of them didn't have it in them. Thane would fight, Jana would do nothing, and the angel would do whatever was best for himself. Their kind always did. It was up to him, to get them free. At least the ones he could. "I can give you someone you want. You get someone you want, and then you let the rest of us go."

"Someone Suriel wants," said Suriel. "And who would you place upon Suriel's altar, a dagger in your hand? Who would you give to him, as alms to buy your freedom?"

"An angel," said Holt. "You can have an angel. The one you were fighting with. The one who tried to get into your compound. You can have him, and you can do whatever the hell you want with him. Just let the rest of us go."

Suriel stepped forward, standing just inches from Holt, his chest well above his head. He loomed over him, a massive giant glaring down with a dismissive sneer. "You would betray him? One of your own, for the lives of all the rest?"

"He's not one of mine," said Holt. He hesitated, inside himself. The angel had never done anything to him. Not this one, anyway. He'd even saved them from his brother, back at the compound, and he seemed to genuinely care for Jana. But he shook aside the thoughts, burying his guilt under a pile of rationalizations. Angels were angels, after all. They couldn't be trusted, not after what they'd done. And he was the leader. If one had to be cut loose to save the many, he'd be the one to do it. And so he did. "He'd give us up in a second, if it helped him. He doesn't give a damn about me, and so I don't give a damn about him. He's an angel. You're an angel. As far as I'm concerned, he's one of yours, and you can have him."

"What if Suriel does not want an angel?" said Suriel. "He has many, and has slaughtered even more this day." He stepped forward, and Holt stepped back, giving way for each inch he took.

"Like I said," said Holt. "I'm here to deal." He put his hands up in submission, backing further away as Suriel kept slowly pressing forward. Soon he'd bumped against the grill of the truck, with Suriel staring down at him and a volatile Thane behind him. He knew he had to get Suriel talking, to find out what he wanted. To find out what he could give him that would save at least some of them. To find the choice, the one that would be the way out, the one that would let him sleep at night without waking up in a sweat, the faces of the lost still on the back of his eyelids. The choice that would save the ones who'd trusted him to lead, at whatever the cost to his soul.

"We can work something out," said Holt. "We'll preach, to the people out there. We'll pray, every night. We're not looking for a fight. Just tell us what you want, and we'll work something out."

"What Suriel wants," said Suriel. "What he wants is a girl." He pressed his hands down against the hood of the truck, denting the metal at his touch and trapping Holt between his arms. "What he wants is her child."

"She's just some nobody," said Holt. "The angel. He hates you. He wants to kill you. We're nobodies, and she's a nobody. We don't matter."

"She is more than that," said Suriel. "Or so Suriel has been told by another. By one who claims to have heard it from her own mouth. Suriel does not believe, but neither does he take chances. Suriel will have them both, and he will have her child. But do not despair. If it is an angel's child, it will have a father. A new father, better than the one who made him, and better than the one who sired him. A father who can teach him the way of things, before he is too old to learn."

"The angel," said Holt. "We'll give you the angel. He's in the back. Just take him. It's a fair trade. A good trade. We won't fight it. We'll give him up."

"You cannot give Suriel what he already has," said Suriel. "Suriel is your god, now. And you cannot fight against a god." He lifted his hands from the metal, then. He grabbed Holt by the throat with one, pressing his back down against the truck's hood as he kicked in all directions. The glass of the windshield exploded outward, and bullets and shouts came from Thane in equal measure. Something stirred in the back of the truck at the commotion, and fire sliced through the tarp covering the back. But Suriel ignored it all.

"No," said Holt. "We'll give you what you want. We'll pray. We'll—"

"Suriel wants a sacrifice," said Suriel. "And Suriel shall have it." He raised his fist, up into the air. Time seemed to slow, for Holt. He tried to shout, tried to think of something that would make the archangel change his mind. But his thoughts were a mess, and all he kept coming back to was Dax. He could almost see him, in the back of his mind. He pointed no fingers now, not like he did in the dreams. He just shook his head, and held out his hand. And then Suriel's fist came crashing down.

CHAPTER THIRTY-NINE

THE BACK OF THE TRUCK exploded into burnt pieces of tarp, blowing upward as Rhamiel tore through them, hovering up above it and looking down on Suriel and the latest of his atrocities. "He joins us," said Suriel. "The prize Suriel was promised." He shook his fist dry of blood, and reached to his side for his sword. "Your army is in ruins, Rhamiel. No one will come to save you. No one will come to save your child. And it is your child, isn't it?"

Rhamiel answered only with rage, filling the air with fire as he attacked again and again. He swung with a fury, driven by the desperate energies of one fighting not for himself but for those he cherished. Even Suriel seemed taken aback by the intensity of it all. He tripped as he moved away, plunging his sword into the ground where it began to turn the dirt into a blackened mud. He pulled it out again in time to parry yet another series of blows from Rhamiel, coming inches from his face before he knocked them away.

"Your child is no longer your own," said Suriel. "He

will have a father. A better father. The Maker and his Son think they can save his creations. They think he will come again, not to end the world but to rebuild it. But if the world is to be rebuilt, why should it not be ruled by an angel? The Maker has been a poor steward, these last centuries. This world needs a firmer hand. And it shall have it."

He whipped his sword upward, battering it against Rhamiel's own and knocking him to the ground. They heard a cry from behind him: Jana, looking out on the battle from beside the truck, being held back by Thane. Suriel just smiled, and pressed his attack. He swung the sword downward, missing Rhamiel as he rolled aside, but barely. The sword caught the front of the truck, cleaving through it and knocking its bumper to the ground.

"Your girl is a pretty one," said Suriel. "But she is Suriel's girl, now. You will be gone, and she will be tamed, given time. Soon she will call out Suriel's name in the night. Every night." That drew another onslaught, and again Suriel was forced to retreat, as blow after blow struck his sword. But he watched, carefully. He was looking for something. Some small delay in the swings, some error in the arc of Rhamiel's sword, or some moment of hesitation. Even Rhamiel knew that was his game. But he couldn't control himself, couldn't tamper the fury, and couldn't stop lashing out at the monster before him. Not with the words he was speaking. Not with how they both knew he planned to savor his victory.

Suriel struck, when he found the mistake. It was just a moment, a tiny second in time, the backswing on one of the strokes of Rhamiel's sword that went just a little too far behind him. It left an opening, before the next attack. And Suriel used it for an assault of his own. He thrust his sword forward, a quick lunge that made it to its target well before Rhamiel could react. He was defenseless, his sword pulled back for the next swing, too far away to block the assault. By the time he looked down, the hilt of Suriel's broadsword was pressed firmly against his chest.

They could see it from behind, Suriel's weapon, as its flames disappeared with one quick stroke. Jana let out a scream, the mournful wail of one who'd lost her love not once but twice. She pushed against Thane, trying to run forward, but he was too strong, and so all she could do was slap at him and cry. There was a sickening pause, as the two angels stood there, staring each other eye to eye. Suriel looked past him, on to Jana, leering at her as he savored the moment. He wanted to see her, to enjoy every one of her tears, the better to make her shed even more in the years to come. He didn't even notice, as his hand was turned and his sword knocked aside.

The cherubs had forged their armor well. Whatever techniques of metallurgy they'd developed had made his replacement armor wholly impervious to fire, even to a weapon as big and as dangerous as Suriel's own broadsword. Its flames had been blocked, as surely as if it had been sheathed, and Rhamiel's armor hadn't even been singed by the attack. Suriel stood before him, hands empty and mind paralyzed as he processed what had happened. He was still standing there, dumb, when Rhamiel gave him a blow of his own.

The sword caught Suriel on the arm, as he held up

his hands to protect himself. It slashed across his wrist, leaving a fresh scar in its wake. The golems pressed forward as Suriel howled, their arms up as bolts of electricity coursed back and forth between them. But they came too close, and came too late. Rhamiel gave Suriel a kick against his chest, knocking him backwards and into their waiting embrace.

Suriel twisted as he screamed in pain, jerking away from the surge of electricity bolting into him from his contact with the golems. He fell to his knees, smoke sizzling from his wings where the power had run through him. His palms pressed against the soil, fingers clenching and then unclenching as he tried to clear his addled mind. He was an archangel, and he could survive things that would have ended a lesser seraph. But still his wounds stung, and still he needed time to regain his composure. And the time he lost to recovery was time enough for Rhamiel.

"Inside. Now!" shouted Rhamiel, and Thane obliged, pulling Jana into the truck. He slammed the door shut, and the two of them found themselves rising, pulled off the ground by Rhamiel. He'd grabbed onto the cab of the truck, dangling it below him as he spread his wings and heaved them all upwards, into the air. They could see the ground growing further and further away, the truck shaking back and forth with each flap of his wings. One of the golems began chasing them, puffing a cloud of steam behind it, but even as encumbered as he was, Rhamiel had the better of it. He pushed forward, gaining ground and gaining distance, and soon the battlefield was on the horizon and the golem just a distant speck, turning away to receive its next orders.

It was terrifying to Jana, being up so high. The truck swayed back and forth as they flew, and for a time she felt overwhelmed with nausea. She couldn't open her eyes, for fear of looking down. But she felt a hand clasp her own, cupping it and holding it tight. It calmed her, and eventually she managed to sneak a peek to see Thane smiling and enjoying the ride. He tried to say something, some friendly word of encouragement, but the wind shouted him down. Still, her courage rose, and soon she was following his example, daredevil enough to lean her head out the window to watch the distant sights below. There were fields, and little buildings, and even a lake, and she thought it all amazing, so small when seen from up so high.

They landed on a hill, in a barren, empty expanse of grassland. Rhamiel set the truck down, gently, and after a little bounce its wheels were settled on the ground. Jana pushed the door open as quickly as she could, rushing back to his arms and back to safety. "You're fine," said Rhamiel. "We've enough distance that they won't soon catch us."

"I gotta go back," said Thane, as he rounded the truck to the others. "I gotta find Faye. She's out there on her own, and she ain't gonna last for long." He slung his rifle on his back, making ready for the long trek back the way they'd come.

"She doesn't want to be found," said Jana. "He doesn't, anyhow."

"You cannot go back," said Rhamiel. "Not now. Not for anything."

"I can't let her die back there," said Thane. "Can't just let her run around on her own out in the middle of a war."

"You would not find her," said Rhamiel. "You may

do as you like, but you know you would not find her. Take a moment. Think on the matter. And then you may do as you please." Thane just gave a grunt, and left the two of them there to pace around the back of the truck with his thoughts.

"All this," said Rhamiel. "Rebellion, warfare, destruction. And all of it mattered not. The Son tried to stop the end, and it came despite his calls for mercy. Perhaps even because of them." He put one arm around Jana, and tested her stomach with the other. He seemed almost afraid to touch it at first, but finally he pressed his hand against it. Jana could feel a little kick inside, and he whipped his hand away before turning back to her with a laugh and a smile.

"Maybe it won't be that way," said Jana. "Maybe it'll all get better. Maybe he'll make it all stop."

"Perhaps," said Rhamiel. "The Maker is unfathomable at times. His Son has bought the world a reprieve from its end once before, at dear cost. Perhaps he will do it again." She leaned into him, and he held her there, standing in silence and safety. He broke it with a few words, and a look of resignation.

"I have to show you, what I left unsaid before," said Rhamiel. "You have to see, what's been done to me. And if it disgusts you, if you cannot look at me the same, I understand. I will still be there as a father, even if that's all you'd have me be."

"Don't talk that way," said Jana. "Don't."

"I'll understand," said Rhamiel. He breathed in, and then reached behind his back, undoing the straps of his armor. He pressed his hands against his shoulders, letting the clasps loose, and then he pulled down the breastplate and showed her what the weapons of men had done to him. The lion was there, traced in the scars, thin lines mapped across his chest. They were pink, still fresh, battle scars that looked more like etchings than wounds.

"What is it?" said Jana, running her finger across it, to a wince from Rhamiel.

"A beast, from heaven's outskirts," said Rhamiel. "Fierce. Angry. They used to batter themselves against the walls, if they weren't driven away, trying to claw their way inside. Angry creatures, but it was for the best to have them there. They didn't tolerate intruders any more than they tolerated us. I took the symbol for myself after we fell. They were courageous to the point of recklessness, and I saw some of myself in them."

"I think it looks nice," said Jana. She pressed her hand against his chest, feeling the bare skin and the little bumps of the symbol he now bore forever. She thought it could have been carved there, the lines were so clean, tracing where his armor had been with precision. She could feel his tension fade away as she stood by his side, and she stayed there until Thane finally rounded the truck, his face torn apart by frustration.

"I can't go back," said Thane. "I want to go back, but I can't. I gotta figure somethin' out, and I gotta find her. But not 'til I have help. Can't do shit without help."

"We must go," said Rhamiel. "Away from here. Somewhere we can hide, and somewhere we can be safe. Suriel will not let us be. He will end his war, and then he will begin looking for us. We must be far away when he does."

"Where?" said Thane. "Where are we gonna go that he can't get us?"

"We have a world to hide in," said Rhamiel. "We will run, or hide, or fly, whatever we must do to make it past the birth of the child. Of our child." He pulled Jana close, and felt her stomach with a hesitant hand, then with a firm one. Then he turned back to Thane. "You need not come. Suriel will not bother with you. One of you is just the same as all the others, to him. But he will scour the ends of the earth for us, and he will not stop until he has the child."

"I spent the last ten years tryin' to kill angels," said Thane. "Now Suriel's doin' my job for me. And you're tellin' me that the biggest, baddest, worst asshole of 'em all ain't stoppin' until he finds her? If I'm there when he does, I'm gonna put him in the ground, right where he belongs."

"You'll die," said Rhamiel. "If you face him, you will surely die."

"Don't care," said Thane. "Gotta die somehow."

Rhamiel looked him up, and looked him down, and then turned to Jana. "He seems a madman, or a fool. I cannot have you endangered, not by someone bent more on vengeance than survival."

"He's fine," said Jana. "I'd still be in there, if it weren't for him and his friends. He's fine."

"You may come," said Rhamiel. "Wherever we go, you may come, for so long as you'd like."

"Got nothin' better to do," said Thane. "Not 'til I figure out how to help Faye."

"Then we must go," said Rhamiel. "And we must try."

CHAPTER FORTY

THE FIELDS AROUND SURIEL'S COMPOUND were strewn with wreckage, twisted hunks of metal that had once been cars and cannons alike. The fences had been pulled from the ground, bent and torn by rampaging golems before the tide of battle had turned. Teams of Vichies and preachers roamed across the field, burning corpses both human and angel. The air was filled with black smoke, billowing up from bonfires all around, and here and there blackened feathers fluttered on the wind.

The battle up above was done, and what few had survived it were huddled together on the ground, all on their knees. They sang, every one of them. Preacher Perry stood at the fore, leading the angels on in the hymn, teaching them the words as Suriel preferred them. Their voices were out of tune, after so many years of neglect. But the songs were still inside them, and they'd spent so many centuries at the task that it was second nature. And so their voices joined and merged, speaking of praise but sounding of sorrow, calling out a love they didn't feel for a master they couldn't stand.

Suriel listened, his face glowing with pride, until he finally grew bored with the affair. He left them at the task, a choir with no audience, happy in the knowledge that they were working at loving him even if he had no interest in the results. He crossed the field, towards another gathering of angels: the cherubs, assembling what was left of their golems, and waiting for a final audience with the victor of the day. They greeted him with bows, and turned their attention towards him as Zephon stepped forward, his face turned human with its expression blank.

"Will you stay, to join Suriel's choir?" said Suriel. "He expects you to attend, as you would have up above. He expects all to attend, if they'd stay in his good graces."

Zephon stared ahead of him and spoke, avoiding any eye contact as he did, though more because he hadn't thought to bother with it than as any insult. "We beg our leave, but only for a time; our studies are a daunting mental climb. But don't think that the cherubs cannot croon; we waited here to beg of you a boon. We'd sing all night if you would grant this thing, and give you all the knowledge that it brings. We ask a favor Heaven would forbid, to help us fathom what the Maker did."

"Then ask," said Suriel. "Suriel will assist you, so long as the request is reasonable. A reasonable god answers his followers' prayers, after all. And Suriel would have the secrets of creation, at whatever cost."

The cherubs all hummed a happy hum, their faces as expressionless as ever. Zephon wrung his hands, over and over, and then he finally looked up at Suriel. "There is a victim of the seraphs' wars, who won't be healed by any hand but yours. There's something valuable inside his head, a knowledge lost when angels' blood was shed. He's too far gone to ever be the same, but light a spark and wisdom we'll reclaim."

"Then bring him forth," said Suriel. "And Suriel will lay hands upon him, and cleanse him of his troubles. Suriel will give you a touch of the spark of creation to study, leaving it within him, and will make him as whole as he can be made. Then you will be about your work, and you will bother Suriel no more until your task is done."

Zephon grunted, and waved to his followers. They called forth one of their transport golems, and it floated down beside them and reached inside itself with its tendrils to retrieve its precious cargo: the body of Zuphias, encased in its vat. The golem let it down upon the ground, gently, and before the vat could connect with the soil it began to hover on its own accord, just a few feet above the ground.

Suriel looked over what they'd set before him, black flesh mixed with metal and growths unknown. He was uncertain what it was, until the stubs of its former wings began to flap, stirring about the fluids inside. "What thing is this, that cherubs ask Suriel to heal?" said Suriel. "A warped body, torn apart by Zephon's scalpel. How is Suriel to mend a thing that has been so tampered with?"

"You need not heal, but only grant your touch," said Zephon. "We ask for but a spark, it's nothing much." He flew to the vat and hammered at the controls. The top slid open, and the liquids sloshed around. The body floated in there, inches below the surface, bobbing up and down along with the fluid.

Suriel frowned, unable to contain his disgust. Then he steeled himself, and went ahead with his promise. "Suriel will mend your broken toy," said Suriel. "As best he is able. This creature will think, perhaps, once it is healed. But the thing before you will never be an angel again." He pulled the glove from his hand, and beneath it was a mess of ruined pink skin. His hand began to glow, and with a last look of distaste he shoved it into the tank, and all at once the body of Zuphias was bathed in both water and in light. After a few seconds, Suriel pulled out his hand, and wiped it against his robe.

He had done something to the body, though as he'd warned, it was no angel. But blackened flesh began to flake away, dropping into the fluid and leaving bright, pink skin beneath. There was life in him, more than there had been before, and strength. The spark had given him power, and even the machines attached to the body began to rumble and stir, the tubes pumping fluids in and out of it at a frantic pace. The speakers on the tank began to sound, shooting out loud bursts of unintelligible static, until one of the cherubs dove towards the controls and cut off the racket with a slap of his hand.

"Now be about your work," said Suriel. "And be vigilant about your promises. Suriel is watching. You have promised him creation, and he expects results. There will be no Lord but Suriel, not on this plane."

"Just give us time, and we'll give you a crown," said Zephon. "We'll lift you up, and tear the Maker down."

They watched him go, as he strutted away, his victory in hand and his place in history secured. There were no more threats to him; no seraphs to oppose him, no golems to strike him, and nothing to worry of but a helpless child in the wilderness. They watched him smile, they watched him swagger, they watched him imbibe the bows and the awe of his human followers. They watched him fly away, back to his compound and back to his women.

Only then did they turn to their prize, the burnt black thing floating in its chemical stew. They all gathered round it, huddling in close to the vat, some perched atop it, others clinging to its sides, others standing on the ground below and reaching up to caress the glass with their tiny fingers. They all began to hum as one, closing their eyes and swaying together to what rhythm was within them.

Then several of them began to tinker, opening up panels on the side of the vat. They crossed wires, they replaced tubes, and they scanned the insides with their tools. They turned knobs and they pressed buttons, and when they were satisfied, they turned to Zephon for approval. He gave them a slight nod, and they closed it back up and stood to the side, watching and waiting.

All was quiet. None of the cherubs spoke, and the only sound was the rustling of wings and the smacking of lips. They were patient, and they sat there for an interminable amount of time, with nothing to entertain them but the vat and what bubbled within it. Each cherub withdrew into itself, and into whatever strange behaviors focused their thoughts. Some spun their heads from creature to creature in a compulsive fury. Others wrung their hands, or buzzed their wings. A few pressed their faces against the glass, slowly licking up and down the sides with their tiny tongues. As for Zephon, he simply closed his eyes and hummed.

Their vigil was interrupted by a slight noise from the speakers. It was just indistinct crackling at first, a minor static that could barely be heard. It rose until it was a voice, but there was something not quite right about it, like it had been torn to pieces and stitched back together again. It modulated up and down, approaching something like speech and then backing away again, and finally it settled on a single word. "Who?"

"A multitude of little angels speak," said Zephon. "Whether through ox's snout or eagle's beak." The cherubs all let their heads fizzle, their chosen form following his words from creature to creature.

"How?" said the voice. It dissolved into static, and then it spoke again. "How, do I hear songs of cherubs?"

"Through speech that's not our own, and amplified," said Zephon. "A fallen comrade who had nearly died. It took the minds of cherubs, ever keen, to meld a miracle to a machine."

"Why?" said the voice. "Why would cherubs go to such lengths, to cry out into the void through the mouth of another?"

The cherubs locked eyes with each other, and let a moment pass in contemplation. They came as close to trepidation as creatures without emotion can, buzzing their wings in agitation. Many of them sat clutching their arms together and violently rocking back and forth, over and over as they tried to hum themselves into a better state. But one by one they each managed to give a nod to Zephon, and he leaned in close to the speakers before he spoke.

"In darkest pits, where banished legions stir," said Zephon, "we call upon the angel, Lucifer."

END OF BOOK TWO.

Liked the book? If you want to get a heads up on the release of the last book in the series, please sign up for my mailing list.

http://www.theywhofell.com

ACKNOWLEDGEMENTS

Thanks to Kathy Dixon Graham and Renee Rearden for taking the time to beta read and to proof the final draft.

OTHER WORKS BY KEVIN KNEUPPER

Cade Crowley, Demon Hunter (Cade Crowley, Demon Hunter #1) – Cade helps a man who's summoned something up from Hell, but didn't have a plan to deal with it.

Dark Hunger (Cade Crowley, Demon Hunter #2) – Cade confronts a demon of gluttony, bent on eating all it can in other people's bodies.

Doors to Nowhere (Cade Crowley, Demon Hunter #3-5) – A man sold his soul for money, but has a plan to keep the demon from collecting. A pastor's son is possessed, and strays from the flock. And a crystal ball foretells the future, with a demon whispering from inside.

They Who Fell – A post-apocalyptic novel set in the aftermath of the fall of an army of rebel angels, intent on enslaving humanity.

Made in the USA
Middletown, DE
03 September 2015